Web of Sh

CW01668785

This historical, romantic novel spans the period prior to ,and including , the Great War of 1914–18.The social and economic background is skilfully presented , but the story concerns Sarah Pearson and her father , their hardships and their joys.Struck down by tragedy , losing her mother and brother , the two are compelled to move to Sidmouth in Devon where Sarah becomes a companion to a lady. There she meets Oliver and romance follows , although the war intervenes and poor Oliver becomes Shell Shocked with resultant personal difficulties.Major events such as the sinking of the *Titanic* are also recorded , the whole integrating to become a fascinating , and moving story.

The Author: A former nurse by profession Maureen Rye lives in Surrey with her husband and daughter Karen.She has always been interested in writing and her hobbies are reading, drawing and crossword solving. Although this is her first novel she is hopeful that more will follow.

ISBN 1-85736-065-6

WEB OF SHADOWS

To Jill & Martin

August 1996.

All good wishes

Maureen Rye.

WEB OF SHADOWS

MAUREEN RYE

Beech Publishing House
15 The Maltings
Turk St
Alton
Hants GU34 1DL

ISBN 1-85736-065-6

First published 1992

Beech Publishing House
15 The Maltings
Turk St
Alton GU 34 1DL
Hants

Dedication

I wish to dedicate this book to David, my husband, for his encouragement and support; to my daughter Karen, for her constructive criticism , and to the memory of my son Stephen.

1

A LONG WINTER

Inside, the room was snug and warm. Sarah crossed to the window and pressed her nose against the pane. The scene out there caused her to shiver, and pull her shawl closer about her shoulders. Drawing the curtains together she turned back into the firelit room. Away from the sight of the swirling snow, and the black menacing trees waving wildly in the wind. Night was falling fast, wintry light was fading into another long black night. Sarah made her way to the cheerful glow of the fire, and placed a log there from the basket at the side. She reached up to the mantle and took down the large oil lamp. Lighting it, she replaced it, causing a soft mellow glow to settle about the room. Giving a large sigh she tilted her head to catch any sound that may come from upstairs, all was quiet for the moment. Father had worn himself out coughing, and hopefully was sleeping. Soon, it would start again, the dry rasping struggle, which left him so breathless and weak. His poor body was quite wasted. Sarah's eyes filled, remembering the good times, when mother and young William had been alive.

It seemed an age ago since those happy times, in fact it was just two years. Sitting on her favourite spot on the fender, and stretching out her hands to the blaze, she remembered how it had been.

Theirs had been a home full of love and contentment. Father looked after the vast gardens up at the Hall, whilst mother helped in the kitchens on certain occasions. Whenever there were guests staying, or large banquets held, she would assist with the preparations, and the clearing up later. On her return home, she would usually have a basket of good things, left–overs from the feasts, and she and the family would enjoy tasty tit–bits for their supper. With father's earnings, and mothers small contribution, together with frequent added food luxuries, life was very comfortable. Sarah recalled evenings when she would wander up the rambling drive of the Hall to meet her mother from her work. Father, already home from his labours, remained with little William. Greeting her mother, the two linked arms and dawdled homewards in contented silence, to find father waiting, son in arms, and the kettle singing on the hearth. The table was set for supper, after which evenings were spent lazily round the fireside, or if the weather was fine, on the small porch outside the cottage. There, they laughed, told tales, and exchanged the days news, until Sarah began to yawn, and had to follow young William up to bed.

One beautiful day in spring, William, nearly two years old, developed a chill. Despite his mothers care, his condition grew worse over the following days. He became listless and feverish. His eyes were unnaturally bright, and his cheeks flushed. Dr. Lindsay was called in from the village, and visited each day. On one such visit after his examining William, mother entered the kitchen, the Doctor following. She was white, her eyes were dark and stricken. She stumbled towards her husband, arms outstretched. She spoke in a flat tone:

"Matthew, the doctor says our son has the galloping sickness."

After the news had sunk in, everyone rallied around in

The Hall where My Father was Gardener

support of the family, and to ensure that little William was kept as comfortable and pain free as was possible. Mother devoted herself to his care. Gently sponging him when he was hot, tucking the covers about him when he shivered. She patiently coaxed nourishment into him, and made certain that he had milk and eggs, which the doctor said might benefit his condition. A large jug of fresh milk was sent from the Hall each morning especially for the boy. The doctor called frequently, and praised mother for her care and devotion. However, he voiced his concern over her own health, observing the dark rings beneath her eyes. She listened to his advice and nodded, and when he had left continued her labours, nursing her son around the clock, willing him to get better. Alas it was all to no avail. William continued to fade. His once chubby frame became wasted, his skin taking on a transparent look. Breathing was difficult for him, the cheeky smile was lost for ever, and the twinkling eyes were dull and lifeless. He responded only to his mother, and was apathetic to anyone or anything else. On the few occasions that father was able to relieve mothers vigil, he appeared to get little recognition from William. Bending low to whisper in his sons ear, or to coax some fluid past the parched lips he was rewarded with the odd glimmer of awareness at his voice, before William drifted back into his fevered state once more.

Sarah recalled that her time had been spent cleaning, keeping fresh linen supplied to the sick room, and attempting to ensure that her parents partook of the meals she prepared. She had been anxious that they did not fall sick themselves. Mother carried on tending for William every need. She insisted that he seemed to be improving each day. Father and Sarah stood by helplessly, realizing that William was unlikely to get well. And so it was, on a hot day in mid

August, the little boy finally gave up his struggle for life, and died in his mothers arms, Sarah and her father standing by.

The next few weeks had been a nightmare. Everyone mournful and silent, each one trying to come to terms with the tragedy in their own way. Sarah and father gradually began to pull themselves together. Not so mother. On the surface, she carried on with life, affectionate to her loved ones, and going about her household tasks with the usual care. But the sparkle that had been and her zest and light heartedness had gone, never to return. Sarah prayed each night for the return of her mother's good spirits, and at last it seemed to be happening, when to everyone's horror and despair, she too fell sick. The symptoms were almost identical to Williams. Father was distraught, and took time from his work to be with her. Sarah tended her mother, nursing her with warmth and gentleness. But, all her efforts were useless, despite fathers entreaties and tears, and Sarah's prayers, mother gave into the illness from the very start, having little desire to carry on living. In late December, the same year of her small son's death, she too succumbed , and died.

Sarah was shocked and bewildered, mechanically attending to the house work and to the needs of her father. His condition concerned everyone, stricken with grief and desolation, he sat, unshaven and wild looking, staring into space. Barely eating, he had to be led to his bed each night, and helped from it each morning like a young child. All that terrible winter it seemed to Sarah that she might lose him too. But, as Spring appeared, so father began to waken with it. His appearance improved, though the stoop of the shoulder, and the gaunt expression remained for many a long month. Still, his spirits lightened, and he spent more time in the gardens at the Hall, than he had for several weeks. Fortunately, his position there was secure.

Neither he nor Sarah could bring themselves to speak of their recent tragedy, but each one knew the others feel-ings, and a deep bond was formed between them, bringing them even closer than they had been before. They supported each other through the difficult times, and there were many, until at last, things took on some sort of normality again.

It was now two years later. Sarah was 13 years old. She had quite naturally assumed the role of caring for her father, and keeping the cottage comfortable and clean. She loved cooking, and also coped with the washing, ironing, and all the other chores involved in keeping house. She resembled her mother in appearance, with large grey eyes, pale skin and a mass of fair hair. Rather serious in manner, due no doubt to her experiences, she had a loving and understanding nature. Father relied on her, and doted on her, treating her with the utmost tenderness. The last two weeks he had worked outside in damp cold weather, and had developed a chesty cough. He was getting very little sleep, and had difficulty in digesting food or drink.

Sarah was very anxious about his condition, and was now awaiting Dr. Lindsay, whom she had called earlier in the day. The mantle clock struck 6 o'clock. Sarah started, disturbed from her thoughts. There was a loud knocking at the door. Scrambling to her feet, and smoothing down her dress, she hastened to answer it. Drawing back the bolt she pulled open the door, letting in an icy blast and a flurry of snow from without. Peering into the darkness, she recog-nized the tall figure of the doctor. He gently pushed past her into the house, removing his hat as he did so. Closing the door firmly behind him, he turned to Sarah smiling:

"Hello there young lady. I'd be obliged if you could take my coat, and maybe dry it off somewhere."

"Of course Dr. Lindsay. I'll hang it over this chair by the fire. I am sorry to bring you out on such an awful evening."

The doctor laid his hand on Sarah's shoulder. She had lost some weight he noted. Her eyes had dark circles beneath them, and her hands were roughened from housework and washing. He observed the clean and shining room, and caught the drift of an appetising smell from the cooking pot on the range. A remarkable child indeed, she certainly could use some good fortune in her young life. So much misfortune had befallen her already. He smiled down at her worried expression:

"No trouble, no trouble at all my dear. I am used to being called out at all times, and in all weathers. It is only a short walk from the village. Now, tell me about your father."

Sarah offered him a seat, and drew a stool up to sit beside him.

"Well, since your visit two days ago, I have tried to get him to take the medicine as you directed, but he doesn't keep it down.It's the same with food and drink, he cannot keep it down. He is so weak, I don't know what to do."

She buried her head in her hands and wept silently, her shoulders shaking. The doctor leaned forward and gently touched her hair.

"Is the cough still troublesome?"

" Yes, it is. Night times are the worst, he no sooner gets settled when it wakens him, and he tosses and turns much of the night after that. Day times are better, but not much."

Thoughtfully, the doctor rose and reached for his black bag from the table.

"He will be all right won't he?" There was desperation in Sarah's voice.

"I will be able to tell you more when I have taken a look at him, my dear. Tell me, is the cough dry, or does he produce any phlegm with it?"

Sarah grimaced. "He does cough up some nasty stuff. I leave a small bowl by the side of the bed. In fact I must empty it. Father has been quiet for a while, and I didn't want to disturb him."

Dr. Lindsay nodded. "His rest is important to him. Now, I suggest that you take me to him please. I will see what I can do for him, and put your mind at rest at the same time."

Sarah picked up the oil lamp, and moved past the doctor, through the door at the foot of the stairs. Holding the lamp high, she went carefully up ahead of him, guiding him into fathers room. Setting the lamp down near the bed, she made her way to the small fireplace and busied herself with the embers there, trying to coax some life into them. The room was warm, despite the rattling of the windows, from the howling wind still raging outside. The fire soon produced a few steady flames with her effort. Sarah went over and joined the doctor at her fathers bedside. They both looked down on him. He lay , a film of sweat on his brow. His hair clung to his forehead, and the face was grey with exhaustion. Although asleep his limbs twitched feverishly beneath the covers. Suddenly, sensing he was being observed, he opened his eyes. His gaze fell on Sarah, then moved to the doctor. With a weak smile, he attempted to raise himself in the bed. Dr. Lindsay gently, but firmly pushed him back onto the pillows.

"No no, please. Don't try to move yourself, just lie still.

I have to examine you, and can manage very well with you lying down."

Before commencing his examination of the patient, the doctor lifted the bowl from the bedside table. Raising the corner of the cloth that covered it, he took a glance at the contents it held, before replacing it.

"Now, young man, lets be taking a look at you."

Delving into his bag he removed his stethoscope, and a notebook and pencil. With Sarah's help, he loosened the patients nightshirt, and placed the stethoscope to his chest, listening carefully for any abnormal sounds. After asking the invalid to turn on his side please, he repeated the procedure at the rear, sounding the lungs from behind. Whilst Sarah set father back into a comfortable position, the doctor wrote busily in his notes. Then, he felt gently behind his patient's ears, under the ears, and finally, asking Sarah to bring the lamp nearer, asked father to open his mouth and say *"AHHH* "

He then peered deeply into his throat, after which he noted down his findings. Closing the notebook, he moved to rinse his hands in the bowl of water that Sarah had made ready for him. Placing his equipment back in the bag, he closed it with a snap, and drew a chair up to the bedside. Beckoning Sarah to come closer, he looked at her, then at father:

"My friends. You will be pleased to know that the worst is over. You , Matthew , are on the mend, and although it may be sometime before you are completely fit, fit you will be. You have the best of nurses here in young Sarah, who will not rest until you are strong and healthy once more. Yes my man, you have many good years ahead of you yet."

Sarah smiled through her tears, and clasped father's hand.

"That is marvellous news Dr. Lindsay. Thank you so much for your trouble and kindness. Now I can look forward to fathers recovery, I will get him well as soon as I can."

The doctor smiled and stood up. He shook father's hand.

"I Shall prescribe a mild sedative which will enable you to get some rest, and also help to soothe your cough. Now, have you any questions for me?"

Matthew Pearson looked up at the doctor with tired, grateful eyes.

"I should like to thank you too doctor. The news is a relief certainly. It would be wonderful to sleep through the night. However I do have difficulty in keeping anything down, be it solid or liquid, so is this going to be any different, this medicine of yours?"

"Your lungs are almost clear now. You have been ridding yourself of the troublesome matter which was causing difficulty in digestion. Your appetite will improve rapidly, and there should be no problem taking the mixture".

Raising his hand in a farewell gesture, he made to leave the room. Sarah blew her father a kiss as she followed his figure out of the door.

On reaching the kitchen once more, Sarah prepared a warm drink for her visitor, before he made his way once more into the winters night. The doctor was already busy with some powders and potions which he had taken from his bag. With his experienced eye he measured the required items, placed them in a small basin, and carefully stirred them for several minutes. Producing a suitably sized bottle, he slowly poured the mixture into it, labelling it with clear instructions for use. Closing the bag, he smiled gratefully as Sarah handed him a cup of tea.

"Thank you dear, most welcome. It still sounds very wild outside. I will be relieved to get home. Hopefully there will be no emergencies tonight for me to deal with."

He finished his tea, and Sarah helped him on with his coat, which had almost completely dried. He buttoned himself up to his chin, and took his hat from Sarah at the door, jamming it tightly onto his head. With a large muffler wound round his neck several times, only the tip of his nose was visible as he stepped over the threshold into the snow.
He mumbled through the layers of clothes.

"Good-night little lady, try not to worry. I will endeavour to call again tomorrow. Now, hurry along inside or you will take a chill too, and that won't do."

"Goodnight Doctor, and thank you. Don't slip on the ice now."

Turning back into the house, she secured the bolt on the door, and went over to the table. Pouring herself a large cup of hot tea, she added two spoonfuls of sugar for a special treat. Making herself comfortable on the fender seat, she relaxed for the first time in several days. A weight had been lifted from her heart, knowing her father would recover. For a while she had been afraid of losing him too, like her mother and William. She reached for the bottle of medicine from the table, and studied the directions on the label. It would be better to wait and give father a dose at bed time, he seemed to be resting at the moment. Glancing at the clock, she saw that it was a quarter to seven. Too early for her bed. She had to be awake to administer the medicine later on. Rising from her spot by the fire, she found her work basket, and sorted out some mending. Shirts of father's needing buttons, and some thick stockings for darning. Turning up the lamp, she worked her way through her tasks, and became so engrossed that when she next looked at the time it was nearly nine–o–clock. Packing away the work, she banked up the fire, and closed it for the night. Going to the window, she tried to determine the state of the weather outside, but she could see nothing but backness. The wind still howled and moaned among the creaking trees, telling her there wasn't much improvement. Pulling the curtains together, she turned and picked up the bottle of mixture. Extinguishing the oil lamp, she lit a candle, and giving a last look around the room, made her way upstairs.

In father's room the firelight flickered, sending shadows dancing on the walls. Checking the label by the light of the candle, Sarah bent and gently touched her father's shoulder. He awakened immediately. Seeing his daughter, he smiled.

"Ah, this is the dreadful medicine then."

"I hope it doesn't taste too bad father, just one spoonful. It will be worth it if you get a good night's sleep."

The spoonful was taken without ado, then, making sure that her father settled, with everything he needed at hand for the night, Sarah bent and kissed him on the brow.

"Goodnight father, God bless, and sleep well."

"Goodnight my little angel, thank you. I hope your night is peaceful too."

He closed his eyes, and Sarah crept from the room. She went straight to her bed, scarcely having the energy to remove her clothes, before climbing between the covers and falling into a deep sleep. The next thing she was was aware of was opening her eyes to a room filled with daylight. Blinking the sleep from her eyes, she hopped out of bed and over to the window, gasping when her bare feet felt the cold linoleum. She drew back the curtains, and scraped the ice from the window pane. The scene that faced her filled her with wonder. A blanket of snow covered the world. White and unspoiled under a pale wintry sun. No sign of the previous night's storm. The sky was blue, scattered with fluffy clouds. It was beautiful!

Suddenly conscious of her bare toes on the cold floor, she darted across the room, and hastened into some warm clothes, finishing by pulling on her thick woollen stockings and ankle boots. Looking at the clock she was concerned to see that it was nine–o–clock. Twelve hours since she had last attended to father. There was no sound from his room, which was unusual at this hour of the morning. With some apprehension she tip–toed along the landing to his door. Pushing it open, she entered and went to the bed.

He lay, his head to one side, breathing easily. He still slept peacefully. Sarah felt his forehead, and found it cool to her touch. She settled the covers around his shoulders, and made to steal from the room unheard.

"Good morning, my little one."

"Father, good morning . I'm sorry if I awakened you, I think you slept very well last night."

"I did indeed. I feel quite refreshed this morning, and even a little hungry."

"That is marvellous! I will prepare something light and tasty for your breakfast. I'll be back directly."

Dropping a kiss on his forehead, she tripped from the room. Once in the kitchen, she busied herself in preparation of an appetizing breakfast for the invalid. Within a short time, Sarah returned to her father, laden with a tray. She had set it prettily with a snowy white cloth. A lightly boiled egg sat in a blue china egg cup, surrounded with thin fingers of buttered toast. A steaming mug of sweet tea, just how father liked it, stood in a, saucer of blue and white. Sarah set it down on the bedside table. She helped raise her father on his pillows to a comfortable position for eating, and placed the tray on the bed, within his reach. She sat beside him, ready to give assistance if he required. But, he managed very nicely, eating, the toast slowly, and taking small spoonfuls of egg. after almost finishing the food, he took up the mug of tea, and completely drained it. Sarah was delighted.

"Oh, well done father."

Taking the tray from the bed, she plumped up the pillows. Dusting any stray crumbs from his chin with a clean napkin, she straightened the covers about him, and with a final sweet smile, she gathered up the tray and left the room.

Matthew Pearson closed his eyes when she had gone. He let his mind drift, as he floated between sleep and wake–fulness. He thought of Elizabeth his wife, as a young wife and mother, with baby Sarah. Later William too, completing their happy family, enjoying their lives, no thought of disas–ter in anyone's mind. Then, when tragedy had struck, doubly, how devastated he had been. Neglectful of everyone and everything around him, even dear Sarah, who had given him total devotion. She was so like her mother, he reflected. Things would be different from now on. He would let her know how much he loved and needed her. He fell into a contented sleep.

Days passed. Matthew maintained his improvement. Each day, Sarah contrived fresh delightful dishes for his nourishment, and was rewarded by an increasingly healthy appetite. The day came when he was allowed downstairs, with Sarahs help. At ease in his arm chair, beside the fire, he smiled at his daughter, fussing around him like a little mother.

On one such day, at around three–o–clock, both were sitting in the flickering firelight. Matthew gazing into the flames, and Sarah at his knee, sitting on the floor, lazily contemplating some unfinished mending in her lap. Suddenly her father spoke.

"Sarah my child, how would you like to visit your aunt in Sidmouth?"

Sarah stared up at him in surprise. About to reply, she stopped as he went on:

"For some time, I have been thinking a trip to the coast would benefit both of us. Your mother has a sister in Sidmouth; I will write to her and suggest that we might pay her a visit. How do you like the idea."?

Sarah remained silent for some time. In fact Matthew was about to repeat his question, when she spoke,

"It sounds wonderful. But is it possible. Can we afford it, and will my aunt mind having us there, and.......?"

"There there girl, one question at a time. We are not without a small amount of savings, thanks to your dear mother's careful management of the household finances. I too put a little by when I was able, so..... all in all, we are quite comfortably off. When I am completely well, I shall find work again, and start earning once more. There is nothing to keep us from going if we wish to. As to your last question, your aunt has talked of little else since your dear mother died, she will delight in having us there. The only question is, how do you feel about leaving all our friends and thc village you have known all your life? If the idea horrifies you please say so, we will mention it no more."

Sarah clasped her hands and looked at him with shining eyes:

"I love the idea Father. How wonderful! Of course it will be hard to leave our friends, but we have each other, that's the important thing and it will feel so good to meet my mother's sister. I know I shall love her, I hope she likes me."

They laughed and hugged each other in anticipation, and Matthew assured his daughter that her aunt would be delighted with her, as everyone was.

The letter was duly written and sent. Days lengthened and Spring showed in the fields and hedgerows. Matthew grew stronger each day, and planning to visit his sister in law with Sarah, gave him some of the sparkle back that had been lacking of late. Friends were told, and agreed that the whole idea was the best possible way to make a fresh start for both of them. There was some sadness at the thought of parting, but some day, God willing, they would meet again.

One day in late March, young Harry raced up from the village and banged on the front door of the cottage. Too breathless to utter a word, he clutched a grey envelope in his grubby hand, addressed to Matthew Pearson, Esquire. All the local post came through the general store in the village, and as letters from any distance were few and far between, this one with a Sidmouth postmark had the locals "buzzing" with the possible contents, even before Matthew had opened it himself. Sarah fidgeted with impatience, whilst Matthew seemed to take an age to read the details. Finally, she could contain herself no longer.

"Well Father, well? Please. I must know what the news is. You have read it so thoroughly, you must know every word."

Father laughed. "All right then Miss. Calm yourself, and I will read it to you":-

My dear Matthew,how delightful to hear from you, and to learn that you are once more in good health. Of course you

will be more than welcome to visit , and bring my darling niece to meet me. I trust you will decide to remain permanently, once you have discovered what a lovely spot this is. There will be work a plenty for you later Matthew, when you feel up to it. Farming and fishing are in abundance here, whichever takes your fancy. I so look forward to seeing you both, at the earliest possible date.

I remain your loving sister,

Laura

He folded the letter carefully, and looked at Sarah.

"I knew that your aunt would welcome a visit from us, all that remains now, is for us to set a date for our departure, and say our farewells, pack our belongings, and be on our way."

"How long before we go Father?"

"Well, let me think now. It should be possible for us to travel in about three weeks. By then Spring will be well on, the journey will be prettier, and the days longer. How does that sound to you my lady?"

"Three weeks! However will everything be ready in time? There is so much to think of. But of course Father dear, you are so right. April, a lovely month, with daffodils in the fields, lambs just born, and everything fresh and new, like ourselves making a fresh beginning."

Sarah ran to him and gave him a warm hug.

"I must make a list of all the things to do, I'm sure to forget something important otherwise".

Sarah ran off, her head full of details and plans, of tasks to be done, and matters to be settled.

Matthew sat down and read his sister's letter once more. He was sure that they were doing the right thing in moving away. This village held too many poignant memories for both of them. He remembered Laura as being a pleasant kind–hearted woman, when he had met her years ago. Sarah needed a woman's influence, she missed her mother sorely. Laura certainly seemed to be looking forward to their visit. He stood up and put the letter in his pocket. Now he too must make some plans, and do some arranging of matters. He smiled to himself. In three weeks everything would be done, they would be on their way to new surroundings, new friends, and a new way of life.

2

MAKING READY

A day was set for the departure. Matthew obtained train tickets, and brought down a large trunk from the attic, for the use of any items which could be packed in advance of the journey. Small items of bric–a–brac with special sentimental meaning to them, family photographs, warm clothes discarded until next winter, several books, including the family Bible, and a favourite cookery book of Sarah's, inherited from her mother. Other items such as linen, curtains and furnishings, pots and pans were sold by Matthew for a minimal sum to the young couple who would now be renting the cottage. The man would be taking Matthews place as gardener at the Hall, and with a wife, and baby on the way , he was only too pleased to be offered such well cared for furnishings for such a low price. His rent would be a paltry amount, as the cottage was tied to his job.

Came the day before they were to leave. The morning was spent calling on friends to say their farewells. A few tears were shed, and Sarah was hugged and kissed so many times she was quite overcome with it all. It was with some relief that they reached the final house, belonging to Dr. Lindsay. Pushing open the gate, Sarah led the way up the narrow path to the front door. Matthew lifted the knocker and rapped sharply. The door was opened by Mrs Wilkins, the housekeeper. Beaming all over her rosy face she ushered them into the hall, and announced them to the doctor who was enjoying a short break from his busy round of patients.

He rose from his chair by the fire, and put down his newspaper. He held out his hands in greeting.

"My dear friends, thank you for calling. Please take a seat. Can I ask Mrs Wilkins to bring you some light refreshment perhaps?"

"No thank you, doctor, we have just come to pay our respects, and to say our farewells."

"Ah, of course, the big day tomorrow. You must be quite excited. All your friends here will miss you very much you know. However, I am sure that you are doing the right thing by making a new life away from here, where so many painful memories must haunt you both. I do wish you the very best of good fortune."

Father murmured his thanks. The doctor went over to a writing bureau standing beneath the window. He unlocked it and reached inside, bringing forth a small package wrapped carelessly in brown paper. Going up to Sarah, he solemnly gave her the packet.

"I hope you will accept this small token young lady, and remember me whenever you should happen to use it."

"Why, Dr. Lindsay, how very kind of you. Thank you so much."

Sarah unwrapped the parcel, quite touched at his kindness. Inside she found a small journal, bound in smart green leather. Opening it to the first page, she read the following inscription, in the doctors copperplate hand:

> *To my young friend Sarah Pearson. May these pages be filled with recordings of happy times, and pleasant thoughts in the days to come. I remain a constant admirer, George H. Lindsay.*

With tears in her eyes, Sarah reached up and hugged

him, thanking him once again. Father also voiced his thanks, saying, that his daughter would get much pleasure from the gift.

"Now, Sarah my dear, we really must be away, there are still things to be done before tomorrow. Come now."

Mrs Wilkins was summoned, to see the pair to the door. The doctor joined them as they stepped outside, and their last sight was of the old gentleman and his rosy faced housekeeper waving their goodbyes from the doorway. Back at the cottage, Sarah brewed a good strong pot of tea. She brought it over to the table, where her father was sitting reading a letter, which had been lying on the doormat when they entered . He drew his breath in amazement at the contents.

"I cannot believe it!"

"Is everything all right Father?"

"Indeed it is. Marvellous! It is a letter of appreciation and farewell from Sir Richard and Lady Mary up at the Hall, they have enclosed a sum of twenty pounds. To help us get started in our new life."

"People have been very kind, haven't they Father?"

"We have some good friends." Father agreed.

While he was still lost in contemplation of the letter, Sarah cleared the cups, replenished the fire, and gathered up her shawl from the table by the door.

"Father, I have to go out for a few minutes, I won' t be long. "

Leaving Matthew to his thoughts, she stole quietly out of the door. Taking the pathway at the side of the house, she wended her way down the leafy track, filled with clumps of daffodils, and wild primroses. Birds chattered amongst the budding branches, and the spring sun shone warmly down.

Cutting across a small field, shutting the creaky gate carefully behind her, she came at last to the churchyard. Entering, she stood for a moment quietly. Then, taking a deep breath, she wandered on, amongst the gravestones. Most were old, and their inscriptions faded. Sarah tried to make out some of the names as she passed by, and picture who they had been, and what they had looked like. Suddenly she came to small plot of earth tended carefully, with a white cross reaching up into the sunlight. Clearing away some dead leaves, she studied the words on the cross:

> ***Here lies Elizabeth Pearson aged 34 yrs. beloved wife and mother, and her son William aged 23 months. May they rest together in peace.***

Bending her head, Sarah said a prayer, then spoke aloud to her Mother.

"I do miss you so much Mother, and little William too. Even though Father and I are going away, you will both always be with us. Our friends have promised to tend this spot, and keep it bright with flowers."

Noticing fresh flowers in the small jar, she realised that father must have visited earlier. She lay her small bunch of primroses at the foot of the cross. Standing up, she stared for sometime at the grave, choking back her tears, before turning swiftly and hurrying away.

After tea Matthew piled the cases together near the door, so that none would be forgotten the next morning. He sat out for the last time on the porch, puffing on his pipe. The evening was pleasantly warm, and passers by called out greetings and good wishes as they made their way home from work. Sarah remained inside. She wished to spend her

The cemetery where Sarah makes her last Farewell

last evening with all her familiar surroundings to herself. She sat, dreaming, every now and then her gazc would travel round the room, hungrily taking in all the old comfortable things, she had grown up with, and learned to take for granted. The wooden highchair in the corner, once hers and then Williams.

She could see him now, his dimpled arms banging the tray in anticipation of his food. And the bright rug made of coloured pieces of rag which Mother had spent hours making patiently. Also the flowered curtains which she had helped her mother to hem, and how proud they had been when they were hung at the window, in all their glory! She rose, and climbed the stairs. Fathers room had once been mothers too, with a large bed in it, and a crib for William. Sunday mornings, Sarah used to make tea for her parents, and take it to their room, where she and William would have a romp on the bed, mother and father joining in, before going downstairs for a filling breakfast, prepared by mother. The sound of father down stairs interrupted her reflections, and she hastened down to get him a hot bedtime drink. It was only nine-o-clock, but they had a long day ahead of them tomorrow, and a good night's sleep was important. They stood, arms about each other, taking a look at this room, which had known laughter and tears, then Matthew turned out the lamp, and they climbed the stairs, Sarah holding the candle.

"Goodnight father, sleep well."

"You too dear, good-night and God bless you."

The big day dawned, bright and beautiful. After a hasty breakfast, neither one being able to eat properly for excitement, Sarah helped her father stack the luggage outside the front door. Mr. Darby the carrier was coming to collect them, and the cases,to take them to the railway station. Sarah checked, to ensure that the house was in order for the new tenants who would arrive later that morning. The fire was glowing, pots and pans shone. Furniture gleamed, and smelt faintly of lavender, and a vase of wild flowers adorned the window sill. Sighing with satisfaction, she turned to leave. A last glance round the door, before shutting it, leaving the keys in the lock for the arrival of the new couple.

In the distance, Sarah heard the sound of a horse and cart, and sure enough a few minutes later she made out the familiar shape of the carrier's conveyance on the brow of the hill. As it approached, Sarah recognised the lean tall figure of Mr. Darby seated leisurely up front, the reins held loosely in his hands. He brought the horse to a halt, and raised his arm in greeting to Sarah.

"Mornin' Miss Sarah, fine bright mornin' for you".

Mr Darby the carrier arrives to take them to Sidmouth

Sarah nodded in agreement. Her father appeared from around the side of the house, having been surveying his small vegetable patch for the last time. He greeted the carrier who descended from his cart to help load the cases. Having secured them onto the rear of the wagon, Mr. Darby climbed up to his seat , reaching down to assist Sarah, father helping raise her from behind. Lastly, Matthew himself stepped up and sat next to his daughter. Sarah felt so proud and happy, up high on the cart, Mr Darby one side of her, and father the other. The carrier took the reins. Glancing at his passengers to make sure of their comfort and safety, he urged the horse into a slow trot.

"Get along there Ginnie, away we go then."

As the cart speeded up, and neared the curve in the road, Sarah and her father both turned for their last glimpse of the home they had known for the past several years. The cottage, small and white, with its chimney smoking, nestled amongst the leafy green trees. Its square windows shone out at them, like eyes. Then it disappeared as they rounded the bend in the lane.

Settling back in their seats, they relaxed. The nearest railway station was several miles away, so the time could be enjoyed, surveying the Suffolk countryside in all its spring glory. It was just after 10 o'clock on a Saturday morning. The road was busy with farmers, and pedlars on their way to the market. Mothers and children in bright bonnets, flower sellers, decorated carts laden with rolls of linen, silk ,and coloured ribbons.

They passed a jolly man selling balloons, all shapes and colours, and a caravan with a beaded curtain concealing "Madame Rosa" the fortune teller. Skilfully, Mr. Darby manoeuvred his conveyance through this crowded stretch of thoroughfare, until once more they were out, among the fields and scattered cottages beyond. The sun shone down, birds sang, Mr. Darby whistled some tuneless air, and the road stretched before them, like a silver ribbon.

Some two hours later, they were standing on the platform of the tiny railway station, the train about to arrive. A friendly porter had charge of the baggage, and all that was left to worry about was boarding the train. The large engine thundered to a standstill, amid clouds of steam. Sarah and Matthew moved to an open door, where a smart lady was alighting. The porter assisted the two of them into the carriage, and slammed the door behind them. Minutes later, the guard blew his whistle, and they were on their way.

The journey was a long one. They had to change trains at London which was quite exciting. The station there was huge, and bustling with people. It was very noisy though, and Sarah was relieved to board the final train with father, and shut out the clamour and dust of London.

Each of them had a doze during the journey, even though Sarah had resolved to keep awake. Their fellow passengers were a quiet, elderly couple, who kept themselves to themselves for the most part. They opened a small food hamper at one point of the journey, and offered Sarah some chocolate, after which the woman occupied herself with some knitting, whilst her husband read his book, and took frequent naps between.

The countryside flashed by. Gradually its aspect took on a change, the green of the trees seemed lighter in colour, the fields and hills rolled into the distance in neat cultivated patterns, and the soil grew reddish in hue as the West Country got closer. By this time, the sun had long passed its peak, and the sky was turning pink, promising a beautiful sunset.

Shadows lengthened across the meadows, and the cattle made their way home for evening milking. Father was asleep, as was the elderly gentleman opposite. The woman leant over and spoke in a whisper to Sarah.

"Not much further now young lady. Have you travelled very far?"

"From Suffolk, a little village called Stowmarket, we've been travelling since ten o'clock this morning."

"That's a long time. We have come down from London. My daughter lives in Sidmouth, and she has just had her first child, a little boy. Our first grandchild. We simply had to make a visit to see them."

"How lovely, we are going to stay with my aunt in Sidmouth, I have never met her. I am very excited."

"Your Mother will follow later on?"

Sarah spoke quietly.

"She died two years ago, and my little brother. We are going to make a new life in Sidmouth with my mother's sister."

" Oh, my dear, how tactless of me, how rude. I wish you all the joy and good health in your new life."

"Thank you, I hope you have a pleasant visit too, with your daughter and your grandchild."

The train gradually changed its rhythm, as it started to slow down. Sarah gently roused father. The pair opposite began to gather their belongings about them, the knitting was folded neatly into a carpet bag, and the gentleman took down his hat and umbrella from the rack above them. Father assisted them with the small hamper basket. He brought down cloaks and a small bag of their own, and Sarah took out a tiny mirror to study her appearance, apart from looking rather tired, and having a black spot of soot on her chin, she would do very well.

They all sat back and waited, as the wheels on the train ground to a halt. Father and Sarah shook hands with their travelling companions, and the woman pecked Sarah on the cheek, wishing them both well.

Standing up, father reached for the door of the carriage. He turned to his daughter.

"This is it my dear, are you ready?"

Sarah nodded, and swallowed deeply, she rose and went and grasped her father's hand in sympathetic accord. The door opened and they stepped out.

3

NEW BEGINNINGS

Laura Fairchild looked forward eagerly to the arrival of her brother–in–law Matthew and his daughter, travelling all the way from a little village in Suffolk to stay with her here in her Sidmouth home. Since his letter a few weeks ago, she had been telling her friends that she was expecting close relations to reside with her for an indefinite period. And now the day had finally come when they would arrive. A tall striking figure of a woman, Laura had never married. She had delighted in her sister Elizabeth's wedding to Matthew, and in the news of Sarah's birth and later William's.

Matthew and she had met some years ago, at the wedding, but she had seen neither of the children, the distance to travel being somewhat great. However she had some pictures of them, taken at various times over the years. That is of course until the tragedy that had taken her sister and the baby so suddenly, leaving poor Matthew and her young niece so bereft. Laura could think of nothing nicer than taking them into her home, after all she had plenty of room, and the place could do with young people in it.

The house itself was tall and narrow, grey brick with red gables. It stood in its own small grounds facing the sea. Until recently Laura had taken paying guests in the season, and had done very well with this, enabling her to finally buy her house outright. Now she was getting older, and did not want the bother of the hustle and bustle of strangers in the privacy of her domain. So, apart from a young woman who came in and cleaned for her, and cooked the occasional meal if dinner guests were expected, she lived alone. A good few years older than Elizabeth, she had always been the protector. There was some similarity in appearance, though Laura had accumulated several grey hairs with her extra years.

The hours passed, the train carrying the visitors was due to reach Sidmouth some time in the early evening, after travelling since morning the pair of them would be somewhat weary. It was now six o'clock, although still daylight, dusk would fall before long. Laura threw a light cape around her shoulders and left the house. Going to the driveway at the side, she unlocked the door of her pride and joy, a small motor car ! Driving had come easily to her, and in no time at all she had mastered it and was a familiar sight locally. Now, she produced the starting handle, put it into place, and skilfully threw the engine into action after a couple of cranks. Quickly slipping into the car, she took the wheel and backed down the drive.

Within minutes the station was in sight. Laura parked the car neatly in front of the small building, which housed the ticket office, and the single waiting room. A few people stood around, and there were some transactions going on at the window where tickets were available. Laura walked through the station to the platform, she found a seat and sat down, glancing up at the large clock as she did so. Nearly a quarter past six. The train was about due. Now the time had come she felt rather nervous, silly, but that's how it was. She was about to come face to face with her sister's husband, and their child, and had no idea what to expect, or if she was doing the right thing in taking them into her home. She sat on the edge of the seat twisting her hands in her lap, and biting the corner of her lip like a young girl. Suddenly the train sounded in the distance, and the platform filled with people. Laura rose to her feet. Within seconds clouds of steam filled the atmosphere, and the large engine ground to a halt noisily. There was much activity, doors were opened, then slammed shut. Porters busily wheeled their trolleys, conveying baggage from the train, accompanied by weary passengers dragging by their sides, pleased to have arrived, but anxious to get out of the station, and to their destinations as soon as possible.

Laura, nerves forgotten, craned her neck and attempted to peer through the thinning vapour.. Then, she saw them coming towards her in the gloom. No mistaking Sarah who looked so like Elizabeth, it brought a lump to her throat. And Matthew, little changed over the years it seemed, but looking thinner and more stooped than Laura remembered. She rushed forward, her arms out stretched:

"My dears!"

"Laura, how good it is to see you, and to be at the end of our journey."

Matthew clasped the outstretched hands, then leant forward putting his arms around her and hugging her warmly. He stepped back and brought Sarah forward, who was standing shyly in the background.

" My dear sister, this is your niece Sarah. Sarah, this is your Aunt Laura."

Sarah took her aunt's hand and looked up at her with large eyes, Elizabeth's eyes. She studied her aunt's face, and seeing the kindly, slightly anxious expression, and the trace of a tear on her cheek, loved her immediately. She reached up to kiss her, and was gathered closely in a fervent em–

brace.

"I am so pleased to meet you, aunt Laura." She managed to say between hugs. Laura at last released her and spoke:

"It is a delight to have you both here at last, I have dreamed of it often. Now I think it is time for home, and supper for you two weary travellers."

With a wave of her hand she beckoned to a porter and the luggage was transferred by trolley through the station to the waiting car. Matthew and Sarah stared in undisguised admiration at the machine. Between them, Matthew and Laura secured the cases with straps to the back of the car, then Sarah and her father were bundled inside, whilst Laura started up the engine. Once in the driving seat she smiled warmly at each of them.

"Right my dears, lets get home."

In a short time they were pulling into the driveway by the house. It was dark by now, so the building wasn't visible, but a friendly light shone through the glass in the door, giving the impression of a welcoming home coming, which indeed it turned out to be. The front door was flung wide open, showing a small square hallway, carpeted and furnished with an elegant coat rack and a profusion of greenery in pots. At one end hung a long mirror, and by its side was a doorway half hidden by a heavy blue curtain.

All the luggage was brought into the hall by father, Laura going ahead, leading Sarah by the hand towards the curtained door. Pulling the drapes to one side, she opened the door and stepped in. Moving toward the brightly burning fire, she reached up and lit the gas mantle over the fireplace. Staight away the room came alive in its golden glow. Sarah still remained in the doorway staring about her, until Matthew gently pushed her from behind. He too looked around at the pleasing sight before them.

Although small, several mirrors placed thoughtfully in the right positions gave the impression of space. Furniture was arranged tastefully, and shone with care. Two comfortable sofas stood in front of the fire on a pretty patterned rug, and between was a low, square table set with refreshment. Crusty white bread, with butter and a large wedge of cheese, and to the side a joint of cold ham for carving. A pot of tea was keeping hot in the hearth.

"Come now, make yourselves at home, this is your home now too. I am sure you must be in need of some food and drink, so please sit down, and help yourselves. And later I will show you your rooms, and you can unpack. Let me relieve you of your hats and cloaks."

Sarah and Matthew moved in a daze. The long tiring day was beginning to catch up with them. And the sight of the pleasant meal in the cosy surroundings filled them with a delightful feeling of weariness. However, on sitting down and beginning to sample the delicious fare, they were revived somewhat, and luxuriated in the warmth of the fire, and being waited on by Laura. Sipping cups of hot tea, after satisfying their appetites, both looked at Laura with gratitude. No words were spoken this night, the pair being too sleepy for conversation. There would be plenty of time for that in the days to come. Now, rest was the important thing. Somehow Sarah found herself with her cases in a cosy room with a slanting ceiling, and an inviting looking bed. In no time, she had shed her clothes, grabbed a nightgown from a case, and fallen into bed, not even thinking to brush her teeth. She fell asleep immediately.

Matthew was led to his room also by Laura, who,

having bade him a very good night, left him to himself. He observed his room with interest, laying his belongings on the bed. He would unpack in the morning, after a night's sleep. Going to the small wash stand in the corner of the room, he splashed his face with warm water from the china bowl there, and dried himself on the towel provided. Then going to the bed he turned back the covers, revealing snowy white sheets. Removing his clothes and , folding them carefully, he placed them on the chair by the bed. Donning a nightshirt, he put his case beneath the foot of the bed, until tomorrow when he could unpack at his leisure. Climbing into the soft bed, Matthew thanked God for their safe arrival, and for the kindness of Laura. He closed his eyes, and dropped into a deep dreamless sleep.

Sarah stirred and opened her eyes, squinting at the shaft of sunlight, shining through a chink in the curtains right on to her pillow. She sat up in bed, a little confused at her surroundings. Ah, now she recalled where she was. Gazing at the untidy pile of clothes she had discarded the night before, she hurriedly arose. Just about to wash herself at the pretty little carved wash stand, she was interrupted by a knock on her door. At her reply it opened and Aunt Laura stepped in with a jug of steaming hot water.

"Good morning Sarah, I trust you slept well. Here is some hot water for you. In future you will be able to fetch it yourself from the bathroom along the passage. But this morning I took the liberty of bringing it to you myself. There will be some breakfast downstairs in about half an hour. Is there anything else you need my dear?"

"Oh no thank you very much , Aunt, everything's wonderful, and I slept so comfortably. I have to unpack, then I will be downstairs directly. Is my father awake yet? It must be quite late."

Laura informed her that it was nearly nine o'clock, and that her father was already shaving in his own room.

Ablutions and unpacking completed, Sarah left her room to look for Matthew. She found him in the next room along to her own, on the point of seeking her out to go downstairs together. He kissed her warmly, and taking her hand, accompanied her downstairs.

"In here, dears."

Laura's voice reached them from a room at the back of the house. Entering together , they found themselves in a tiny dining room , filled by an enormous polished table. One end of this was set with two places for breakfast. An appetising smell drifted along the hallway from somewhere beyond the dining room, evidently the kitchen. Matthew and Sarah couldn't help sniffing appreciatively. Laura saw them seated at the table, and left, returning with a fully laden tray. Matthew hastened to relieve her of it, and set it down on the sideboard as she directed. Bidding them help themselves, she concerned herself with pouring three cups of tea. Placing them in front of each one, and including one for herself, she sat alongside whilst they ate a hearty breakfast. At last they pushed the plates aside with satisfied sighs. Re-filling the cups with tea, and taking a sip, Laura spoke.

"It does my heart good to see food enjoyed so much, it feels so right to see you both sitting at my, at our table I should say. I hope you feel just as content."

Matthew arose from the table, and went to her, taking her hand in his , replied:

"Indeed we do my dear, you have made us feel so welcome, and , in fact , I am so well fed, I think if I ate another morsel I should burst."

They all laughed. Rising, Sarah began to clear the

dishes from the table, but was halted gently by her Aunt.

"Leave that dear, young Millie will be along at ten o' clock, and will see to things, come along both of you, we will be comfortable in the parlour. The fire kept in last night, so it is warm in there."

The room they had eaten in the previous evening, looked surprisingly different by day. Sunshine pervaded the scene, and the result was bright and cheerful. Laura gave the fire a poke or two, and it sent fingers of flame darting amongst the coals. Patting the seat beside her on the sofa, she invited Sarah to sit down. Matthew took his place on the opposite side of the fire. He spoke first:

"You have a beautiful home, Laura."

She inclined her head in thanks.

"I think so. My home is now your home, we must establish that. I want you to be happy here, and to get to know you thoroughly, after all , you two are all the family I have. I neglected seeing my sister for too long, and then, it was too late. I cannot forgive myself for that. Therefore the very least I can do is to share my home with you both, her beloved family."

Matthew sat silent in thought, and Sarah ventured to speak:

"We will be happy here, I know we will. Mother spoke of you often, you look a little like her."

Here Sarah swallowed with emotion, and her aunt drew her close in comfort.

"Time enough for chatting, all the time in the world. I want to hear all your stories, and about the village you were so happy in, and the cottage, and all your friends you had to leave behind. Everything, but not now. When you feel more able to talk to me, and know me a little better. The important thing is, how would you like to spend your first day?"

Before either could answer, there was a light tap at the door and a young slim girl entered the room, giving a slight curtsey.

"Morning Miss Laura, madam"

"Good morning , Millie. I would like you to meet my dear brother, Matthew, and my niece Sarah, from now on this will be their home. My dears, this is my good friend Millie. She cleans for me, and cooks the occasional meal, and fills me in on all the local gossip."

"Ooh, Miss Laura! Pleased to meet you , Mr. Matthew and you too,Miss Sarah, I'm sure." She gave another little bob and left the room. Laura excused herself and followed Millie, to give some necessary instructions for the day. Sarah and her father were left alone.

"Aunt Laura is wonderful isn't she Father?"

"Yes, she is, a lovely lady. We are lucky. Well , what shall we do today ?"

"I think I have to look at the sea, will you come with me?"

"Try to stop me. We must collect our cloaks and hats from upstairs, in case the sea breeze is fresh. And take our leave of your aunt, let her know our plans."

Father and Sarah donned their walking clothes and met with Laura in the hall, on her way from the kitchen. She approved of their idea to visit the sea, and informed them it was but a hundred yards from the front of the house. Saying their goodbyes, Laura reminded them there would be a light lunch for them at one o'clock. Stepping out into the sunlight, the two of them breathed deeply, and took in the good salt air from the ocean. On reaching the gate Sarah turned and looked at their new home. She thought it beautiful !

The First Glimpse of the Ocean was a Magnificent Sight

Tripping alongside Matthew, she hadn't felt so light–hearted in months, and looking up at her father saw that he too looked relaxed and happy.

Crossing a narrow road, and rounding a bend, they suddenly came upon the ocean. Sarah gasped. She had never seen anything so vast, or magnificent. Matthew was taken aback also, as he had not seen the sea since he was a small boy, and could not really remember it. Hand in hand they stepped down on to the narrow strip of shingle, and walked slowly toward the shining mass of water. Standing at its brink they remained silent, not wishing to spoil the magic of the moment . Gradually Matthew became aware of small fishing craft a little way out at sea. He watched with interest, noting how skilfully the nets were cast over the side, and how the fishermen sang, and called to their friends on the other boats in jovial fashion. He smiled to himself. How happy they all seemed at their work. He took in another lungful of the clean pure air. Sarah had bent down and was examining some interesting pebbles on the beach. Matthew picked up one with a certain shape to it, and telling Sarah to watch, sent it skimming and bouncing once, twice, three times across the water. She clapped her hands, delighted. Linking arms they continued along the beach at the waters edge, until they came to such a narrow strip that Matthew led Sarah up the steps to the esplanade. Here, they found a seat facing the sea. Lifting their faces to the sun, they basked in contented silence.

Around them more and more people appeared. It being a Sunday, most were lucky enough to have the day free from work, and took the opportunity to spend some time with their families, strolling on the sea front before lunch. Beside the parents with their small children trailing, or their babies being wheeled proudly in their bassinets, there were older children with a day away from school, boys, hands in pockets, kicking the odd pebble as they shuffled along, and the girls tossing their heads and giggling in twos and threes, telling secrets and eyeing the lads who walked nonchalantly by, seemingly unaware of the interest they caused.

The sunshine shed a gentle warmth on everyone. Ice cream vendors appeared with their gay carts, and did a brisk trade with the many who felt they had a penny to spare on a cooling ice cream cornet. For two pence one got an enormous double portion of ice cream, but very few could afford that luxury! Matthew and Sarah treated themselves to an ice cream, and walked contentedly along the esplanade, observing everything and everyone with interest. Having taken the last delicious mouthful, Matthew drew out his pocket watch and studied it. It was nearing twelve o'clock already!

"Sarah, I think we had best turn about and make our way back to your aunt's, by the time we reach home and freshen ourselves up, lunch will be ready. What do you think of the seaside after your first taste of it?"

"It's beautiful! I didn't imagine it would be so lovely as this, the sea is so..... large. And the air is sweet. Back in the village the air was good with all the smells of the land, but here the scent is sharp... and clean smelling. I'm sure it is very healthy."

Father laughed and agreed with a nod. Taking her arm he tucked it beneath his, and they continued on, until they came to the spot where the small pathway through the trees led them once more to their new home. Approaching it, they both had an excellent view of its front features. It looked tall compared with the tiny cottage they had left, just yesterday. Grey brick with thick ivy clinging across much of it, and neat, white painted shuttered windows six in all. One of these was high, set into the roof. Sarah realized that it was her room there, and vowed that at the first opportunity she would go to that window in her bedroom and look out. Maybe if she stretched herself, she might even glimpse the ocean.

By now, the pair had reached the front gate, Matthew unlatched it and stepped aside for Sarah to enter before him. The front garden was very small indeed, but was tended well. A bed of daffodils and tulips produced a riot of colour, and two shrubs in full bud adorned each side of the front porch, leading up to the door. Painted green with a large black knocker, it had squares of coloured glass forming a window at the top. Stepping up onto the porch Matthew reached and lifted the knocker, letting it fall gently with a single rap. Immediately the door was opened by Millie looking neat and trim in her white cap and apron. She bobbed, and waited for them to enter, whereupon she relieved them of their hats and cloaks, and closed the front door. At this moment Laura appeared, her face flushed, and her hands covered in flour. Her hair was drawn back into a knot, though some strands had escaped, and strayed onto her cheek. She gave a broad smile and wiped her hands briefly on her apron.

"Hello dears, I must say you have a glow about you that wasn't there when you left this morning. I take it that you both enjoyed your walk, and breathed some of our good salt air. I'm glad the sun shone for you on your first day here."

"The morning was most pleasant thank you, Sarah and I took great delight in the ocean. I am sure that she will spend much of her spare time on the beach, gathering sea shells, and even dipping her toes in the sea, when the days are hot enough. Now, I feel we must freshen ourselves if you will please excuse us for a moment."

"Of course. A light lunch will be awaiting you in the dining room when you are ready." With that, she returned to the kitchen and her pastry.

Sarah and her father each went to their rooms, and attended to their toilet. Sarah glanced in the vanity mirror above her wash bowl. She smoothed down her hair, which immediately sprung back again into its soft fine waves. She pouted and let it have its way. About to go from the room, she suddenly remembered. The window! Moving across and around the foot of the bed, she came to the window seat. Lifting her skirt, she climbed and knelt there, resting her elbows on the narrow ledge beneath the casement. Stretching to her utmost, and pressing her forehead against the pane, she strained to see as far as she could. ,But, although the view was very pretty and interesting, the ocean itself wasn't visible. A little disappointed, but not unduly, Sarah moved down from her position, straightened her clothes and returned downstairs. Her father, and aunt were already in the dining room, and they all enjoyed a pleasant lunch together.

The rest of that day passed in a relaxed and comfortable atmosphere. The afternoon saw father snoozing in the parlour in front of the fire, occasionally stirring enough to glance momentarily at his newspaper, before nodding off once more, his head resting easily on the back of the sofa. Sarah took the opportunity to spend the time in the garden at the back of the house. First informing Laura of her intentions, she sped upstairs to collect a shawl. Reaching in to a top drawer in the small chest beside her bed, she brought out the leather journal that Dr. Lindsay had given to her, together with a pencil, she clutched it to her, and made her way to the garden.

Leaving the hallway by the door that her aunt had pointed out to her, she discovered herself on a large terraced area, with garden seats and tables scattered about. Ornamental shrubs and climbing foliage adorned the surrounding low stone wall, beyond which, five steps led down to the garden proper. Placing her journal carefully on one of the tables, Sarah ventured down the steps and walked slowly through the grounds. The lawn was green and thick beneath her feet, and, all around, flower beds, well cared for and abundant with growth, promised a blaze of colour in the months ahead. Here and there, little rockeries. And a patch of bright, varied coloured heather stood out against a dark privet hedge. Sarah was entranced. In the far corner was a tiny wooden building. Drawing near to it, she found it to be a quaint round shaped summer house, complete with wooden seats covered by soft bright cushions. How delightful! Near the entrance to this wonder, another discovery! A pond with lily pads, and rushes growing. Leaning over, Sarah peered down into its depths, and was thrilled to see some small fish, and two young frogs darting about.

On the surface and above, insects hovered, and all around birds chirped and sang. It was almost like being back in the country village. Dreamily, Sarah dawdled back to the terrace, sat down with the journal in her lap, and stared for several more minutes down into the little paradise she had just explored. Then, taking up her journal, she opened it at the first page, and began to write down everything that had occurred since leaving the cottage. Every so often she paused, tapped her chin with the pencil, frowning slightly, before finding the words she needed and setting them neatly down in her book. Thus the afternoon passed. Shadows lengthened, evening approached. Once more inside the house

A Fish Pond provides an interest

Sarah entered her room to wash and prepare for the evening meal. Returning the journal to the drawer, she took out some family pictures and arranged them on the top of the chest, turning them to face her bed. One showed mother and father laughing casually, and the second was a formal family portrait taken by a photographer. Mother with William, a babe in arms, and behind her chair father, his right arm about Sarahs shoulders. She leaned toward her mother with her hand on the back of the chair. Sarah remembered the occasion clearly. She sighed. Perhaps her aunt could lend her some suitable frames, she would ask her.

After a sumptuous meal, cooked entirely by Laura, Sarah helped her aunt to clear and wash the dishes. And all three spent an evening in the firelight, quietly chatting, and becoming more acquainted. Laura told tales of her childhood with Elizabeth, and how close they had been to each other, especially when their mother had died. The girls had been fourteen years, and five years old. They were left with a father who lost himself in the bottle, and cared nothing for his home, or his daughters. Laura became a mother to Elizabeth, teaching her what she herself knew, simple writing and figures she had learnt from her mother. She had scraped enough to clothe and feed her young sister, by cleaning and taking in laundry. Her father had some private means, which the girls never saw. This was squandered on drink. Their father's food came entirely from Laura's small earnings.

At fifteen Elizabeth had a simple , but steady situation as a maid up at the vicarage, in the Kentish village which was their home at that time. When the Vicar and his family moved to Suffolk, Elizabeth went along too, there she met Matthew. Two years later they were wed.

"And you know the rest, dears". She finished with a smile. There was silence for a time. The clock struck ten o'clock. Stifling a yawn, Sarah rose and excused herself. She stooped and kissed her aunt, and then her father. Exchanging their goodnights, she left for her bedroom, pleasantly drowsy.

Ready for bed Sarah knelt and said her prayers. For her mother and brother. For father and aunt Laura. And gave thanks for a wonderful first day in Sidmouth.

4

SUNNY DAYS.

Spring turned into Summer, days grew long, and nights became warm and stifling. Windows were left wide open, with blinds drawn , allowing whatever breeze there was to cool the inside of the house. In the full heat of the day , Sarah would wander amongst the trees in the garden, and come to rest in the shade of the summer house, she would spend many happy times here. Sometimes her journal would accompany her, or maybe a reading book. Or she may work on some embroidery, which she was very clever at. With bare arms, and sometimes bare feet, a large floppy sun hat protecting her head, she became suntanned and strong that summer. Her body rounded and developed, and she became taller.

Matthew himself delighted in her beauty and good health. He had recovered his strength completely, and was looking fit and handsome with all the time he spent in the fresh air and sunlight. He had drifted back into garden work. It started with Laura's own garden, which she had always worked in herself, with occasional local help. Matthew insisted on doing the heavy jobs, and anything else required. He would ask his sister's advice, and go along with her wishes regarding flower beds, and colour schemes. She seemed to have a natural flair for this. Visitors to the house one day remarked how impressive the garden looked. Discovering it was mostly due to Matthew's labours, asked if he would possibly be available for work on their property. He accepted the offer with enthusiasm, and word got around about this pleasant, hard working brother of Laura Fairchild, and before he knew it, Matthew was employed up to six day each week , in different situations. He loved his work, had a feel for planting, and the soil. It pleased him that he was able to contribute some of his earnings to Laura's household, and not be beholden to her generosity, as well as her good nature.

Much of Sarah's time was spent helping her aunt prepare the meals, she washed and pared the vegetables, and learned the art of creating tasty sauces to accompany various meat and fish dishes. Laura enjoyed teaching Sarah , and passing on her knowledge of cookery. She was an apt and willing pupil. Together, they produced tasty and varied meals, greatly appreciated by Matthew especially, who returned at the end of each day with a hearty appetite. Mealtimes were happy occasions, breakfast tended to be a bit hurried, on account of Matthew getting ready to go to his work. He took bread and cheese for his lunch, with a flask. But at seven–o–clock or thereabouts, in the evening, was the main meal of the day. Matthew, washed and changed from his working clothes, sat at the head of the table, whilst Laura and Sarah served up the food. Then, they all sat down and savoured whatever pleasing dish was in front of them that particular evening. The time passed with chat and laughter, and later, when the table was cleared, a quiet hour sitting out on the cool terrace with tea or coffee. Listening to all the sounds of the evening from the garden, and watching the moths fluttering near the lighted windows of the house. In a drowsy, contented silence, the day wound down to its close. Sarah usually went up to her bed first, leaving father and her aunt to enjoy a little more time to themselves.

Her bedroom was gradually showing signs of Sarah's

influence, her family photographs,now framed were arranged along the top of her chest of drawers together with a vase of fresh flowers. On frequent visits to the beach, she was forever finding interesting shells and pebbles, which were brought home and examined, before being set to adorn the shelf below her window. Matthew had built a narrow wardrobe to fit in one corner of the room. After a shopping trip with her aunt in order to buy clothes to replace her outgrown ones, it was decided that hanging space was required for them. Hence, the wardrobe. Sarah had never had anywhere especially for her clothes before, and felt very lucky with the new piece of furniture. Her father painted it blue, and it brightened the corner considerably.

Among her garments she had some pretty petticoats in fine white cotton, and a light grey cape with matching hat for cool evenings. They made her feel quite grown up when she tried them on in the privacy of her room.

One especially hot day in July, Matthew was at his work, and Sarah had spent the morning at the beach, sitting on the breakwater reading , her feet dangling in the water. On her return home she had a cold lunch and some home-made lemonade. It was now three o'clock. Laura was expecting some friends to call for afternoon tea, and as Millie had been given the afternoon off, was preparing this herself. Sarah was assisting. A lace cloth was spread on one of the tables on the terrace underneath the shady branches of an old apple tree. The best cups and saucers were produced, and plates of savoury sandwiches, wafer thin and daintily cut. By the side of the table stood a handsome cake stand with all manner of cream and chocolate delights, cooked by Laura that very morning. At half past three the visitors arrived. Laura brought them through to the terrace, where Sarah greeted them politely. She then left for a moment to bring a fresh pot of tea from the house. On her return both ladies were seated with her aunt at the table. Placing the teapot on its stand for her aunt to pour, she sat down herself , a little way back from the table. Laura saw that her guests had re-freshment, and bade Sarah take some as well.

"How are you and your father finding it here in Sid-mouth, child ?"

The elder of the two spoke to Sarah:

"Very well , thank you. It is a beautiful town, and the sea is especially interesting."

After a while, the conversation turned to the plight of a mutual friend of the three women. Recently widowed, and in her sixties with no family, she was suffering from loneli-ness and depression. Despite her friends concern, she had withdrawn from all social occasions, and spent most of her day sitting alone reminiscing , or sleeping in her chair. Apart from an elderly cook, who ensured that she ate, and a maid who did the cleaning, she saw nobody. Acquaintances had stopped calling on her, as she always had an excuse for not seeing them. Laura spoke:

"It is such a pity. She is a pleasant lady with a lot of character. The answer is a companion of some sort , I would think."

"That is just what she needs. A person to sit with her, and talk, or read. Take her out of herself."

The younger women agreed with the idea. The other visitor was nodding her head thoughtfully, she spoke with some doubt.

"I am sure you are both right in what you say. But what young person would choose to sit with a melancholy old woman all day? It would take a very special and patient dedication for that task."

The chat continued until it was time for them to leave. After Laura had seen them to the front door, she and Sarah began to clear the table.

"Sarah."

"Yes, Aunt Laura ?"

"Let me be clear, how old are you now?"

"I will be fourteen at the end of this month , aunt."

"Of course, I wonder how you feel about the idea of us finding you some sort of employment?"

"I am not skilled at anything, I don't know what I should do."

Sarah spoke apologetically. Laura hugged her niece.

"I am not trying to push you out to work dear, but for your own sake it would be good for you to learn some occupation, and earn a shilling or two to save."

"Have you anything particular in mind? I could maybe learn to be a kitchen maid."

Laura smiled.

"I think you are capable of more than that. I do have something in mind, but we will discuss it more when we have spoken to your father."

With this Sarah had to be satisfied. Not until father had come home, changed and eaten, and was sitting comfortably with his cup of coffee out in the garden, was the subject raised again. After Laura had made the suggestion, there was a long silence.

"It's not possible! My little girl, employed! But of course my dear Laura , you are right. Sarah, my love, are you agreed with us? We have to think of your future, my dear . Will you tell us what you have in mind for my little girl.?"

Beckoning to Sarah to come and sit beside her, Laura

dressed both of them.

"A very good friend of mine has recently been wid-ed. She cannot come to terms with her situation, and has withdrawn into herself, refusing any contact or help from her friends. We, her friends that is, feel very concerned about her. And the idea has come to us that a young lady companion would be a perfect solution. After some thought on my part, I feel that Sarah might be the ideal young lady."

Sarah gasped:-

"But Aunt, I can't imagine how I would be suitable for a position like that. I have no experience of such things, and have had very little to do with elderly ladies. The few I have known though, I have liked very much." She added quickly.

"Exactly. Also, you have some experience of losing a loved one, so would be sympathetic and understanding to Mrs Davenport's (that's her name) feelings. Matthew, you have not said a word. Do you think Sarah will be capable of such responsibilities ? Speak up please , Brother."

Matthew smiled, and answered quietly:

"She will be perfect. As you say , she has sympathy and understanding of others feelings, especially on bereavement. She is kind, quiet and capable, and has a heart of gold." He spoke with pride.

"I'm glad you feel that way, I was sure you would agree with me. Tomorrow, my intention is to accompany you , Sarah , on a visit to Mrs. Davenport, and try to persuade her that she would benefit from a lady companion."

"You mean she doesn't realize what you have in mind?" Sarah was horrified.

"Don't worry , my dear, before our visit is done the lady herself will think the idea was hers in the first place, trust me."

On that, the subject was closed, and soon afterwards Sarah said her goodnights and departed to her bed.

The following afternoon found Sarah and her aunt dressed ready for visiting. Sarah looked quite grown up in a pale blue cotton dress with white collar, and short white gloves. She wore a straw hat with blue trimmings, and white shoes and stockings.

Mrs Davenport lived within walking distance, and in ten minutes the large impressive house was in sight. It was surrounded by a tall privet hedge, and rose trees in full bloom led up to the front door. Pulling the bell handle, Laura stood back. She gave Sarah a reassuring glance.

The door was opened by a tall woman, dressed in cap and apron. She enquired as to the callers' names, and invited them into the hall. Laura asked if Mrs Davenport was at home for visitors. The maid hesitated.

"I'm not sure , Madam , if it is convenient to visit, I will enquire, if you will please wait for one moment."

"You may tell the lady that Mrs Fairchild will wait in the hall if necessary., until such time as she will consent to receive her. "She smiled broadly at the open mouthed maid.

"Yes, Madam, I will tell her."

With that , she bobbed and disappeared through one of several doors leading off from the hallway. After a moment or two she returned, and asked them to follow her. Stepping into the room, with the visitors close behind, she announced their names, stood aside , bobbed and made her exit.

After the bright sunlight outside, the room appeared quite dim. The large windows were partially darkened with heavy curtains, giving the whole chamber a shadowy, ghostly atmosphere. Laura and Sarah peered through the gloom, trying to discover their hosts whereabouts. Suddenly a movement on the far side of the room drew their attention.

"Well now , Laura Fairchild, you have managed to gain entrance to my drawing room. I'm afraid you will find me a poor host, I have lost all heart , when it comes to entertain-ing. I find my own company more to my liking. It is good of you to take the trouble to call on me though. I see you are not alone, are you going to introduce us?"

"Indeed I am my dear Celia. This is my beloved niece Sarah who, with her father now resides with me."

"Really, and what is your mother doing all this time, letting her husband and child live away from her?"

"My mother is dead."

"Oh, I am so sorry, you poor child! Laura, you should have told me. Letting me upset the girl so."

"Sarah is coping very well with the loss of her mother, as well as losing her little brother. She is my sister's child, and brings light and youth into my home. I didn't tell you because you gave me no chance."

Celia remained silent for a moment.

"I too have lost a loved one my child; you, it seems have lost two .Perhaps we have something in common, you and I. It is good to talk to someone who understands ones true feeling's of grief."

"Mrs Davenport, I understand your feelings too well. But I also believe that our dear ones would want our lives to go on, and us to enjoy them. I am so sorry to hear of your loss."

Laura intervened here.

"Sarah is so determined to go on with her life, that she is seeking employment of some kind."

Celia Davenport appeared to have little interest in Laura's remark. She sat, hands in her lap, idly twisting her wedding ring, a remote expression on her face.

Undeterred by the lack of response, Laura spoke again:

"Yes, Sarah is interested in becoming a companion to some mature lady, who would benefit from her sunny disposition and caring ways. I think she will make an admirable lady's companion. She is very capable, and doesn't mind attending to any tasks that she may be given."

"I trust she will be successful in gaining a suitable position, she seems to be a pleasant young person."

Celia endeavoured to close the subject, but Laura persisted:

"What is needed ,in fact , is a chance for her to have a trial period, a month maybe, with some kind person who could advise and help acquaint her with all the duties expected of her. I wonder...but no, it would be too much to ask of you, still grieving for your dear husband. Sarah is only just emerging from her own grief and to think of both of you sharing hours in close contact.....it may not be the ideal situation. A pity though, you , being the friend I know so well could have started her on her first steps to being a successful lady's companion, never mind, it was a just a thought."

For some time Celia remained silent, until Laura was sure that either her remarks had gone unheard, or had not been understood. She was about to repeat the whole thing once more when her friend replied :

"A companion is the last thing I crave at the present, I am satisfied with my own company. However, I feel it would be charitable to start this young woman on her vocation. I have a kindred feeling for her, having suffered similar experiences. We may be good for each other, who knows."

gave a sigh after such a lengthy speech, and lay back in chair, closing her eyes.

Laura and Sarah exchanged glances of satisfaction. After establishing the fact that Sarah was to return the next afternoon to discuss some terms of employment, they both left Celia resting, enjoying her accustomed solitude once more.

That evening after dinner, Matthew was acquainted with the latest news, and was delighted for Sarah. He hugged her closely, and told her now proud he was of his girl, and that he had every confidence in her success. Soon after, Sarah went to her bed, tired after the day's events. She said her prayers padded over to the window and gazed out at the night sky, full of twinkling stars. Taking a deep breath of cool night air, she pulled the curtains together, and went to her bed, where sleep came almost immediately.

The following afternoon found Sarah once again entering the Davenport residence. On admission to the house by the same maid as previously, she was straight away shown to the drawing room.

Today the curtains were open wide, and sunlight streamed through the tall windows, revealing an elegant room filled with ornate and expensive looking furnishings. Celia Davenport sat near a window in a high wingbacked chair. Her feet rested on a footstool, and on her lap was a large white cat, purring loudly and staring at Sarah with its green eyes. Mrs Davenport waved an arm vaguely, beckoning her to approach. Sarah walked over and stood beside the chair, looking down at her host, able to see her features clearly for the first time. Her face was a gentle one, with high cheekbones and pale blue eyes tinged with sadness. A fair complexion was accentuated by her black hair, barely showing any signs of greying, drawn back carelessly into a bun. The full mouth broke into a slight smile at Sarah's scrutiny. A faint aroma of violets exuded from her person. She bade her visitor sit on the chair at her side.

"Well now young lady, since your visit yesterday with your aunt, which took me rather unawares, I given have much thought to the subject we discussed."

"You haven't changed your mind about my becoming your companion, for a trial period that is?" Sarah spoke anxiously.

Celia gave a little chuckle.

"On the contrary, I have decided , that I like the idea more and more. I think you and I should talk a little. How would you feel if I paid you five shillings each week? Your hours of duty will be nine o'clock until six o'clock everyday, except Sundays which will be your day off. Does this sound satisfactory to you?"

Sarah nodded, her eyes shining. Five shillings a week! It sounded so much.

"It all seems very agreeable, thank you. When would you like me to start?"

"Today, being Friday....... I think you should enjoy a free weekend, and I will see you on Monday morning at nine o'clock. Now, if there is nothing else, I will say goodbye to you, until Monday".

Sarah politely took her leave, and left the house. Skipping lightly all the way home, she slipped through the front gate to find her aunt kneeling, her garden gloves on, and her head shaded with a floppy, well worn sun hat. She was pulling weeds from the fine dusty ground, between her flowers. She raised her head as Sarah bounded into the garden.

Excitedly the girl gave her the news, stressing the fact

that she would be earning **5 shillings** each week, and would be able to contribute to the household, like everyone else. Laura got to her feet, and turning Sarah to face her, insisted that the money she earned should be put aside for the future.

"Since you and your father came to live here, my life has been far more interesting and worthwhile. Also, your father pays a generous amount towards expenses from his earnings, I am not completely without means, and have no difficulty in managing the household budgets. So , my dear Sarah, the matter is settled. The money you will earn is yours to use as you please. Though I feel sure that you will dispose of it wisely".

Sarah hugged her aunt and nodded. They went indoors, arm in arm, and prepared for the evening meal.

After dinner, when all three were sitting in contented silence in the twilight, surrounded with the night sounds of the garden, Sarah told her father the news. He kissed her soundly, his eyes moist, and was most impressed with her earning "five shillings a week!"

Sarah sat up later that night. After Laura had departed to her bed, she remained with her father. Sitting in the now dark garden, with just the lights from the house shining into the night , in a contented silence, together. He lounging in the restful chair, with Sarah at his knee, just like the old days. He stroked her hair affectionately. Between them were unspoken images of the past. Mother and William loomed clearly in their thoughts. No longer overcome by sadness, they were able to enjoy their memories silently together. Eventually, the hour grew late, Matthew was yawning, and Sarah's eyes had difficulty in keeping open. Time for bed. With a final tender caress for his daughter, he sent her off to bed and, after some silent reflection, made his way to his own bedchamber.

The next day being Saturday, Matthew was finishing his work early, and had the afternoon free, so Laura made the suggestion at breakfast, that they should all take a picnic out that afternoon. It was agreed. The morning was spent preparing tasty pasties and cold meats, together with crusty bread and cheese. Apples and oranges were added, and delicious homemade blackberry tart with a pot of cream. For a special treat aunt Laura slipped in a bottle of wine. All the items were packed into a hamper, and loaded into the car.

By two o'clock the three were ready to leave. With Millie waving them off at the gate, they all piled into the car and were on their way. Laura knew the area in and around Sidmouth well, and her competent driving soon had them way out on the country roads of Devon. It was the first time that either had seen anything of the beauty of the hills and vales, with the famous red coloured soil in contrast with the lush green of the fields. On and on they drove, around the winding lanes, up hills and down again, until at last Laura came to a halt in a small clearing at the side of the road. Parking the car beneath the trees, she helped Matthew with the picnic basket from the back seat. Then, with Sarah and her father carrying it between them, Laura led them down a narrow pathway into some woods. After about ten minutes the trees thinned out, and they found themselves on the bank of a rippling stream. Here, the cloth was spread out on the thick green grass, and the food and drink unpacked and set out on plates, with glasses ready to receive the wine which Matthew had already got chilling in the shallow water of the stream. Soon they were tucking in to all the good things before them. Sarah felt quite light headed after being al–

Through the woods and they were all set for the Picnic in the Clearing

lowed two glasses of wine. After the meal Laura and Mat–thew lay back on the cool grass, he to have a nap, and aunt to lose herself in her latest novel. Sarah took the opportunity to go and explore the stream, divesting herself of her shoes and stockings, she gingerly dipped her toes in the water. It was icy cold! Gasping, she let her feet slowly get accustomed to the feel of it, soon it didn't seem quite so cold, and Sarah dared to move around, gazing down into the clear depths to see what she could discover. Minute creatures darted about, and once a silver fish flashed by, close to her toes. A pleasant hour or two soon passed, then came the time to pack away the few remaining scraps of food, and knives and plates, fold the table–cloth, and wend their way back through the darkening woods to the car. It was a quiet journey home, each one clinging to the joy of the afternoon. By the time the house was reached it was nearly six o'clock. Millie had long departed , but had left the table set, and a dish slowly cooking in the oven for the evening meal. The day had been a good one. No one was too late to bed that night, being tired and full of fresh air and good food. A satisfying sleep was had by all.

Sunday saw everyone refreshed and ready for ten o'clock church. The tiny church in the middle of the town was always packed. Sarah and her aunt and father walked the short distance from the house. The service was enjoy–able, and hymns rousing. Later at home they had a leisurely lunch, followed by a lazy afternoon in the garden. Matthew caught up on his newspaper, and Laura wrote some letters and read her book. Sarah made her way to the summer house, and sat down to work on her journal which had been rather neglected of late. There was so much to write. When she had finished she lay back on the chair in the sunlight.

Tomorrow she would be starting her employment, and in a few days' time she would be fourteen. Life was very exciting at the moment. Father seemed well and content. Aunt Laura was wonderful. Sidmouth was a delightful spot to live in , and Sarah was determined that she would endeavour to be a good companion to Mrs Davenport, and ensure that her position would be a permanent one. She hugged her knees in anticipation of the morrow, when a new stage of her life would be starting.

5

A NEW FRIEND.

At nine o'clock precisely on Monday morning , Sarah stood in the hall at Mrs. Davenport's house, having been admitted by the usual maid. Jennie, the maid, acting on instructions, showed the new employee upstairs to the mistress's room. On entering Sarah discovered Mrs. Davenport on the point of rising from her bed, having been served breakfast there.

It came naturally to Sarah to assist the lady into her robe, and help her along to the bathroom, where a tub of hot water was already waiting. Whilst her new employer was in the bath, Sarah laid out some suitable attire for the day, and straightened the bedroom. Drawing back the brocade curtains and securing them with the silken cords, she flung the windows wide open, letting in the early sun and a sweet smelling breeze from the ocean. Glancing at the ornate clock on the bedroom mantelpiece, she made her way back to the bathroom in time to help the lady back to her room, where she was assisted when required, to dress and ready herself for the day.

"Would you care for me to brush your hair, Madam?" Sarah offered timidly.

"That would be nice , my dear. I'll have none of this "Madam" business, Mrs. Davenport will do very well, thank you. You are not a servant to me, you are a companion."

She handed the silver backed hairbrush to the young girl, and seated herself in front of her dressing table. Sarah began to brush, firmly but gently. She had often brushed her mother's hair in the past, so was experienced in creating a soothing effect with her efficient and even strokes. Celia Davenport found herself thoroughly enjoying the experience. On completion of the brushing, Sarah gently drew the long fine hair back behind the ears, where she skilfully wound it into a neat bun and secured it with several hairpins. After applying a little rouge to her cheeks, and dabbing some perfume onto her handkerchief, which she then tucked into her bodice, Celia motioned that she was ready to go downstairs. Instead of entering the room which Sarah was familiar with, they went in through another door from the hallway to a small cheerful room with a large easy chair, and a tall bookcase full of books in all sizes , all beautifully bound in red, green and brown leather. Celia made straight for a handsome writing bureau standing near the single window of the room. Rolling back the lid she exposed delicate notepaper and envelopes, and a brass ink stand and pen.

"I have the tiresome task of writing some letters. If you can amuse your-self whilst I do this, then we shall take a stroll and post them off. You may look at the books if they interest you."

"Certainly, Mrs. Davenport."

Sarah left her to her correspondence, and went over to the glass fronted bookcase. Turning the key she gently opened the door. She examined some of the titles of the many books. Some, she had never heard of. However, her mother had introduced her to several well loved tales from a very young age, teaching her to read at the same time. Here and there on the shelves were titles that were familiar to her. Reaching up,she removed a particular one that caught her eye, *Jane Eyre* . It had been a great favourite of hers, and she and mother had read it together many times.

Sarah opened the volume carefully, and began to read the first page. Soon, she became quite engrossed with the story, familiarizing herself with the characters once again. Without realizing it, she moved to the arm chair and curled up in it comfortably, still absorbed in her reading. Celia, having finished her letters, closed her desk and turned to see how Sarah was occupying herself. She smiled to herself, seeing the girl reading so avidly.

"Sarah, if you are ready, we can go now."

There was no response from the chair.

"Sarah!"

The girl jumped, and looked up in bewilderment, her mind still on the story. Suddenly, awareness dawned. Reddening in embarrassment, she leapt from the chair, closing the book with a snap.

"Mrs. Davenport, I am so sorry. I will just return this to its shelf, and I will be ready to accompany you directly."

"No need for apologies my dear. It was good to see you enjoying the book so much. Tell me, which book was it that was so absorbing?"

Sarah smiled:

"Jane Eyre. It was always a favourite of mine. My mother and I read it together."

"Ahh. You must miss her very much. There was a time when I was always reading a book. Now, I can't seem to concentrate too well. But perhaps you will read to me aloud at some time, *Jane Eyre* would be nice to listen to. We shall consider that for sometime in the near future. Now, my girl, we must hasten to catch the post , come."

The morning passed pleasantly. During the walk Celia was greeted by several acquaintances, and a few acknowl–

edged Sarah also.

On their return to the house, Jennie was instructed to serve refreshments in the conservatory. This was a lofty, spacious room at the rear of the house, furnished with a number of small chairs, and some glass topped tables. Green ferns, and other more exotic looking plants were in abundance. The atmosphere was very warm. At Celia's request Sarah opened wide some double doors which led onto the terrace, letting in a refreshing breeze. Sitting at a table nearest the door they enjoyed cool lemonade, and a slice of cold cheese pie with tomatoes and homemade chutney. There were grapes and peaches at the side, if desired. After the meal, Celia informed Sarah that she would take a short rest on her chair in the drawing room. Ensuring that she was content, with a cushion at her back, and Trixie settled on her lap purring, Sarah left her, with instructions to be back within half-an-hour.

Returning through the conservatory, she wandered into the garden, amongst ornamental fountains, stone maidens and bird baths, intermixed with brightly coloured flowers and shrubs. Sarah thought it was very nice, but preferred her aunt's garden really.

At half past one, she went to awaken Mrs. Davenport. They remained in the drawing room, Celia worked on a piece of crocheting, which fascinated Sarah. She enquired shyly if her employer could instruct her in this.

"Of course. It is quite simple really, see here."

She demonstrated how to place the silk around the finger, whilst hooking the loop through with the crochet hook. She was making a centre place mat, and her fingers moved deftly, producing intricate stitching, which quickly grew into a patterned square as Sarah watched. While she worked, Sarah gained the confidence to talk a little. The words started slowly and quietly, but , as she felt more at ease, became stronger and more detailed. Celia said not a word to interrupt. She had taken a liking to this girl, and enjoyed listening to her pleasant tones. She was beginning to think that a companion was not such a bad idea after all. Mostly, Sarah talked of her life before she and father moved to Sidmouth.

Celia gathered that before the family tragedy, life was exceedingly happy. Sarah went on to tell of the months following their misfortune, when father had fallen sick, and she had been in fear of losing him too. And later the excitement and preparation of the move , at the end of which was Aunt Laura's loving welcome into her home. She concluded by saying how the months since had been wonderful, and although she sometimes missed the cottage they had left, father and she felt so close to Aunt Laura, and loved the ocean, that it was clear that they had done the right thing in coming here.

At last, she paused and took a deep breath, lost in her thoughts, she sat at Celia's side, her hands in her lap.

The woman spoke quietly, continuing with her crochet.

" I am glad that you and your father are happy here in Sidmouth. You have suffered some hard times, and deserve some good fortune. Laura and myself have been good friends for some years. She is a remarkable woman, and would have made an ideal wife for some lucky man, but that is by the way. We were very close at the time of Robert's(that was my husband) final illness. He suffered greatly, and if I hadn't had the support of your aunt to take some of the burden from my shoulders, I don't think I could have coped. But I am sure she takes as much pleasure in your company, as you appear to have in hers."

She laid down her work, and took Sarah's hands in hers:

" I have taken a liking to you, child. I hope we can be friends, and that this arrangement of ours will be successful, and long lasting. Now, if you feel inclined, I will give you a tour of the rest of the house."

Happy in a new found friendship, Sarah took Celia's arm and walked with her throughout the house. It was very large, with many rooms, some apparently unused, but still kept in immaculate condition. Outside one door on the upper floor Celia hesitated. Taking a key from her pocket she unlocked the door and stepped in, Sarah following.

"This was my husband's study."

She stood still in the centre of the small room, twisting the key about in her fingers. Sarah went to her and touched her lightly on the arm, expressing sympathetic understanding.

"Until today, I have never entered this room, since he died. Jennie opens the windows, and runs the duster around it once a week. She has strict instructions not to touch or move anything. It is a strange feeling, here with his things about me, I almost expect him to be seated at his desk!"

Here, her voice wavered, and she dabbed at her eyes with her handkerchief.

"Let us leave now , Mrs. Davenport, this is too upsetting for you. I feel very privileged to be here with you in this special room. If you don't mind my asking, how long is it since Mr. Davenport died?"

" A year, in August. The longest year of my life, my dear. But then you understand my feelings exactly."

Sarah nodded. She took Mrs Davenport's arm, and led

her gently from the room, watching whilst she locked the door. Together, they went back downstairs. Jennie brought in a tray of tea and biscuits at four o'clock, and after that the time simply flew by. Celia showed Sarah her collection of pressed dried flowers, and Sarah spent half-an-hour playing games with Trixie and a ball of wool on the rug. Celia laughed to see their antics, and the mantle clock striking a quarter before six surprised them both.

Sarah took her leave, each said farewell, and both looked forward to the morrow. It was not yet dark when she left the house. Closing the garden gate behind her, she hastened down the lane to home.

Tiredness caught up with her finally during dinner. She barely had energy to finish her meal, before her eyes began to droop. Stifling yet another yawn, she protested :

"But father, Aunt Laura, I wanted to tell you so much; it's been a wonderful day. Mrs Davenport is really sweet, and .....oh my!"

With another yawn, she gave in, amid chuckles from Laura and Matthew. Giving each a swift kiss, she climbed the stairs to her room, and after a hurried wash, she brushed her hair with the compulsory 50 strokes, mumbled her prayers, and collapsed on the bed, drifting into the dreamless sleep of the young. Whilst downstairs, her father and Laura came to the conclusion that her first day of employment had been successful.

The next two days passed in similar fashion for Sarah. Her relationship with Celia Davenport was a comfortable one. Each found that conversation came easily, they would sit and sew, or look at scrap books, and photograph albums from Celia's past. At one time she had been a dancer of some renown. Often the two shared a time of companionable silence, which proved how their friendship was growing.

Thursday dawned, Sarah's fourteenth birthday. She awakened, arose as usual about half–past seven, and was able to enjoy a hot bath, before going down for breakfast. The first thing she noticed on entering the dining room was that there were two small packages by her plate on the table, together with several envelopes. Excitedly , she unwrapped the first parcel, which was from her father. Inside was a tiny box containing a gold chain with an engraved locket. Sarah studied the words :

Sarah, with my love, Father

Tears pricked her eyes, it was so beautiful ! She carefully fastened it around her neck. The second packet, from her aunt contained a pretty velvet purse, with 10 shillings inside. Delighted with the gifts, she started to undo the envelopes. They all contained greetings cards for her birthday.

One was from father, one from Aunt Laura, and the others were from friends left behind in the village. It was very touching that they should remember. Included was a message and card from Dr. Lindsay :

> **"A very happy day to you, I hope you and your father are well. Keep working on your journal, and if you can find the time to write a line or two, with news of your goings on, I would be only too pleased to hear from you. All the very best. George Lindsay. "**

Sarah pondered on this with much affection.

Suddenly her aunt and father burst in the door with loud greetings, and there were hugs and kisses all round. Sarah thanked both of them for her gifts, and showed off the locket that she was wearing. Father had a hurried breakfast before setting off to his work, and Sarah left soon afterwards. Aunt Laura was sipping a second cup of tea, and reading her newspaper, when Sarah departed from the room.

On arrival at Celia's house, she left her cloak in the hall with Jennie, and went straight upstairs. Celia Davenport was still in her bed. She welcomed Sarah, and bade her sit down for a minute or two. She was reading her post which had just arrived. When she had finished she removed her gold rimmed spectacles, and placed them with the letters beside the bed. Beckoning the young girl closer, she pressed a small hard object into her hand:-

"Happy fourteenth birthday, my dear."

Sarah opened her hand and saw the most delicate of cameos in pink and white. She had seen it on Celia's dressing table, and knew it to be quite valuable. She was lost for words.

Celia spoke:

"I only found out by chance that your birthday was today, so had no opportunity to choose a gift for you. The cameo , however , is quite beautiful. It was my mother's, she gave it to me when I was sixteen. Pink and white are colours more suited to a young person. And so, my dear, I thought of you, and how you might like it for a birthday present, I hope it pleases you for many years to come."

Sarah stepped forward, bent and kissed Celia Davenport firmly on the cheek.

"It is really beautiful, and most kind of you to give me a birthday gift. I will treasure it always. My father gave me this locket, isn't it lovely? And I had the sweetest purse, and some money from my aunt. I have been so lucky."

Celia agreed.

"As the sun is shining, and it is your special day,

perhaps we might stroll along the promenade. I may even be tempted to buy an ice cream for each of us. It is some time since I went so far as the sea front, it will make a pleasant change."

It was late morning when they finally left the house. The days were still warm, though the height of summer was past, and evenings were starting to draw in earlier. Soon, Autumn would be here, so it was a good idea to enjoy a walk by the sea, whilst the good weather prevailed. The two of them dawdled amiably along the promenade, arms linked.

They found a seat and sat down, taking pleasure in watching the ocean, and the passers by. Sarah was sent off to an ice cream vender, and returned with two enormous cor–nets. Celia felt quite light–hearted sitting with this young girl, licking an ice cream, and watching, as the seagulls strutted to and fro, waiting for a crumb to fall.

Most of the day they remained there, on the sea front. At one point when hunger nagged, Celia bought two small bags of potato chips with salt and vinegar added, and they meandered homeward relishing the taste of each one. After–wards, they laughed and licked their fingers delightedly. When six o'clock came, and Sarah was preparing to leave, she again thanked Celia for the gift, and for a most enjoy able day.

"I , too , had a marvellous day, child. Better than I ever dreamed. You are good for me. Now, go home and enjoy your evening with your family."

After dinner that evening, Laura brought coffee into the parlour, and drew the curtains against the darkening sky. She lit the gas lamp, and poured three cups of coffee. Hand–ing one to Sarah, she asked:

"Did you have a memorable fourteenth birthday my dear?"

"Lovely, really lovely."

Sarah replied, and told of the day's events. She showed them the cameo brooch. Both Laura and Matthew admired it very much.

They chatted until the clock struck ten, then Laura cleared the tray, Matthew turned off the lamp, and another day ended. Sarah lay in her bed, going over her day, and thinking how exciting it was to be fourteen. She fell asleep, her mind still active. And the night spread all around.

6

GROWING UP.

It was the month of January, in the year 1912. Sarah and her father had lived in Sidmouth for nearly two years. This year Sarah would be sixteen. Life was good. Father still had plenty of work, gardening in the summer months, and repair jobs throughout the rest of the year. He maintained his good health, and seemed content with his life. Sarah remained working as a companion to Celia Davenport. The arrangement had worked out so successfully, that her place of work was more like a second home to her, and Celia a second aunt. Aunt Laura considered Sarah and her father her responsibility, and made their welfare her concern. She saw that they were nourished in the most appetising ways, ensured that they returned at the end of the day to warmth and comfort, and lavished affection on both, in every possible way. Christmas had been celebrated traditionally. Dinner with all the trimmings, and friends dropping in for sherry and mince pies. Even Celia had been persuaded to visit, and had enjoyed an evening of carols around the fireside.

Sarah was enjoying the last few minutes in her warm bed, before having to rise and make the cold dash to the bathroom, and hot bath. She wallowed in her comfort for two more minutes, then, in one movement, was out of bed, into her robe and down the passageway to the bathroom.

At breakfast, conversation was cheerful. Father spoke of his present work, which was replacing some shelves for one of the local trades people. He was thankful the work was indoors, as outside the snow lay heavily , and the sky promised more to come. Sarah looked forward to her day . She was well into reading *Little Women* aloud for Celia. She had not read it before and found it most enjoyable. Laura fussed and listened , and advised , as she replenished their cups of tea before they departed into the winter's morn.

On arrival at Celia's , Sarah's heavy cape and hood were taken by Bridget , the latest edition to the household. Jennie had left a month ago to get married and Bridget , her replacement , was proving to be the perfect maid in every way. Celia and Sarah were most impressed.

The relationship between Sarah and Celia was a special one. Sarah had coaxed Celia out of her solitary state , back into the real world. This was accomplished quite unintentionally . With her natural frank and understanding perception, she had drawn Celia from her deep depression , into life once more , and Celia would be eternally grateful.

Winter days were spent mostly around the fire, in the drawing room. Sarah would read aloud , or she and Celia might sew. Often, if her employer dozed, Sarah would spend time playing with *Trixie*, who was always ready for a game. The cat loved Sarah, and followed her everywhere about the house when she happened to be there.

Today's game consisted of Sarah pulling a small piece of paper across the rug with a length of string and *Trixie* chasing it, and eventually being allowed to catch it, whereupon she tore it to shreds triumphantly. Celia continued to sleep peacefully in her chair and Sarah studied her face at rest.

Her appearance had lightened over the last year. She now used a little colouring on her cheeks each day and wore her hair in a less severe fashion than in the past.She tended to wear pale pastel shades in her dress. Well cut and styled , her clothes complimented a trim figure. Her arms now hung over the side of the chair, long slender fingers showed to perfection the fine wedding band, and large ruby ring worn on her left hand. Her favourite perfume was faintly noticeable . As Sarah watched , she stirred and opened her eyes. Smiling she smiled and stretched her arms above her head.

" Fancy that , I was sleeping quite deeply , it must be the warmth from the fire. I see you have worn *Trixie* out."

The cat lay at full length along the fender , tired at last, from fighting the piece of paper.

Sarah laughed and said: "Finally ! She still likes to play even though she not a kitten any more. How old is she , Celia ?"

(Christian names had been suggested by Celia. She felt that Sarah should be counted as a friend rather than an employee , and therefore entitled to address her in an informal manner. At first the girl was reluctant and embarrassed and made mistakes, but after correction by Celia she graduallybecame accustomed to her new privilege.)

Replying to the question , Celia suggested that Trixie must be about 6 years old.

There was a knock on the door and Bridget entered with a tray. "Tea Madam." She placed the tray on the table , gave a small bend to the knee and left.

"I will pour if you wish." Sarah poured two cups of tea , adding sugar and milk to Celia's. Handing it to her, she walked over to the window, looking out at the swirling snowflakes. Drawing the heavy curtains against the weather, Sarah returned to her seat by the fireside, shuddering. She took a sip of hot tea.

"The snow is falling thicker than ever I believe."

"What is the time dear ?"

Sarah stood to get a closer look at the clock in the darkening room.

"Ten minutes to five."

"I think you should leave for home a little earlier tonight, as it is so bad outside. The snow will be quite bad by now, and you will have difficulty in walking. Go now, and if you cannot get here in the morning, don't worry , I shall understand ."

Sarah thanked her , and assured her that she would do her utmost to be there on time the next day. Picking up the tray she made for the door, saying farewell to Celia as she went.

Stepping outside, Sarah pulled her collar up around her ears, and slid both hands deep into her pockets, her ankle boots sinking in the soft snow. It was a difficult walk home, even though the distance was only a short one, not a soul was in sight, though she did see a friendly constable standing beneath a street light, stamping his feet, and blowing into his hands. He bid her good evening, and trusted that she would reach home safely. He could walk with her if she preferred.

"Thank you, no, I have not far to go. Thank you again for your offer."

Almost at once she was at the front door of the house, with its friendly light shining forth through the glass. Using her latch key, she stepped into the warmth of the hallway. Aunt Laura came from the kitchen to greet her.

"Sarah, dear, I'm so glad you are home. I presume Celia let you leave early, that was good of her. Come here. Off with those wet clothes and boots, and get yourself in by the fire."

She assisted Sarah in removing her coat, shaking the wet droplets from it. Then whilst the girl sat on a chair, took her boots, as they were tugged off one by one. Sarah thankfully went into the drawing room, where she dried her long hair with the towel that Laura brought in. Curling up by the roaring fire, she allowed her tresses to hang down in the warmth of the blaze, until they were completely dry. She then rose and sat in the corner of the sofa gazing at the flames. A few moments later Matthew entered, snowflakes on his hair, and ruddy cheeks glowing. He made straight for the fire, stretching his hands towards it.

"Hello, my girl, how are you? What a terrible night out there! Not fit for man or beast! I had quite a job getting home, the snow is very deep, and it is still falling heavily. I must say I am glad to be working inside, there would be no possibility of outside work in this weather. Mrs Davenport let you home early then, I'm grateful to her. It may not even be practical for you to go to work tomorrow, if it keeps on like this all night."

"We'll see, Father, what the morning brings. I did say I would try to go. She, Celia that is, gets quite lonely, and enjoys some company. If it is possible, I shall turn up as usual, after all it is only a short distance."

Father smiled, and ruffled her loose hair, knowing her determination, and regard for Celia. Laura called that dinner was on the table, and they left for the dining room, arm in arm. Next morning , Friday, Sarah rose at the usual time, switched on her new electric light, and went to the window, to ascertain the state of the weather this morning. She could just make out that it was no longer snowing but the world was covered in a white blanket, beneath the still black sky.

Within the minimal time, she took her bath, dressed in layers of warm clothes, brushed her hair, catching it into a casual coil at the back with a comb. Then she tripped down-stairs as usual for her breakfast. Matthew was just leaving. He dropped a kiss on Sarah's head, and went to the hall to don his topcoat and muffler, before venturing out. Sarah left the house soon after, and with some difficulty and effort , came to the Davenport residence at last. Celia was engrossed in her mail, which had , remarkably , arrived before Sarah. The girl quietly busied herself, leaving Celia in peace, reading.

"Well well , how remarkable, fancy that , marvellous ! "

*The **Titanic** regarded as unsinkable ,although events showed something different*

Celia voiced her remarks aloud, and Sarah was most curious as to the contents of the letter. She was not kept in ignorance for long. Celia folded the letter, took off her spectacles, and looked up at Sarah, standing by the bed.

"Good morning , Sarah, I am glad that you were able to come this morning, I had my doubts, but you are a good girl. I have received this letter from my younger cousin, Rose. She and her husband live in Scotland. For some months Sam, her husband , has been unemployed. They are reasonably wealthy but not enough to remain permanently idle, so, they are sailing to America to seek a new life, and work. Sometime in April it seems, on a luxurious new ship in the last stages of construction, what's it called? The*Titanic* . Sounds wonderful. The best thing for them both, a comfortable cruise to an exciting new land, I'm sure it will work out well for them. They do have a son. But he has decided to stay, as he has steady employment.

If I were younger I would think about joining them, I must admit."

She sighed and arose from her bed, allowing Sarah to cajole her into making ready for another day.

The long days of Winter slowly eased into an uncertain Spring. March roared in like a lion, with high winds, and squally showers, then went out with quiet, still, hazy days filled with birdsong , and blossom, awaiting April.

Celia had replied to her cousin's letter, wishing both her and her husband "Bon Voyage." The ship was due to sail on April 10th so time was fast approaching for their departure.

There had been much talk in the news of this wonderful *Titanic* . It had been pronounced unsinkable, and was equipped throughout with every luxury for its passengers. Bookings for the maiden voyage were a sell out. Celia was quite envious of her family's trip.

Days continued in the usual way, the weather becoming warmer and more settled. Spring was well apparent everywhere, and birds were busy with their nest making.

On the day that the Titanic was due to sail, Celia and Sarah took a stroll down to the seafront. They stood for a while gazing at the vast ocean.

"Just think, travelling across all that sea, and finding another land, another life really. Marvellous, but a little bit frightening too".

Sarah nodded, agreeing with her.

"I don't know whether or not I will ever wish to leave England. Not to live anyway. I think it is rather a special country, green and pleasant, just like the hymn".

"Well my dear, Rose and Samuel would rather have remained in their native land , I'm sure, but circumstances drove them to the big decision.

No doubt if they do. well in America, Oliver, their son will join them in time. Or they may return in a few years, having made their fortune, ensuring security and comfort in their old age. Whatever, I wish them well".

"Me too!" Sarah spoke whole-heartedly.

A few days later, the Fifteenth of April to be exact, Sarah was walking to Celia's as usual, at the beginning of another beautiful spring day. As she drew near to the street corner, her attention was caught by the shouting of a newsboy, selling his papers. He was surrounded by a small crowd of onlookers. As she came nearer to him, she made out more clearly the words he was shouting:

"Read all about it , read all about it.
Unsinkable Titanic hit by iceberg. Lost. Hundreds dead.
Read all about it."

Sarah raised her hand to her mouth in horror. People jostled about her, pressing forward to purchase a paper. The crowd were noisy, some women were weeping. Pulling herself together Sarah escaped the throng, and continued on her way. She wondered to herself whether Celia had heard the news yet. She had. Sarah found her in her writing room preparing to write to Oliver.

"I must write to him. He will feel so alone. We will not know for sure names of any survivors, for some days. We must pray that they have been spared. Meantime Oliver must know that our thoughts are with him at this time."

The letter was dispatched, and some two weeks later Celia received a reply. It was confirmed by this time that neither Rose nor Samuel had survived the disaster. Oliver wrote on grey notepaper, in a scrawling hand:

My Dear Aunt,

I realize that you are not really my aunt, but feel sure that

you will not mind my addressing you thus. Thank you for your kind letter, and condolences. At this time my feelings are both sad and angry. Sad, because mother and father did not live to fulfil their dreams in America. And angry because of the sad lack of safety measures provided by such an expensive liner, measures which should have been a normal procedure. My parents, and hundreds of other people might have been saved for instance, if sufficient lifeboats had been available. However it is useless, and too painful to dwell on what might have been. My thanks again for your kind thoughts. My work here as a clerk keeps me busy, which is a good thing. I would like to pay you a visit at some future date, maybe in the Autumn when I will have more free time. Mother spoke of you, and Uncle Robert with great affection. I look, forward to meeting with you.

I remain your faithful nephew.

Oliver McGregor.

Summer arrived, and departed. Sarah had her sixteenth birthday in July. She had made some local friends over the past few months, friends of her own age. Walking on the beach one evening, after leaving Celia's, she was standing at the water's edge, deciding whether or not to slip off her shoes and stockings, and go for a paddle. She became aware of two young girls walking towards her, their shoes were in their hands, and their skirts hitched up over the knees, they giggled and squealed each time a small wave threatened to reach above their ankles. Suddenly they saw Sarah, and sensed her wavering over the idea of a paddle. They approached, the tallest of the two, a merry faced girl with abundant brown curls spoke to her :

"Hello, my name is Jane, and this is Dorothy my best friend. If you are wondering how the water feels, it is marvellous. Not too cool, but so refreshing. Do join us, what is your name? "

"Sarah. Thank you, I will join you. I had almost decided to

paddle anyway. My poor feet are so tired and hot, ahhh, that's better."

She removed her shoes and stockings, and picked them up in her hand, making her way to Dorothy and Jane through the shallow water. She gasped at the sudden chill, but soon got used to it. The three girls laughed and splashed together, and became quite well acquainted in the short time they had, before they all parted and made their individual ways home. They promised to meet up again at the same time and place. And so, a friendship grew between the three. Jane, the pretty one was also sixteen, a real chatterbox. She worked as a waitress in a tea shop in Sidmouth. Dorothy, not so dazzling perhaps, but attractive in a quieter way, was pale with long dark hair, and the bluest of eyes. She hoped to train to be a nurse, as she was only fifteen, she had to wait a few months until she was the right age to begin her training. So, she helped her father in his general store, until such time when her career could commence.

On her Birthday Sarah asked her aunt if her two friends might come for tea. As the birthday fell on a Wednesday , Laura suggested that they come to the evening meal, when father could meet them as well. And that is what they did.Laura cooked a special treat in celebration and later with coffee she produced a beautiful cake, complete with sixteen candles. It was a lovely evening, father got on well with both girls, and at nine o'clock walked them both home, Sarah accompanying them. She had been lucky with gifts and cards once more. A new outfit from Laura, a bicycle from her father, which she had long wanted. Twenty pounds from Celia, and handkerchiefs and chocolates from her two new friends.

Now, with the bicycle at her disposal, Sarah travelled many miles in, and around Sidmouth, sometimes one or both of her friends would borrow a bike and ride with her, but usually she went alone, and took great pleasure in finding new lanes, and exploring unfamiliar country trails. Up hills and down dales, her pedals flew round, and her hair streamed behind her, as the wind caught it.

In mid September Celia again heard from Oliver. He requested a visit, saying in his letter that he hoped to be able to travel down from Scotland the following weekend, which happened to be in four days time. There was no time to reply to the letter, but of course he must realize that Celia looked forward to meeting him, and having him stay at her house. The next day or two was spent preparing the best guest room : Bridget hurried and scurried with brooms and dusters, and lavender smelling furniture polish, Sarah helped her make the bed up, with crisp white cotton sheets, and lace frilled pillow cases, stone hot water bottles were refilled constantly and placed in the bed to air it thoroughly, as it had been years since anyone had slept in it. Fresh soap and face towels were laid by the ornate wash stand, and Sarah gave the final touch by standing a vase of cream coloured roses on the bedside table.

On Saturday, Celia looked in and gave a nod of approval at the sight of Bridget and Sarah's handiwork. Everything gleamed, and smelt sweet. The fire was ready laid for lighting, as the evenings were chill at times, and a small selection of books were set near the bed for his pleasure, if he so wished. Sarah would be on her day off when the visitor arrived, so it was with some curiosity that she arrived at Celia's on Monday morning. Her friend was already up and in the garden , Bridget informed her.

Sarah went straight through the house, out of the conservatory door, gazing around her in search of Celia. Suddenly, she came face to face with a very tall young man with unruly red hair. Both stopped in their tracks, staring and waiting for the other to speak. The young man recovered his composure and spoke first.

"Good morning, you must be Sarah. I am pleased to meet you. My aunt hasn't stopped talking of you. I am Oliver McGregor by the way."

He held his hand out, Sarah took it and they shook hands firmly.

I am Sarah Pearson, yes. Nice to meet you Mr McGregor. I hope your visit will be an enjoyable one."

Oliver raised his hands in protest.... "Please, please, not **Mr**, that makes me feel quite middle aged. In fact I am only twenty three, little older than yourself. If you call me Oliver, that will please me."

Sarah laughed and agreed. Just then Celia approached them, face wreathed in smiles when she discovered that they had become acquainted.

The day passed very pleasantly. Oliver absented himself for most of the morning, taking himself down to the sea shore with a promising book. He returned for lunch, and later they all sat together in the drawing room, where Bridget had lit a small fire against the Autumn chill. After some time chatting, Oliver perceived a piano in the far corner of the room. It was locked, and all the music tucked away in the base of the piano stool. On request, Celia rummaged around and produced the key. Lifting the lid, Oliver ran his fingers over the keys. Then he searched for a suitable sheet of music to play. He came across *Greensleeves* and *Lass of Richmond Hill* and proceeded to play them with gusto, gaining loud applause from his audience.

"It is some time since that piano was played with such feeling, that was most enjoyable, what do you say Sarah?"

Celia turned to her friend, her face smiling with pleasure. Sarah nodded in agreement. The young man had certainly brought some sunshine into the house. Celia had taken him to her heart, and was visibly enchanted with his youthful charm, and pleasing manners. As well as this, he had proved to be a gifted pianist. Robert, Celia's husband had been very fond of playing the piano, and many hours of listening to his light-hearted tinkling on the ivories, had given her a sentimental ear for music, especially the piano. The instrument had been kept locked the past three years, although regularly tuned professionally. Oliver's delight and talent for the keyboard, had opened yet another door into reality for Celia.

With just a matter of days before returning to Scotland, Oliver was treated to every local pleasure available in the shortest possible time. He visited the promenade (several times) and was bought numerous flavours of ice cream. A boat trip around the bay took care of an afternoon, accompanied by Sarah and Celia. All three returned, wind blown and ravenous, finishing the day with a large portion of fish and chips wrapped in newspaper. Strolling home in the late afternoon, cheeks aglow and eyes sparkling, no three people could have felt more content with life that day.

One day, Oliver accompanied Sarah home to Laura's for dinner at the end of her day. They chatted easily on the way home, and entered the house laughing at some small joke between them. Laura studied them when they were not aware, and was conscious that they shared a special understanding of each other. She said not a word but was secretly delighted.

Oliver met father, and an instant rapport was formed between them. They found a mutual interest in the game of cricket. The rules and technicalities kept them in deep conversation for some time. Come nine o'clock, Oliver reluctantly said his thank yous and farewells, and Sarah saw him to the gate. He leant over the gate towards her.

"I have had such an enjoyable evening Sarah. Your father and aunt are lovely people. Which must explain why you are such a pet. Thank you for inviting me, see you tomorrow. Goodnight."

Sarah remained at the gate long after Oliver's departure, deep in thought. What had he meant, such a *pet* ? What a cheek! Still, she supposed it was a compliment of sorts. Smiling to herself she went indoors. The last two days went swiftly. Laura took Celia, Oliver and Sarah out in the car one day. They covered many miles of countryside, autumn leafed lanes, and the smell of burnt stubble from the corn fields surrounded them on all sides. The air was filled with the scent of bonfires, and red and golden leaves drifting down from the trees. Laura parked the car high on a hilltop, allowing a marvellous view of the Devon country side.

Celia and Laura climbed out of the car, strolling to a nearby tree stump to sit and chat, and take in the scene. Oliver and Sarah climbed to the highest point, from where they could look down on rolling landscape in four different directions. And way beyond the hills and vales, the dim blur of the distant ocean. They stood together, he, tall and lean beside her slight womanly form, and they shared a feeling of carefree, breathless wonder at the sight laid out before them. In the awe of the moment Oliver put a friendly arm around Sarah's shoulders, it seemed the natural thing to do. And so they stayed for several minutes, in an intimate world of their own, oblivious to everything but the cool air on their faces, and the brief contact with each other.

Laura called from somewhere below them, causing Oliver to release Sarah from him. They gazed at one another dazedly, then both gave a secret smile to the other, before ascending the steep slope to the car, and the waiting adults.

The journey home went far too quickly. Oliver led them all in a sing song, filling the car with a joyful sound. Though Sarah joined in, her mind was not wholly on the singing. She was aware of the close proximity of Oliver. He turned every so often to her, giving her the warmth of his smile, and the unconcealed admiration of his eyes. Too soon they arrived home. Laura dropped Celia and Oliver off first, then sounding the car horn, she turned in the direction of their own house.

Sarah was quiet that evening. Father thought she maybe was sickening for a cold, but something prevented him asking her what was wrong. Laura kept giving him strange looks, which he could not interpret. So he kept his silence. No doubt it was some woman's business, and he would be told in time. At ten o'clock Sarah kissed them both and departed for bed.

In her bed she lay, eyes wide open, thinking back over the day. Oliver crowded her mind. Her heart raced thinking of his tender glances. Tomorrow he was going back to Scotland, and she may never see him again. But somehow she knew that they would meet again, someday in the future, and then..... with this thought she happily fell asleep.

The next afternoon Laura drove them all to the station to see Oliver onto the train. He bent and said goodbye to Sarah, giving her a swift kiss at the side of her lips, then, he was on the train leaning out of the window waving and shouting farewells to them all. They all watched until the train was out of sight, around the bend. Many months would pass before they would all meet again.

7

DARK TIMES

After Oliver's departure, life went on as usual. Christmas came, and went, and the New Year, 1913 was welcomed in with much celebration. Sarah and Oliver had corresponded regularly since his return to Scotland, and at Christmas,they had exchanged cards. It would be some time before he could make another visit, but he sent Sarah a snapshot of himself, requesting one of her in return. She kept it by the side of her bed, along with her family photographs. Every so often she would gaze at it, trying to recall the happy time they had shared, but it was difficult. Nevertheless, he had a special place in her thoughts, and she wished for his return to be sooner rather than later. It was with some excitement that she received the news from Celia, that Oliver hoped to visit during the summer months for a week.

He arrived in the heat of late June, and there were wonderful days spent on the beach, taking country picnics, walking through leafy lanes, and sitting in the garden at twilight beneath the stars, just talking. Celia joined them on some occasions, but found the heat quite taxing, so was content to let Sarah keep her guest occupied, which suited the young pair very nicely. One such day, the two had cycled far into the countryside, Oliver carrying a small picnic hamper, strapped to the back of his machine. They reached the arranged spot, and rested their bikes against a tree, before taking a stroll to discover the delights in and around the tiny glade, where they had decided to have their picnic.

They walked, hand in hand, among tall heavily laden trees, and lush green undergrowth beneath, birdsong surrounded them, though not one was to be seen. And sometimes, there was a rustle in the undergrowth, and a moving of the foliage, without any apparant cause. Here, in the sheltered bower of green, with slants of sunlight trying to penetrate into the cool shadows, Oliver turned Sarah gently to him, and kissed her long and sweetly. Later, they retraced their steps to the picnic spot, arms now about each other, in a warm contented silence. The picnic was spread out, and the food eaten automatically, between secret warm glances, and accidental, or not, touching of hands. After the meal, Oliver sat resting against the tree, with his face turned slightly from Sarah. He spoke softly.

"I love you, dear Sarah, it would make me very happy if you will wear my ring, and one day become my wife, please say you will?"

Sarah moved towards him, and turned his face to hers. Looking into his clear grey eyes, she smiled and consented to becoming engaged. They kissed, sealing their promise.

Celia, father, and Laura were delighted at the news. The engagement was to be officially announced on Sarah's seventeenth birthday, two days before Oliver was due to leave once more for Scotland. Oliver purchased the ring from a select jewellers in the town. Sarah wished him to make the choice, and he took a long time making his decision, before finally settling on a single diamond, set in sapphires. He was anxious as to whether Sarah would like it, but had no need for reservations. Sarah adored it, and proudly showed it off, stretching out her hand with slender fingers, and gazing at it from all angles.

Dorothy and Jane warmly congratulated the pair, meeting Oliver for the first time, and giving him the nod of approval, as a suitable fiance for their friend, Sarah.

Once more time came for parting at the railway station. This time it was more poignent, and after his fond farewells to his aunt, Laura and Matthew, Oliver drew Sarah to one side, to take his leave of her in some privacy. They clung together, and kissed in a desperate need to prolong the moment. At last, as the whistle was blown by the guard, Oliver gently, but firmly removed Sarah's arms from around his neck. He turned her fact up to his, for a last sweet kiss, murmuring his love for her. Then he turned swiftly on his heel, and boarded the train just as it was moving from the station. Soon, it was out of signt, and the platform was empty once more, apart from a sleepy looking porter, and the station cat sauntering past them with his tail in the air.

The next months passed slowly, and Sarah awaited the weekly letter from her beau eagerly, and wrote back with every detail of news. The letters between them were tender and loving. Oliver wrote of his impatience to be near to her once again, and always signed his name passionately with many kisses.

That Christmas was bittersweet for them both. Sarah adored the traditions and festivities of the season, but missed Oliver so much. They had exchanged gifts this year. Hers was a carved wooden jewel box, with her name engraved inside the lid. Sarah sent him a pair of fancy cufflinks in a leather case. Father and Laura encouraged her to join in the merry-making as much as possible , but realized that her thoughts were else-where most of the time. She visited Celia on Christmas day with a gift, and they talked in the firelight of Oliver, and his next visit the following Autumn. Sarah professed that it seemed a very long time. Celia laughed in a sympathetic manner , and promised that the time would pass eventually, and before she knew it, they both would be wed, and on their way to

Scotland.

"I shall miss you so much, my dear. You brought light into my life at a time when I had begun to think that my life was over. I hope I can expect frequent visits from you both".

Sarah bent and hugged her friend, and assured her that she would be "sick and tired of their visiting" they would come so often.

Winter passed, and Spring also. Long hazy days of Summer were here again. Father continued to work at his gardens, and led a contented life, cosseted by Laura, who remained constant in her care and affection for the two of them. They were resigned to the fact that Sarah would be moving to a new life with Oliver in the near future. They both admired Oliver, so felt no qualms at the prospect of the pair marrying. However, Matthew knew that he would miss Sarah dearly, but prayed that she would find the happiness she deserved. He would remain content if he was certain of her well being in the years to come.

On July 28th 1914 Austria declared war upon Serbia, accusing that country of the murder of their Archduke Ferdinand, and his wife a month before, during an inspection of troops on the occasion of Serbia's national day. The war seemed to have no great significance for the people of Britain at that time. However by the month of August, Germany had become involved, and invaded Belgium, causing Britain to intervene.

On the 4th August, Britain declared war on Germany. This had all happened so quickly, and over the next few weeks young men were offering themselves to fight for their country. Military clad men were familiar sights in the streets, and recruitment posters plastered all available spaces in town. Otherwise, life went on much the same for Sarah and her family. She was looking forward still, to Oliver's return in a few weeks time. At the end of August she opened a letter from him, before leaving for Celia's. As she read the words, she paled, and her heart sank within her. He wrote:

Dearest Sarah,

I know you will understand, when I tell you that tomorrow I am going down to enlist in the armed forces.

After much heart searching, I feel that it is my duty to fight for our future together. Many of my friends feel as I do, and we wish for nothing more than to bring this war to a satisfactory finish in the shortest time. Please give me your blessing my love. I long for the day when I will return victorious, and you will become my wife. I am sure that in a matter of weeks, we will be together again. Until then my love, please wait, and pray for us all.

I love you dearly,

Oliver. x x x x x.

Thereafter, Sarah followed the news avidly. Letters continued regularly from Oliver, now in army uniform.

Then, in the Spring of 1915 letters became infrequent, when Oliver was sent to France. For several weeks there was no news from him, Sarah was frantic with worry, with terrible accounts of injuries and fighting conditions reported in the papers, and on the wireless each day. At last a disjointed letter came. Written in an untidy hand, with smudges, and blots aplenty. Oliver told of endless days, surviving in trenches, constantly wet, and cold, of being weary beyond belief, and of witnessing the appalling injuries and dying of his comrades in arms. He however was determined to survive, and return to his love. So, Oliver told her to keep her chin up, in readiness for his return, which he was sure would be very soon.

Signs of the war spread across Britain. Zeppelins were seen over the English coast, and dropped bombs first on Yarmouth, and later on London. Sarah and Laura offered their services locally, helping to nurse war wounded victims, in a specially improvised ward at the local hospital. There were some horrific sights, but Sarah was a natural.

Quiet and efficient, she carried out instructions handed down by the harassed doctors. She had a sweet smile and gentle hand for many a suffering soul, as she went about her duty. It made her feel closer to Oliver, knowing that she was doing something to help young men, who like himself, had been separated from their loved ones in order to go into battle. Which had little meaning to them personally, other than causing them to witness, death and destruction, to become agressive in attack, and to know panic and fear like they had never imagined. Little more than boys, some around the age of Sarah herself. Many had limbs missing, or severe burns, from gas warfare.

The ward was filled with silent moans, or louder wails, even screams at times. Doctors and helpers worked around the clock, trying to alleviate the suffering where they were able. Often death came, giving the victim eternal respite from all pain at last. Laura and Sarah worked so hard that they were scarcely aware of days or nights passing. Sarah still visited Celia when she had the time, but her main concern was the hospital work these days. Celia busied herself with her knitting for the forces. Each week a fresh pile of scarves, gloves and socks were packaged and taken down to the military sorting office in town, from whence they were dispensed to grateful servicemen fighting in dire conditions, for their King and country.

Father remained working on the land. Now, however he did more than tend the local gardens in the area. He purchased a small commercial van, and travelled further from the town, helping on the farms. Many were shorthanded due to most young men away fighting. Matthew still faced the possibility of conscription, though he was now approaching fifty. Meantime he did his part, working long, back breaking hours on the land, ensuring that basic crops produced food, and animal feed for the winter months ahead, which were just around the corner. He came home each night, weary in his body, every muscle aching. But he felt satisfaction in his job. The men he worked alongside had become his friends.

They were a team. They toiled all day, with willingness and good humour, and finished the day with a jug of ale at the local pub. Matthew, though a likeable man, had never had men friends as such, being too wrapped up in family life. He found himself enjoying the companionship, and the lighthearted banter exchanged over a drink, after the days work. 1915 was fast drawing to its close.

November brought sleet, and biting winds. News was still grim, with no sign of an early end to the war. There had been no word from Oliver for some weeks, and Sarah and Celia hoped for a letter each morning. At last, an official brown envelope arrived at Celias, delivered one gloomy windswept morning by a miserably damp postman. She opened it up as she walked into the drawing room. Switching the lamp on, by her chair, she sat down and read:

> **Dear Madam,**
> **It is with regret that we have to inform you that your nephew Oliver McGregor, has suffered such injuries during the course of battle, that, on medical advice, we are discharging him herewith. He will be escorted home into your care at the earliest possible date.**
> **Yours sincerely,**
> **Major Phillip Thompson.**

Celia sat in silence for some time, part of her relieved to know that Oliver was alive, and coming home, but also worried as to the extent of his injuries. Had he been blinded, or burnt, and if so, how badly? Perhaps one or more of his limbs were damaged, leaving him crippled for life. Her imagination was running riot. She steadied her thoughts and stood up. Sarah must be told, and prepared.

A ground floor room must be made ready for Oliver's return. Motivated into action by these ideas, her first move was to instruct Bridget to prepare the large light room at the rear of the house. Leaving her to make a start on the arrangements, Celia donned her thick waterproof coat, and wellington boots and left the house grabbing an umbrella from the stand as she passed through the hall. The rain had eased somewhat, which was fortunate, as the high wind would have made it difficult to use the umbrella. Holding the collar high around her chin, she squelched through the damp, dismal streets to Laura's house. Laura herself admitted Celia into the house, and relieved her of the damp coat and boots in the hallway. They went straight to the parlour, and Celia was made to sit down by the fire and calm herself, whilst Sarah was called from her room.

Laura took herself to the kitchen to brew a fresh pot of tea. Sarah entered the room, going over to Celia she knelt beside her and took her hand.

"Celia, what is wrong? Please calm yourself, and try to tell me. It is to do with Oliver isn't it? Something awful has happened to him, I know, I can feel it. Celia, he's not... tell me, he's not.....nooo!"

She stood, hands clenched together, staring at her friend. Laura had come quietly through the door with the tea tray. She remained in the doorway, motionless, the tray held rigidly in front of her. Celia spoke to Sarah.

"My dcar. Oliver is alive, thank God. But he is wounded, I don"t know to what extent, but they are sending him home to us. Here, here is the letter I received this morning".

She handed the envelope to Sarah. Sarah did not open the letter. She held it loosely in her hand. For some moments she gazed into the flickering flames of the fire, lost in her thoughts. Then suddenly, she buried her head in her hands, bursting into tears. Laura deposited the tray and rushed to comfort her, and Celia rose from her chair, reaching towards her.

"It's all right really. The truth is, I am so relieved that Oliver is alive and actually coming home. I realize that he is wounded, but we will care for him, and nurse him back to his full health. The thing is, he will be among the people who love him most in the world, and I can't wait for him to arrive".

The room was ready and waiting for Oliver, prepared with loving care by Bridget, with advice and assistance from Celia and Sarah. It was a spacious room on the ground floor, previously used for storing disused or spare furniture. Now, it held a comfortably sized bed, with suitably masculine furnish–ings of chests, and a wardrobe, complete with robe and slippers. Tall windows opened onto the terrace, and draperies of blue velvet toned in with patterned rugs, and the heavy blue quilted bedspread. The bed was kept aired, and the fire laid, ready for lighting. Celia was notified of the arrival day.

The 4th of December. That day found Celia, Sarah and Laura at the station anxiously awaiting Oliver's arrival. Laura had the car parked nearby, for easy conveyance. At three o'clock a train steamed in to the platform. The steam cleared to reveal two figures approaching. One, a stocky capable looking individual, with a peaked cap, and a handsome moustache, leading the other tall, slightly stooped uniformed, clean shaven Oliver. Sarah rushed forward to greet them, closely followed by Celia. The military escort bowed his head politely, and clapped his heels together. Oliver stared straight ahead, blankly.

"Mrs. Davenport, Madam? Mr. Oliver McGregor, safely

handed over to your care, according to my instructions. I was asked to give you this letter also. I'm afraid Mr. McGregor is rather weary after the journey, and in need of rest and refresh–ment. I have to leave immediately. I therefore hand my charge to you Madam."

He then turned to Oliver, and gave him a swift affection–ate grip of the shoulder, before standing to attention and bowing his head respectfully to Celia, who thanked him sincerely for his safe deliverance of her nephew.

After his speedy departure, Sarah and Celia supported Oliver on either side, whilst Laura opened the car doors for them. On arriving home, the invalid was settled comfortably into his room. Assisting him in the removal of his clothes, Celia was aware that his mind did not respond to his surroundings. In fact, he seemed oblivious to any thing, having a blank look in his eyes. She put it down to weariness, and lost no time in getting him into pyjamas, and snugly into the bed. His eyes remained open, she drew the curtains together and left him staring at nothing.

On her way to the drawing room she asked Bridget to leave a cup of hot tea by his bed, but not to disturb him. Sarah rose when she entered the room, an anxious look in her eyes.

"How does he seem Celia? I thought he looked so tired, poor dear, he was too tired even to speak. A good sleep will do him the power of good."

Celia replied, some doubt in her voice:

"I'm not at all sure that sleep will be sufficient in making him more like the Oliver we all know and love. I seem to think that the trouble lies deeper than that. Perhaps this letter will throw some light on the matter."

She took the envelope that the military escort had handed to her at the station, and opened it up with a single movement.

She read aloud to the other two:

Mrs. Davenport.

By the time you read this letter your nephew Oliver McGregor will be safely in your keeping. You may be wondering as to the extent and nature of his injuries, causing him to be invalided from the army. This letter may help you to understand. Oliver's injuries are not of the physical kind, and therefore not visible. His mind however has been affected by his experiences on the battlefield. Before his trauma overcame him, he carried out his duty bravely, and had a great many companions, being a pleasant and friendly young man.

Two or more of these companions were felled in battle, one died right by Oliver's side. This affected him deeply, though didn't cause any change in his behaviour at the time. However, the lack of sleep and constant deprivation of comfort plus continued death and injury of comrades about him finally began to take its toll on his health. Towards the end, he would cower in an immobilised state, covering his eyes and ears, against the sound of the gunfire, and bombs.

This condition is unfortunately common, and is known as *Shell Shock*. The treatment is patience understanding, gentleness and loving care. One cannot specify whether or not there will be a complete recovery, or, how long it may take. However, it has been stated that at least 20% of those affected, have made a reasonable recovery. I therefore wish you complete success, and Oliver the joy of a full recovery.

I remain yours sincerely,
Dr. Jonathan Barnes.
Medical Officer of Health.

Celia finished reading, and folded the piece of paper slowly. She looked up at her two companions. There was absolute silence for several minutes. Eventually Sarah spoke quietly : "Shell shock, of course. I should have recognised it from all the other cases I've seen at the hospital. Poor dear Oliver, such terrible things to go through. I should like to see him please Celia, if possible."

"Of course you may dear. If anyone can get any response from him, you can, I'm sure. Go ahead, and stay as long as you like."

Sarah left Celia and her aunt talking together, and made her way to Oliver's room. Tapping the door gently she entered and crossed in the gloom to this bed. He now had his eyes closed, and Sarah gazed down on him, her heart full of love. She bent and softly kissed his brow. He remained asleep, but his face twisted as if in pain, and a deep furrow lined his forehead. Sarah gently tucked the covers around him, and settled back in a chair at the bedside to keep watch. He slept fitfully.

Both Celia and Laura offered to relieve Sarah, but she was content in her vigil, and sat for 3 hours just familiarising herself with his dear face. Suddenly he jerked himself awake. His grey eyes blinked away the sleep, focussing on their surroundings. They came to rest on Sarah, and gazed without recognition at her. She drew closer to the bed, and switched on the bedside lamp. Taking Oliver's face in her hands, she looked straight into his eyes.

"Oliver, it is I, Sarah. Your fiancee. Please try to remember my love. Look, look at me. Now, say you recognise me, please." Oliver stared back at her.

He frowned in concentration, then shook his head dazedly, closing his eyes in exhaustion. Sarah let his head fall gently back onto the pillow. She sighed, and brushed a tear from her eye. Celia entered the room at that moment, and Sarah was persuaded, at last, to leave the bedside watch to her, whilst she had a break, and took some refreshment. That first night was a long one. Laura had returned home to see to Matthew's needs, leaving Sarah and Celia to share the task of sitting with Oliver. Celia forced some broth between his lips during the evening, and he took frequent sips of water at intervals during the night, whenever he awoke, which was often. His sleep was troubled, disturbed by bad dreams.

At times he shouted out, and thrashed about. Much of the night was spent remaking the bed, the devoted carers smoothing the sheets, and securing the blankets time and time again. Sarah jumped, hearing the hall clock strike 8 o'clock. She had dozed in her chair. Stretching wearily, she reached over to look at the invalid. He was awake. Lying perfectly still with his eyes wide open. He did not even blink as she leaned over him to adjust the covers. She went to the window and drew back the curtains.

Another grey day outside, but not raining at the moment. Celia came in with a welcome cup of tea for Sarah, and a light breakfast for Oliver. Together they raised him to a sitting position, and Sarah supported him, while Celia coaxed some nourishment into him. Then they assisted him out of bed, and into a robe and slippers. Celia escorted him to the bathroom, whilst Sarah replenished the fire in his room. He returned, walking unaided, and went straight to the bed, climbing in and pulling the covers over his head. The women left him to himself. In the drawing room Celia spoke :

"I am going to get the doctor in to give me some advice on Oliver's general care. Also I feel that there should be someone qualified to look after him for a few hours each day. What do you think? We have to spend some time away from the house, especially you, with your work at the hospital. And I am often out visiting, or involved in relief work in the town. I for one will be easier in my heart, if I know that our dear boy is being cared for properly in our absence. At night, if you are willing and able, we can take turns to sit with him, until such time as he is

able to be left alone. "

Sarah agreed with her friend, and later that day the doctor visited. He spent some time with Oliver, before joining Celia in the drawing room, gratefully accepting a cup of tea. Sarah was working at the hospital. Dr. Grant sat down, at Celia's invitation, and drew up his chair to face her :

> *"Mrs. Davenport, may I say how sorry I am to see your nephew in his present state. Very sad. However, I have spoken to the young man, and will try to advise you as to the best possible treatment you can give him. Firstly, do not treat him as an invalid. See that he rises from his bed and dresses, each day, just like everyone else. He may take his meals at the table, try to encourage him to feed himself. Most importantly , speak to him, and draw him into discussions and conversations as often as possible. If he has an interest that you know of, attempt to introduce him to it once again. Keep his mind active if possible, but on the other hand avoid stress or any emotional upsets. Apart from that, just plenty of loving care, which I'm sure there is no need for me to mention."*

He rose to take his leave.

"Thank you for coming so promptly Doctor, and for your advice. I was thinking of employing a nurse for a few hours each day, to ensure that Oliver isn't left alone at all. Do you think this is a good idea?"

"Excellent, company is good for him. Company, and quiet conversation may encourage him to unlock his mind, letting all the horrors out that haunt him. I think I may know of a suitable lady for the job, she is a retired nurse, lovely disposition. I am sure she would welcome a chance to earn a little extra money for herself. If you wish, I will enquire, and get back to you."

He shook Celia's hand and departed. Sarah arrived in the evening to find Oliver and Celia sitting by the fire together. Celia was knitting, there was soft music coming from the wireless, and Oliver sat, his chair drawn back into the shadows. Perched on the edge of his chair, his two arms wrapped around himself, he looked tense and uncomfortable. Sarah was just about to remark that he should be in bed, when Trixie the cat, tiring of her spot on the floor, made a graceful leap right onto Oliver's lap. Celia froze, her knitting clenched in her hand. Sarah gasped, and made to rush forward. She paused and stared. Trixie had entwined herself through Oliver's arms, and was making herself snug across his knees. She purred and fixed her green eyes on him, willing him to move and give her a wide expanse of lap. Slowly, Oliver eased himself back into the chair, laying his hand gently on Trixie as he did so. Once there, he commenced a regular stroking motion, to the cats obvious delight. She purred loudly, and burrowed deeper into his lap. Then suddenly:

"Trixie."

Sarah and Celia looked at each other. There was no mistake. He had spoken the cat's name. The voice was low and hesitant, but he had spoken. Sarah moved over to his chair. She bent down and tickled Trixie behind the ear, studying Oliver's face as she did so. He looked at her.

"Hello Oliver dear, how are you feeling?"

He stared at her, then dropped his gaze once more to the cat without replying. She squeezed his hand gently, and moved away toward Celia. He didn't speak again that evening.

8

PICKING UP THE PIECES.

Christmas 1915 was dismal for most people in Europe that year. Men continued the fight overseas, and many were maimed in battle, or lost their lives on some foreign field, far from their homeland. At home, wives and mothers coped in the best way they could without their men to fend for them and their children. Most of the larger cities were bombed to some degree, and many were homeless that Christmas season. Voluntary organisations set up various community shelters, which were homes for bewildered and bereft souls, offering them warmth, bread and hot tea, and the company of others in similar positions. Sarah and her family were not in such dire circumstances, still having their home. Celia too had her house, although some of the windows there were boarded up, as they had been shattered during a specially heavy raid, causing the whole area to shake, damaging the panes. Other than that, and the usual shortage of rations, they were comparatively lucky.

They planned to spend Christmas together. Celia invited them to her for the day. For months she and Laura had put small amounts of flour and sugar aside, and both had stores of fruit and jams, and chutneys from before the war. Matthew was able to provide vegetables from his farm work, and also begged and obtained six eggs from a friend who kept chickens. The two allowances of meat were combined to produce a reasonable piece of pork. So all in all they would all enjoy a substantial Christmas dinner.

The week before was spent mixing and baking, eking out the ingredients as far as possible. Laura provided the mince pies, and the pudding. Celia the cake, which had been baked weeks ago, and sealed in a tin to mature.

Oliver's health continued much the same, with little apparent improvement. However, with encouragement, he rose and dressed each morning, and attended to his own toilet. His appetite was small, but then he had little activity. Sarah read to him from the newspapers each day, avoiding items to do with the war. Music was played a lot on the radio, and the piano was kept open, in the hope that he may be tempted to play. This hadn't happened yet.

Trixie got the most response from him. She would sidle up to him, and arch against his leg, until he bent to fondle her. The the cat rolled onto her back in delight, until such time as the caresses ceased. Oliver would relax and smile at her antics, and for a short time seem his old self. Until, suddenly, the shutter would come down once more, and his eyes darken, his mind lost in its private horrors again.

Christmas Eve was a busy day. Celia rummaged around and found some decorations of bygone days, tinsel and glass baubles. Not having a tree to decorate, she gathered some evergreens from the garden, and stood them in a tall vase beside the window in the drawing room. Bringing Oliver to assist her, she encouraged him to fix the novelties on the tree, as she handed them to him. He managed quite well, and stood with her and admired the handiwork, when completed.

Celia had found some tree candles, which she placed carefully on certain points of the branches. With a last glance of satisfaction, she left the room, leaving Oliver, seated in his usual chair at the fireside.

In a moment she returned with wrapping paper and boxes

Sitting at the table, she commenced the task of folding, and cutting, and parceling several small gifts to place under the improvised tree on Christmas day. She switched on the radio, and *Silent Night* rang out into the room. Glancing at Oliver, Celia saw him turn his head towards the music, a rapt expression on his face. Then, wonder of wonders, he attempted to join in the chorus. Only a couple of lines he managed, but for that moment his face showed joy and awareness. Celia was delighted. Sarah spent Christmas Eve morning at the hospital, which was busier than ever.

The afternoon found her calling on friends in the town with small gifts and greetings for the season. She visited Jane at the tea rooms, and exchanged good wishes with her. She too was engaged to be married, to a handsome young policeman, who was posted in Exeter. Their friend Dorothy was now nursing, training at a large hospital some miles away. Every now and then they would receive a letter from her, full of happy news of her new life.

Matthew worked throughout the day, ensuring sufficient animal feed was at hand for the next two days. The farmer thanked them all at the end of they day, and bought everyone a pint of ale at "The Kings Head" a small public house down the lane from his farm. It was late evening, and snowing lightly when Matthew arrived home. He parked his motor behind Laura's car at the side of the house, and went indoors.

Laura and Sarah were seated around the fireside. They both greeted him fondly as he entered the room. Sarah rose and kissed him, bidding him sit down while she refilled the teapot. He stretched wearily enjoying thc warmth from the fire.

"This is good. It has been a long day. You look tired Laura, have you had a hard day too?" Laura smiled, stifling a yawn.

"I always seem to be tired these days, as does everyone. It has been a busy day, busier than usual with two days to prepare for, but I don't mind. I only hope we have a night free from raids, and a peaceful Christmas Day to follow."

Matthew nodded and observed his sister in law admiringly. She looked drawn these past months, and her hair was white in places. But her spirit never faltered, and her energy and affection were as strong as ever. He sighed. The last year had taken its toll on all of them. He was aware of several grey strands in his own head, though the hair was as thick and plentiful as ever it had been. Sarah too suffered in her own quiet way, through Oliver's pain. He sighed again. What would become of the pair of them? Would they ever find the happiness they deserved? Sarah came in, and poured her father fresh tea. They all chatted for a short time, before going to their beds.

There was one brief raid during the early hours of Christmas morning, but it was over before anyone had chance to respond to the warning, and the next sound Sarah was conscious of was the distant bells celebrating Christmas day. Matthew brought cups of tea to both she and Laura as a treat Shortly afterwards they all assembled in the dining room for hot porridge, and toast, washed down with strong tea. In a festive mood coats and hats were donned, and gloves and scarves, and all three set off to meet Celia and Oliver, and walk with them to church.

The church looked beautiful. Somehow red and white flowers had been obtained. Together with greenery of holly and ivy, a splendid display adorned various parts of the church. Carols were sung with enthusiasm, Oliver singing along most of the time. Prayers were said , especially for the bereaved, and war victims, suffering or dead at the hands of the enemy. Prayers were also said for the enemy.

Afterwards, the five strolled home, their feet crunching in the light snow beneath them. Sarah walked behind with Oliver, gently tucking her arm in his. He appeared to be happy with this, looking down at her and giving a smile of contentment. Sarah was very happy. Arriving at Celia's, all made for the drawing room, and admired the decorations, glinting and glowing in the light from the window. Celia had found a bottle of sherry in the cellar, and everyone, even Oliver raised a glass in celebration. Celia bustled to and fro, and then at one o'clock pronounced dinner was ready.

The dining table had been set with care. Celia had unearthed crystal glassware, and silver cutlery from the attic, and they shone to perfection together with snowy white napkins held in silver rings. The centre of the table was dominated by a silver bowl filled with holly, firs and pale green ivy. Tall white candles in silver holders stood at each end of the table. Everyone gasped in admiration. Celia accepted their compliments with pleasure.

Matthew was placed at the head of the table, opposite Celia. On her right sat Oliver, next to Sarah who was across from Laura. Dinner was served by the women, Celia bringing the joint of pork in last of all, steaming on its platter. Grace was said, and Matthew carved, allowing each a generous portion. Together with potatoes, roast and boiled, carrots and sprouts, thick dark gravy and homemade apple sauce to compliment, a veritable feast was enjoyed.

A bottle of red wine from the year 1901 accompanied the meal. All took their time to savour the food. Oliver cleared his plate, and accepted the offer of second helpings. At last everyone sat back, replete. But, as Celia informed them, they had yet to sample the pudding, before they could think of leaving the table. Rich and dark, with a sprig of holly in the top, it was borne in and placed on the table. All were persuaded to have a small helping, without too much effort, and helped themselves to hot custard, pouring it on to their pudding. It was pronounced perfect. The last mouthful complete, everyone sat around the table sipping the wine, and chatting easily. Oliver was drawn into the conversation quite naturally, responding with a nod, or occasional monosyllables. He appeared happy enough, his cheeks were flushed from the wine, and his eyes were shining as they flitted from person to person, following the animated conversation. Sarah studied him often, and smiled, squeezing his hand affectionately when he turned her way.

Lunch over, everyone made short work of clearing the table, and washing the dishes. Celia made a large pot of tea, and all of them adjourned to the drawing room, settling themselves comfortably in the warmth of the fire. Sarah poured out the tea, handing round the cups.

They talked and laughed, it was time for opening the presents. Gathering everyone around the "tree" until Celia commenced handing out the various packages. Sarah had quietly placed some of her own there on arrival, together with one or two from her aunt and Matthew. The next half hour was spent amidst discarded wrappings and ribbons, each one showing delight, and exchanging thank yous with the other. Oliver seemed rather bemused at all the goings on, but voiced his appreciation at his gifts. He received a wollen scarf from Laura, a box of handkerchiefs from Matthew, and a pair of carpet slippers from Celia, which he donned straight away. Sarah had saved long and hard for just the right gift, and at last had found the very thing.

Everyone looked as Oliver unwrapped it, the last parcel. Inside, hidden among layers of paper was a handsome wrist watch with a silver band. Turning it over for Oliver to read,

Sarah pointed out the inscription on the back of the watch.
"Oliver dear. Christmas 1915. from your beloved Sarah."

Everyone paused, awaiting his response. For a moment or two there was none, he remained gazing at the gift in silence. Then, he turned to Sarah, tears in his eyes, and kissed her gently on the cheek.

"Thank you dear Sarah."

He murmured, his voice husky with emotion. Sarah helped him to put the watch on, and after that, the parcel wrappings were cleared, the fire was stoked up, and they all settled back to enjoy a relaxing exchange of stories, old and new, festive jokes, and good friendly conversation. Someone then burst into a popular song, and was soon joined by the others. This was followed by another favourite, and so on. In the middle of the sing song, Oliver rose from his chair and left the group, Sarah thought nothing of this, until suddenly from the far side of the room the piano was heard, its notes in accordance with the song they were singing. At first the notes were hesitant and faint, but as the player gained confidence, the tune became louder and more impressive. Noone stopped their singing, but at a sign from Celia, they moved silently over to the piano, where Oliver sat, now totally rapt at the keyboard. He finished the tune and paused. Matthew started to hum another well known air, and Oliver quickly picked it out on the piano. The evening went on like this, until no one could think of another song to sing.

Everyone clapped Oliver on the back, and praised his playing. He smiled in contentment, though did look rather drawn and tired. Celia suggested that it was time to end the proceedings, as it had been a long day. They all took the hint, as everyone observed how weary Oliver had become. Going into the hall Matthew handed the coats and scarves to the ladies, they donned them with their snow boots and thick gloves and said their goodbyes to Celia and Oliver.

Sarah hung back in the doorway as her father and Laura walked down the garden path. She kissed Celia, and thanked her warmly for the wonderful day, then she turned to Oliver.

"Goodbye my dear, until tomorrow. It was so grand to hear you playing again I am so happy, and I do love you. Bye."

She kissed him tenderly, turned and hurried away into the night, after her aunt and Matthew.

The next day they entertained Oliver and Celia at Laura's house. *Bubble and squeak* was on the menu, and fruit punch which Sarah and her aunt had concocted, and which proved to be very potent. Jane and her "intended" came around at tea time for a short visit. The Christmas cake was cut and sampled, and Jane showed everyone her ruby ring shining on her engagement finger. Oliver said a few words to Ted the fiance, who talked easily, and drew him into the conversation by talking about cricket, which he knew Oliver loved. Later when all the visitors had left, Sarah sat with her father and aunt gazing into the dying embers of the fire. She sighed, a long contented sigh.

"A lovely Christmas, don't you agree? I do think Oliver is showing some improvement, what do you think?"

Laura nodded.

"I think you are right, but we must still be very gentle with him, he has a long way to go yet before he is himself again. Patience is what is needed right now."

"Yes of course, I am trying to be as patient as I can, but I'm sure that he is showing more awareness, and the way he played the piano last night was so encouraging."

Matthew reached for Sarah's hand and squeezed it.

"Time is the healer dear, your aunt is right. We must all be understanding and tolerant, and let things take their course.

Oliver certainly appears brighter of late, but it would be disastrous to rush things. I know everything will turn out well for you both in the end, once this awful war is over."

Soon after this, they said their goodnights, and made their way upstairs for sleep, after a tiring day.

The following weeks found life returning to the normal day to day toil, and struggle to survive the shortage of rations, the bitterly cold weather, and the nights disrupted with raids from the air, which left chaos and devastation afresh each morning. The hospital still stood, undamaged, and was full to capacity. Sarah worked for up to 6 hours most days, and Laura only slightly less. Some evenings they were so weary on reaching home, that it was all they could do to prepare some sort of substantial meal ; if it hadn't been for Matthew coming in hungry from his farm work, the women wouldn't have troubled just for themselves. However, Sarah endeavoured to visit Celia at least twice a week, and to spend some time alone with Oliver.

One Wednesday afternoon during January, Sarah had a few hours off, before returning to her work. The previous night had been particularly violent, with everyone getting little or no sleep at all. A number of bombs had hit the town, and smoke still filled the air, rising from the blackened snow, and chartred remains of buildings. Sarah picked her way around the piles of rubble, as she made her way through town. She saw many familiar faces as she passed by, acquaintances she had become friendly with in her day to day walk to and fro work. Some of those she saw had lost their home altogether, and stood around in small groups, lost and dazed, watching the smouldering ruins of what had once been their domain. Men were attempting to salvage anything which looked vaguely useful, by moving and lifting items like doors, or wooden beams and placing them to one side. Women concentrated on pots and pans, and the tin bath if it was reasonably intact, with no holes.

On the other hand, the children tended to treat it all as a game, hopping and skipping between fallen bricks, and playing amongst the blackened boards that had once been their home. Sarah hurried on, hands in pockets against the cold of the wind. It was starting to snow again, and would soon hamper any work started, as already a clean carpet of snow was settling over everything. She noticed that the town Tea rooms had gone, along with adjoining shops either side. Poor Jane wouldn't be working today or for a good many days come to that, Sarah thought to herself.

After a while she left the damaged part of the town, and continued until she came near to Celia's. Looking ahead at the house, it was hard to believe that things were any different from that first winter, when all had been at peace in the world. Snow covered the roof, and surrounding trees and hedges, hiding any signs of damage which would otherwise be visible. The walls were all standing still, though some windows had been blasted out, and were boarded up. Sarah knew for a fact that the garden, once so carefully tended, was now overgrown and negelected. At the rear of the house, the ornamental grounds were no more. Stone maidens and bird baths lay broken, amid fallen debris, and weeds had taken over, where exotic blooms had once flourished. However, today the house actually looked beautiful, all its inadequacies hidden beneath a soft snowy blanket. Sarah sighed for past times as she plodded up to the front door. She fumbled for the key in her pocket, and turned the lock, letting herself in.

Divesting herself of her coat and boots in the hallway, she glanced in the mirror, and ran her fingers through her wayward hair, attempting to control the fine wisps. To no avail, it sprung back into its own sweet way. She continued into the drawing room, calling as she went :–

"Hello there, it's me, Sarah. Celia,! Oliver,! Where are you?"

No reply. She went on, opening doors and peeping in, looking for any sign of her friends. It seemed they were out. Sarah was puzzled. It was most unusual for them to be out this time of the day, already the afternoon sky was darkening. She came at last to Oliver's room. Knocking gently, she entered. Everything in here was dark, the curtains still drawn across. She switched on the light, and at first saw nothing out of the ordinary. Then, there came a faint whimpering sound from the other side of the bed. Sarah hurried to investigate.

Oliver lay on the floor, curled up in a ball on his side, his arms were covering his head in a protective attitude. He was wedged between the bed and the chest nearby. Bending down, Sarah spoke quietly to him.

"My dear! Oliver! It's alright now, I am here, Sarah. Come, let me help you up."

She made to take his hands from his face, but they held fast. He lay still, but for an occasional shudder, and a constant pitiful whimper. Sarah covered him over with a blanket, as he felt so cold, and went to continue her search for Celia. Something was very wrong. After an unsuccessful scour of the entire house, she at last found herself in the conservatory. Most of the windows here were broken, and were boarded up. Dust lay thickly around, and it was bitterly cold, the door was creaking to and fro in the draught from the winter wind. She walked over to close it, nearly tripping over a dark shape on the floor. Gasping, Sarah leaned over, to discover Celia's crumpled form lying awkwardly on the cold stone surface.

Remembering not to move her, in case of broken limbs, Sarah felt her pulse, it was weak but regular. Her appearance was ashen, and her breathing shallow. It seemed that she may have suffered a heart attack. Goodness knows how long she had lain there. After covering her with a blanket, she left Celia and rushed out of the house, without bothering to put coat or hat on. At the gate she frantically searched the wintry aspect, her eyes peering through the gathering gloom. To her relief she spotted a young boy dragging a sledge along the pavement towards her. She hailed him, and ran out of the gate.

"Excuse me young man, I have some trouble. A friend of mine has been taken ill in this house, I would be much obliged if you could find a doctor.

"All right Miss, I'll go right away, don't you worry."

"I think the best place to go will be the hospital. Ask for Dr. Brooke, if he's not there, any doctor will do. But please hurry."

The boy ran off, and Sarah rushed back into the house. The next half hour was spent flitting between Celia and Oliver, who still remained uncooperative in his bedroom. After what seemed an age, the door bell rang, and Sarah admitted Dr. Brooke with relief. She took him through to Celia first. He examined her briefly, and carried her to her bed. Injecting her with a stimulant, he advised Sarah on her treatment, stating that she had suffered a minor heart attack, which had been complicated by prolonged exposure to the cold. Then they visited Oliver who remained as Sarah had left him. It took much gentle handling and persuasion by the doctor to finally coax Oliver from the floor into his bed. There he lay, staring at the doctor, fists clenched at his side, terror in his eyes. The doctor was marvellous. He spent at least half an hour just talking to Oliver, quietly reassuring him and calming him. Then, he gave him an injection to sedate him which worked almost immediately,and lead Sarah from the room.

"He will be fine. I think the bombing last night revived bad memories for him. Being alone, with his aunt in a state of collapse, caused him to hide, and protect himself in total fear of the enemy. Thus, the curled up position, behind the bed. Unfortunate, as I think some improvement was beginning to show."

Sarah nodded, tears in her eyes:

"It was. At last, he seemed to be responding to those who cared for him. Now what"?

"Ah all is not lost my dear. Keep up the good work. It is only a temporary set–back. I assure you, with rest, your friend Celia will recover. And your very good friend Oliver will respond to your care and devotion, and patience."

"Patience, of course." Sarah sighed.

"Now, is there anything else I can help you with, before I return to the hospital? There should be somebody here at all times, can that be arranged?"

Sarah replied that she could sleep there that night, if a message could be got to Laura. But plans would have to be made for the daytimes.

"There was a lady who watched over Oliver for a few hours each week when he first came home. She is a retired nurse, and Dr. Grant recommended her. Mrs. Davenport has recently dispenced with her services, as Oliver seemed so much better in himself, that is, until today."

Here Sarah swallowed her tears.

"Can you recall her name?"

"Yes, Mrs. Harrison."

"Right, I do know the lady, and will contact her accordingly, to see if she can manage some full time duties here. It may be better if she lived in, is that possible?"

"Of course. I can prepare a room for her. I will also ask Bridget if she can come in just to prepare a meal each day. She used to work here as a maid before her marriage, and gets on very well with Mrs. Davenport."

"Excellent. That is settled then. You will be here tonight, and I will ensure that your aunt is told. Both of your patients should sleep through until early morning, after their injections. I will leave a tablet for Mrs. Davenport for whenever she awakens, and I don't think the young man will need anything other than the reassurance of knowing that someone is nearby.

"Thank you doctor for coming so promptly, I realize how busy you are."

"Not at all. Happy to be of service. Now however, I must dash back to the hospital. I will call on your aunt first. Will she be at home?"

"She may not be. I will write a short note for you to drop through the letter box, if you will be so kind."

Sarah scrawled an explanatory note, which she folded and handed to the doctor. He picked up his bag, and was shown out of the house. Checking on the two invalids in her care, Sarah first visited Oliver's room. He slept peacefully, and deeply, benefiting from the sedation he had received from the doctor. She left him, opening the door into the softly lit hallway, in case he should awaken and call out. Entering Celia's room, she found her to be in a restless sleep. The clothes had been thrown off, and the pillow was wringing wet with perspiration. Sarah fetched a thermometer and took her temperature, it was high. Bringing a bowl of tepid water to the bedside, she proceeded to sponge her friend from the face downwards with damp cloths, drying as she went with a soft towel, finishing with the feet.

Finding a fresh night gown from the drawer, she gently and expertly eased it over Celia's head and shoulders, and pulled it right down, making sure it lay smoothly beneath her. Taking the temperature again, she was relieved to find that it had dropped a little. After removing the bowl, and setting the covers straight, she prepared herself a tray of tea, with a sandwich, and made herself as comfortable as possible in the armchair by Celia's bed. Sarah knew she would hear Oliver if he awoke, and felt that Celia was in the more serious state of the two of them. If she awoke Sarah wanted to be near at hand.

The rest of the evening passed without any further disturbances. Every so often Sarah checked Celia's temperature, and breathing. They remained stable. Her sleep was more peaceful, and her colour had improved. Once in a while Sarah crept down to Oliver's room, and looked in on him. He slept like a baby, remaining in the same position each time she visited.

Night drew on. The whole atmosphere grew more chilly. Not wishing to use any of the fuel, which she knew was in short supply, Sarah curled in her chair, feet tucked beneath her, and a thick eiderdown wrapped about her. Some how the cold still reached her, especially her feet, which became numb from time to time. Every hour throughout the night, she rose from her slumberous state to check on Oliver, and to stretch her limbs. At 3 a.m. an air raid warning startled her out of a doze. Seconds later a distant blast caused the whole house to shudder. Jumping to her feet, she threw her cover to one side, hastening to observe Celia. She still slept deeply. Hurrying down the stairs, she made for Oliver's room, and was just in time to prevent him from leaving his bed, dragging bedclothes with him, to find refuge, in a dim corner somewhere.

With much difficulty, Sarah restrained him, and pulled him back on to the bed, talking softly to him all the time. His terror made him very difficult to manage, but at last he lay in some sort of reasonable position on the bed. Retrieving the covers from the floor, Sarah was tucking them around him, whilst he lay tense and distressed, when there was another tremendous explosion, this time much closer. Throwing herself across Oliver, to prevent his rising in sheer panic, she held tight to the bed posts to give her stability. Beneath her, Oliver was straining to escape, and sobbing pitifully. After an age, the **all clear** sounded, and very slowly, Sarah eased herself up from the bed. Oliver had his eyes closed tightly, and his hands gripped the covers. Sarah spoke to him.

"It's all right now dear. All quiet again. I'm sorry if I hurt you, I was trying to keep you safely in bed. Are you recovered? Oliver!"

No response. Sarah continued to reassure him, gently laying her hand on his forehead "Oliver, you can open your eyes now. I am here, and you are safe. Try to relax, and trust me dear."

Suddenly he did open his eyes, but they were so full of terror, that he didn't see Sarah at first. Slowly, he calmed down, and his vision at last focussed on her anxious face. Giving a deep sign of relief at the familiar sight of her, he managed a tremulous smile. Sarah bent and kissed his lips.

"Now my love, if you feel able to make us a nice hot cup of tea, I would be grateful. Your aunt is also unwell, and I must go and make sure she is all right. Do you feel strong enough to join me upstairs for a short visit with her? I don't want her disturbed if she is still asleep mind."

At the news of his aunt being unwell, Oliver immediately pulled himself together, as Sarah had anticipated, and started to climb out of the bed. Sarah laid her hand on his arm , saying: "Don't worry my dear. Take things steadily. I will go on to your aunt's room, and you can bring some tea and biscuits in when you have prepared them. Just remain calm, things will be a lot easier if I dont have you to worry about as well."

Oliver nodded, he reached for her hand, and put it to his lips. Then, he steadily rose from the bed, and reached for his dressing gown. Sarah left him and went back to Celia's room. She had woken up, but lay quietly resting. She looked up as Sarah entered the room.

"Sarah!What has been going on? Why am I here in bed? Where is Oliver?"

Sarah laughed and shook her head.

"Celia, Celia! One question at a time please. Oliver is fine. You will see him shortly, when he brings us all a cup of tea. You are in bed because you suffered a mild heart attack, and lay in the conservatory for some time exposed to the elements. I discovered you when I visited yesterday afternoon. The doctor carried you to your bed, and said that you will be completely well with rest."

Celia snorted.

"Rest? How can I rest, when there is so much to do? Oliver has to be watched over. My voluntary work in the town, I can't just abandon it. You cannot be here, you have your work. It's impossible to rest."

Sarah quietly explained the arrangements that had been made; that is, if Celia was in agreement. She was.

"Thank you dear girl, for arranging things so well. What would I do without you? If you hadn't found me lying there yesterday, why I could easily have......."

She shuddered at the thought. At that moment Oliver entered with a tray of hot tea and biscuits, and the mood lightened. Oliver was relieved to see his aunt in a reasonable state of health, and Celia felt likewise when she observed him.

They all enjoyed their cups of tea. Sarah then sent Oliver back to his bed, and made Celia comfortable, ensuring that she took the tablet prescribed by the doctor. She placed the tray in the hall, to be cleared in the morning. Glancing at the clock, she saw it was nearly five o'clock.

****

Another hour or two, and the night would be over, Thank God. Leaning back in her chair, Sarah fell into a deep sleep, and was unaware of anything else until the grey light of morning filtered into the room.

9

CHANGES AFOOT.

The following week or so was spent in organizing some sort of day to day routine for the household. The nights were no problem. Either Sarah or her aunt slept in at Celia's, in case they were needed, though after that first night, both Oliver and Celia had relatively peaceful periods of sleep, apart from any disturbances caused through air raids. These times were still bad for Oliver, filling him with deep terrors. Whichever one was keeping vigil, when these attacks took place, sat by his side for as much as an hour at a time, reassuring him, holding his hand, and constantly speaking works of comfort and affection. Eventually the episode would pass, slowly his eyes cleared, and his limbs would relax, until finally he ended up by sobbing weakly in the arms of his nurse.

Celia progressed, with no further signs of repeated heart attacks. She slept deeply, reassured by the presence of one or the other of her friends. Even the air raids failed to awaken her most times, although if the house actually shook, she might just turn over in her sleep! Mrs. Harrison gladly moved in for a period. Her own family were grown up and away from home with their own families, and her "dear Fred " had passed on these last 4 years leaving her somewhat at a loss as to how to fill her time. She had nursed for many years, and was now in her sixties, voluntary work occupied her a little, but she was secretly delighted to be asked to work full time once more, nursing Mrs. Davenport, and young Mr. Mcgregor, lovely people.

The money would come in useful too. Her nights were

undisturbed, as Sarah or Laura took over, but from 8 a.m. until around 7 o'clock in the evening she was on duty. Very little nursing care was required, as both patients were up and about the house. Mrs. Davenport had to be prevented from doing the housework, or running around fetching and carrying for Oliver, as was her due. This was a task in itself for the efficient Mrs. Harrison as Celia proved to be a very stubborn lady. However, she respected, and took notice of the advice, contenting herself with reading, and writing her letters, and knitting, if her arm didn't pain her too much. Bridget supplied a hot meal each day for the three of them. She cooked it at home, and brought it the short distance to the house. It arrived hot, and delicious, at one o'clock or thereabouts, and was welcomed by them all.

After two or three weeks of these arrangements, Laura and Sarah were quite exhausted. They still both gave several hours each day to the hospital, which was tiring enough in itself, then one of the two would go home and cook a meal for Matthew at the end of his day, whilst the other made her way to Celia's, for her period of "watch". Winter was waning at last. Snow gave way to dirty grey slush, and trickled down the gutters. Heavy skies showed patches of blue, and fields, shrub and hedgerows appeared once more from beneath their wintry blanket.

One Sunday afternoon in late March, Laura and Matthew called around to Celia's. Sarah joined them later from the hospital. Celia made some tea, and Oliver toasted some bread at the fire. Laura spoke, glancing at each of them :

> *"For some few days, I have been trying to come to some solution with regards to easing the situation of this household. Sarah and myself, as you all know, are more than willing to give our time and energy to you, Celia and Oliver our dearest friends. However, as you must realize, we are both near exhaustion, by the time our hospital work is through*

as well. Mrs. Harrison does an excellent job, but cannot be expected to have her nights disturbed, after working an eleven hour day. So, after a lot of thought, I have come up with an idea. I trust that you all will think about it carefully, before coming to any decision?"

Everyone remained silent, their eyes fixed on Laura. Celia prompted Oliver to remove the toast as it was burning, and they waited for Laura to continue.

"I think it would be ideal if you Celia, closed up your house, and moved in with us. Our house is smaller, and less work to keep clean. I can cut down my hours a little at the hospital, and be there to cook the evening meal. Now, I also think it may benefit Oliver to have a change of scenery, and think that Sarah and he might visit her old village in Suffolk, I know she has long had thoughts of her past friends, and how they are faring. Now would be a good time to find out."

She took a deep breath, and waited for the outburst. Celia laughed aloud.

"You are incorrigible Laura, all these little schemes you have been hatching up. Actually I have been concerned for yourself and Sarah lately, you both look so fatigued, all of the time. I would certainly feel less guilty over your health, if easier arrangements can be made. The idea of shutting the house up is sensible, if you are sure that you have room for me at yours. But of course, the idea of Sarah and Oliver taking a trip will be entirely up to them."

She looked enquiringly at the two in question. Sarah moved towards Oliver, and put her hand in his. He was frowning in perplexity, at all this talk of shutting the house, and taking a journey. It was hard to take in. Seeing Sarah smiling up at him, he shakily attempted a smile back. She addressed them all.

"If Oliver is agreed, I will be delighted to accompany him, and show him all my favourite haunts. I am sure there will be someone who will give us board for a few weeks. Tell me Oliver, does the idea please you?"
Oliver thought deeply, and finally nodded with a smile. Every–one gave a cheer.

Later that evening, Sarah sat with her father at home, whilst Laura took her turn at Celia's. Matthew asked her what her plans were.

"Well, I have more or less kept in touch with Dr. Lindsay over the years. I think I will ask his advice on accomodation for myself and Oliver. He will know the most suitable place to stay, I'm sure. And I will try to find some voluntary work for a few hours each week, I will feel useless doing nothing after my work at the hospital."

"It would be wonderful if you would actually stay with Dr. Lindsay, he is a good friend to have, I have always had a special regard for him since his kindness to us in days past. I'll be interested to hear of his reply to your letter, whenever that might be. It will be an excellent idea for you both to get away together, I believe the bombings are somewhat less in that part of the country, also you two need time to yourselves."
Sarah hugged her father, grateful for his understanding. That very same week, the letter was written. Sarah filled the doctor in on all the news, including Oliver's progress, which he always asked about in his letters to her. Not until the very last page did she mention the fact of the intended visit to the village, adding that she would be grateful for any possible information on boarding houses in the area, which would be suitable for a few weeks stay.

Two weeks passed without an answer to the letter. Life went on in its usual hectic manner. Celia remained at her own house, until such time as Sarah and Oliver knew their plans for certain. All the snow had gone now, and work went on daily in the town clearing rubble, and attempting to provide temporary shelter for the homeless, and there were many. Some charitable families kindly took in friends or neighbours, sharing their table and fireside, and offering sleeping space, if somewhat cramped. Small cousins and friends slept alongside each other, and brothers or sisters doubled up to make more room. This worked as a temporary arrangement, but tended to cause some family disagreements after a time, but all in all a strong united feeling prevailed amid the gloom and desolation of the war strewn town.

The slightly warmer weather made life a little easier. Willing workers achieved some return to the everyday functioning of the town: the streets were cleared to enable free passage for traders, pedestrians and the like and, those shops still standing opened for business, though their stock was very limited in most cases.

The basic diet for many people consisted of potatoes, or other root vegetables, with the occasional paltry ration of mince or sausages when obtainable. Bread, when one was fortunate enough to buy it, was eaten dry, or with margarine. And cakes and sweets were a thing of the past, sugar rations used only for special events such as birthdays, where "fancies" and biscuits were baked. Sarah descended one Wednesday morning from her room to find a letter on the doormat. Taking it to the kitchen with her, she tucked it in her pocket whilst she set the kettle on to boil for the morning pot of tea. She loaded the tray with cups and saucers, and a platter of fried potatoes, which would suffice for father's breakfast, and took it into the dining room. Calling to Matthew that it was ready, she at last sat down and opened the envelope.

My Dear Sarah,
It was good to hear from you again, and all your news. I cannot believe that the little girl I once knew is approaching her twentieth birthday. Thank you for bringing me up to date with word of your father, and Oliver. You will both stay with me of course, no worries there. Let me know when you will be travelling up, and I will arrange for you to be met at the rail-way station. You will find a few changes here, no doubt, though all in all we have had little in the way of bomb damage, to date. I am as busy as ever, with no chance of retiring yet awhile. I look forward to seeing you once again, with your young man. Write with details of your arrival, until then I remain your very good friend,
George Lindsay."

Sarah waved the letter at her father who had just entered the room, she handed it to him to read whilst she attended to pouring the tea. He finished it and gave a sigh of relief at the news that their old friend was offering accommodation to the young pair.

"That is good news, I am relieved that you two will be staying with such an old and trusted friend. You can begin to make your plans now, my dear."

"Yes. The first thing to do is to tell Oliver, so that he has plenty of time to adjust to the idea, and make his arrangements. He can't be hurried in any way without getting into a panic, it seems. Then, I must see my friends, and take my leave at the hospital. That will be hard, I'm very attached to my work. Maybe we will be able to leave in a week's time, if all goes smoothly."

Sarah had work that morning, and informed her colleagues, and patients, that she would be away for a short while from her duties, but looked forward to returning in two or three weeks time. After leaving the hospital, she visited her friend Jane, who lived with her parents in a small terraced cottage in the centre of town. Jane of course, no longer worked at the tea rooms, they having been entirely destroyed by a bomb. However, her bubbly charm and attractive appearance made her an ideal helper in the voluntary situation of tea lady at the town hall.

The hall had been made into a temporary "Restaurant" for the needy. For a small sum, an adequate two course meal was supplied, with a cup of tea. Jane worked at the tea urn. With her sunny disposition, and merry smile, she cheered many a desperate mother, with her brood, who came to take advantage of the one wholesome meal they might enjoy that week. Sarah found her, at the end of her busy spell, helping with the dishwashing, in her usual chirpy manner. Both seated with a cup of tea, and a slice of vegetable pie, the girls exchanged news. Sarah admitted that she had not yet told Oliver of this morning's letter. "I intended to tell him first, but somehow I broke the news at the hospital this morning, and now, you. I hope Oliver is pleased when I tell him."

Jane reached over and held her hand. "He will be. I know he will. Tell him quietly and gently, and hold his hand. It will be so good for you both to get away, so good for Oliver. I will miss you, Sarah, but have a good rest. Come back in time to be my bridesmaid in June. We have finally set a date. Dorothy is taking time off from her busy hospital life to be bridesmaid number two, so you simply must be there too".

The time came to break the news to Oliver. In her own way Sarah waited until she was alone with him. Then, slowly and gently, with his hand in her own, she gave him the news of the planned journey, of the promised welcome of a trusted friend, and a well deserved rest. Oliver sat seemingly disinterested until Sarah had finished, and sat awaiting the response. Suddenly, Oliver turned to her, anxiously fixing his grey–green eyes on her clear grey ones. He gazed for a time, then feeling somewhat reassured by Sarah's expression, spoke :

"If you think it will be good for us to go away for a while, that is good enough for me. I trust you dear Sarah. I would go to the ends of the Earth if you bade me."

Sarah laughed.

"That won't be necessary my darling Oliver; only to Suffolk. I hope that we both will benefit from the rest, and change of scenery. I love you so, and only wish to see you completely well again."

Oliver's eyes filled, and they held each other desperately. Farewells were said, Dr. Lindsay notified, as to arrival times, and the day of departure finally arrived. Laura drove the pair to the station, accompanied naturally by Matthew and Celia.

After a rather emotional scene on the station, Sarah and Oliver were at last alone in the railway carriage. It being a Sunday, they were likely to have a reasonably peaceful journey. As the train steamed its way through the Devon countryside, stopping at small village halts, then proceeding on into hills and vales, decked for spring, with daffodils bending in the breeze, Sarah was taken back in time to her journey down here nearly six years ago. She regarded this as her home now, her childhood village just a pleasant memory. Sleepily she regarded the green fields flashing by, dotted with the first spring lambs. She glanced at Oliver. He sat, eyes staring but unseeing at the passing beauty. Hands clenched, knees together, he spent the hours in a mixed world of his own, torn between the beauty outside and horror, in his own mind. However, as the countryside changed with the passing miles, so he seemed more aware of his surroundings, and the varying aspect outside. He smiled faintly at Sarah's offer of some chocolate, declining with a shake of his head. Soon, the train entered more populated areas, houses became less individual, and more inclined to terraces, long rows of identical looking grey brick buildings, packed together, with their shabby front doors and small square windows. Bomb damage was very apparent. Blocks of buildings were razed to the ground in places, and large areas of land were littered with debris, and items of damaged furniture, or belongings desecrated by the war. They drew closer to the city of London, where they would have to change trains. As the train steamed into the large station, Sarah reached up to the rack for the cases, but switftly Oliver intervened, and easily lifted them down with his long arms.

Alighting from the carriage, Sarah was amazed at the number of military uniforms milling about. Many a serviceman was taking a tearful farewell from his family, others were arriving for a welcome leave, looking gaunt and weary from their duties. Sarah was worried at the effect of all the uniforms on Oliver, but his responsibility to her seemed to occupy his mind, thank goodness. They each took a suitcase, and he gently but firmly propelled her along the platform, his hand beneath her elbow. Sarah anxiously looked about her, searching for whoever might supply some information on which platform they were to go to for their train for Suffolk.

Once again to her amazement, Oliver took over. Beckoning a likely looking porter engaged in unloading large crates from the luggage van, he politely inquired as to the exact time, and platform number where the train would depart. Finding out that they had nearly an hour to spare, Oliver steered Sarah to the station refreshment room, depositing her at a table, and ordered two cups of tea from the lady at the counter.

"Thank you, just what I need."

Sarah smiled at him, and sipped from her steaming cup of strong tea. Oliver stared about him at the assorted throng of

The Countryside changed as they proceeded

people. Some were in pairs sitting at the round wooden tables, others lounged against the counter making small talk with the counter assistant. Several servicemen filtered in and out, some with families, enjoying last moments of comparative normality before once more embarking on their journeys into Hell.

Fathers held tiny tots close to them, savouring the moment. Older children attempted braveness, knowing that the time for parting was close. Wives and mothers talked loudly and brightly, inwardly dreading the final farewell, and the thought of uncertain and lonely times ahead. Seeing how his mind was reacting to so many people inside the small confines of the cafeteria, Sarah encouraged him to finish his tea, and led him outside to the coolness of the station platform.

Half an hour had passed, and by the time each had visited the cloakroom, and freshened their appearance, it was near to the moment of arrival of the train to Suffolk.

Departure was punctual. The final stage of their journey progressed, out of smoky, ruined London, away from the built up areas of drab, narrow streets filled with lines of dingy washing strung between the houses, into a gradual, almost subtle change, with fewer, more tasteful residences in tree-lined avenues, and fields of green once more to be seen, with the colours of spring, dotting the countryside. Sarah relaxed, leaning back in her seat.

Oliver watched the passing scenery. He looked weary, Sarah thought. Poor dear, it was quite a strain for him, this journey, in his present state. Another two hours yet, then hopefully, some time to relax and gather themselves together.

A mother and her young son sat in the far corner of the compartment. The boy was fidgeting, as young children will, and his mother was trying to occupy him by reading to him from a book of fairy tales. The story was of the princess and the frog.

Sarah smiled, remembering how she had loved that tale as a young child, glancing at Oliver she saw that he too was smiling in recollection of happier times. Sleepily, her mind drifted, while the woman's soft voice continued in the background.

Suddenly, she started forward in her seat, opening her eyes. The train halted with a final grind. It seemed that for the last two hours Sarah had slept deeply. Smiling sheepishly at Oliver, she was rewarded with an assured grin, and an air of composed responsibility. Once again he brought down the cases, including those of the young woman, and assisted them all to step down from the train.

Immediately, an agreeable man in a smart blue suit came up to them. He introduced himself as Jonathan Lewis, assistant to Dr. Lindsay.

"I assist the good doctor in his practice, hoping to qualify myself some day. Although he is still very active in his work, he is not so young as he would wish, and the duties don't get any less, so, I was fortunate enough to be taken on to help him out in small ways. He is a marvellous teacher, and person."

"You had no trouble in picking us out from the crowd." Sarah smiled.

"The doctor described you perfectly. Although you have not met for some years, his image of you was very accurate. Also, there aren't too many young men and women travelling together these days, civilians that is."

Sarah nodded.

Oliver had again taken a back seat in the proceedings, after the initial introductions. It was Jonathan who now took over. Oliver picked up his own case, Jonathan took Sarah's, and they made their way from the station to the small square outside, where a car was ready and waiting. Not a lot was said on the final stage of the journey. Jonathan was intent on his driv–

ing, and on getting his passengers to their destination swiftly and safely. Oliver was deep in thought, staring out of the window as they rattled along the winding roads in the rather ramshackle old car. Sarah was lost in her memories, hungrily seeking out familiar landmarks along the way. There were a few. The old windmill, high on the horizon she recognised, and the tower clock in one small market town, as they passed through speedily.

The surrounding areas to the villages hadn't altered a great deal, though some factories had been built, and many farms had gone to ruin with no one to tend them. Sights grew more familiar as the small village of Stowmarket was neared. Sarah felt an inner excitement, and a lump in her throat, as she recognised the old general store, and then the low school building, which she had attended for a while before her mother's death. In no time at all the small cluster of cottages was reached, at the end of which stood Dr. Lindsay's dwelling.

The time was now nearing 5 o'clock although it was still daylight, the sun had gone, and the air had a chill to it. Jonathan braked, and the car halted at the gate. The front door opened, and the gentleman himself appeared, walking down the path to greet them. Sarah scrambled out of the car, and ran into the doctor's arms, laughing and crying in turn. Turning, she pulled Oliver forward, and put his hand into her friend's. Holding them both together she spoke shakily.

"Oliver, my dear, this is a truly wonderful friend I have long wanted you to meet. Doctor, this is my fiance, Oliver."

The old gentleman clasped Oliver's hand fervently, and shook it with vigour. The three thanked Jonathan for the safe conduct of the visitors, and Sarah looked forward with pleasure to their next meeting. The young man waved and sounded the car horn as he drove off. The Doctor placed an arm around each of his friends and walked them up to the house. Jonathan had deposited the cases at the front door, and Oliver took both of them inside, whilst their host closed the door behind them. Suddenly, a small stout figure bustled out of the kitchen towards them, hands raised in welcome. Looking much the same as she had all those years ago.

Sarah was enfolded in her expansive arms, and Oliver, when introduced, was treated similarly, Mrs. Wilkins reaching up to his height and pulling his head down to be clasped to her bosom. He straightened from her embrace, his face flushed. Gaining control of himself, he laughed awkwardly and busied himself with the cases, waiting for directions to their allotted rooms. The doctor smiled, and bade Mrs. Wilkins lead the way upstairs. Sarah followed behind her, then came Oliver with the bags. The upper landing was neat but roomy, with a bathroom and three bedrooms leading off from it. A fourth exit opened onto a short flight of steps up to a further two rooms, which were occupied by Mrs. Wilkins. Passing by the first bedroom, which was the doctor's, the housekeeper led Sarah into the next one along. Oliver placed her case inside the door, and gave a quick glance around, before being shown to his own room opposite. Sarah, left alone, took stock of her surroundings. Mrs. Wilkins had worked hard to make the room welcoming and cosy. Chintzy curtains hung at the tiny window, and a bright rug covered the floor.

The bed was feminine with frills and flounces of pale blue edged with white lace. A polished chest stood beside the bed with a brass lamp and a vase of daffodils on top. A blue and white wash stand with matching bowl and jug completed the furnishings, standing in the far corner to the side of the window. Sarah sighed with pleasure. Laying her case on the bed, she left to find Oliver. He was standing by his bed, his suitcase open.

His arms were full of clothes. Sarah smiled, and went over to him, kissing him she relieved him of the folded garments, and started to put them away in the chest, which was an exact replica of her own. The unpacking complete, she sat down on the bed taking Oliver's hand and pulling him down to sit beside her. They studied the room together. Predominately green, it was a cool soothing room.

Heavy drapes in dark green velvet were tied back from the window, and the bed furnishings were in cream with a light green pattern, toning in with a pastel coloured rug on the polished floor. A marble toilet stand with accessories was in the corner of the room. Sarah squeezed Oliver's hand.

"How do you like your room dear?"

"It's lovely, very tasteful. Your friends have done us proud."

"I knew you would like them. Now, if you feel ready I think we should go downstairs and rejoin the doctor."

"Certainly. Sarah?"

"Yes my dear."

"You do realize that I love you dearly, don't you?"

Sarah reached out to him, and he took her gently into his arms, kissing her on the lips. Drawing apart relunctantly, they left the room hand in hand and made their way downstairs.

10
THE PAST REVISITED AND STRENGTH RENEWED.

Waking on the first morning of their visit, Sarah wallowed in the luxury of a lie in. Burrowing further beneath the covers, she sighed in contentment. Lazily, she thought back to the previous day, the long journey, the warm welcome from her friends, and to Oliver's unexpected show of affection last evening. It had been many months since he had been so forthcoming with his feelings, and had to mean that his state of mind was improving. The evening had continued downstairs with a cosy tea in the front parlour. Seated around the fire, Mrs. Wilkins did the honours, serving piping hot bowls of her special vegetable hot pot with freshly baked oatcakes, followed by generous slices of fruitcake stored by from Christmas. With cups of tea at their sides, and satisfied stomachs, a fresh log was put on the fire, and everyone settled back in their chairs. The curtains were drawn; the lamp lit. Mrs. Wilkins made short work of clearing the dishes, and was away to the kitchen to wash them. Sarah offered to help her, but with a gracious smile from the lady, the offer was politely declined. The doctor turned to Sarah when Mrs. Wilkins had left the room.

"Her kitchen is her domain my dear, even I have to knock before I enter there. Besides, you are here for a rest, not to do household chores."

"I don't think I can spend three whole weeks without some form of occupation. I am used to being busy you see. If there were some sort of voluntary duties I could help out with, just a few hours a week, that would be splendid."

The doctor glanced over at Oliver, sitting quietly in his chair : "How do you feel about that young man? Will you find it tedious by yourself, whilst your fiance is out and about helping the less fortunate?"

Oliver hesitated, then spoke earnestly.

"I could never prevent Sarah from the work she does so well, it is in her nature to help people, and I wouldn't have it any other way. I love and admire her for all that she is, I certainly won't be bored, there is so much to familiarize myself with from Sarah's past. I do sometimes wish that I might do something worthwhile. I have proved that I can't be a fighting man, most certainly." His voice shook, and he cleared his throat. Rising from his chair, he strode from the room.

The doctor and Sarah looked at each other. Sarah rose, and made to follow Oliver, in order to calm him down, but Dr. Lindsay laid his hand on her arm, halting her. "Best if you leave him to himself for a while, about half an hour. Then go to him by all means. He spoke up well, but is starting to feel ashamed and somewhat frustrated at his inactivity, when he sees all around him "doing their bit" for their country. These are all good signs. With your approval I may involve him in some of my visits in the community, during the time that you are occupied yourself. It will do him good to meet some people, maybe worse off than himself. Do I have your backing on this?"

Sarah flung her arms about him... "We are so lucky to have you for a friend, you are very kind, and clever too, what a marvellous idea."

"Well, that remains to be seen my dear. But I am sure that no harm can come from his accompanying me on a few visits. If I feel they cause him too much distress, I shall stop them immediately. Now run along, and see your young man, he should be calmer by now."

Dropping another kiss on his forehead, Sarah straightened up and made her way to Oliver's room. The door was ajar. Tapping gently, she entered. He was sitting on the bed with his back to her, facing the window. He was unaware of her presence, and started as she came up from behind him. He reached for her hand. "I'm sorry to have made a scene in front of your friend, I don't know what comes over me sometimes. I just feel so useless, and so unworthy of your love."

Sarah put her finger to his lips. "Don't ever say anything like that again, do you hear me. You have more that proved yourself, with all that you have suffered on the front line. I am thankful that you lived to return to me, you don't have to prove yourself to me. I love you, and if you love me, that all that matters, that and getting you completely well. But I think you are making progress."

For some moments they sat in silence, holding each other close, until Sarah gently disengaged herself, and went over to draw the curtains. Lighting the lamp, she reminded Oliver that they had both been through a long, tiring day, that she was weary, and was sure he was too. There was so much to do on the morrow. They kissed tenderly, and she left him to his rest. Climbing into her bed, she said a swift prayer of thanks, and fell into a peaceful sleep.

Now, the following morning, with sunlight spilling through the chinks in the curtains, Sarah lay peacefully contemplating the past 24 hours. A knock on her door interrupted her dreaming. At her response, Mrs. Wilkins cheerful face appeared around the door with a tray of breakfast. Sarah sat up to receive the tray. "Really, you shouldn't have done this Mrs. Wilkins. We aren't used to having our breakfast in bed, you know. You will get us both into bad habits."

The housekeeper laughed. "I'm only acting on the doctor's

instructions miss. Just this first day, from now on your breakfast will be waiting for you downstairs.

After an enjoyable breakfast, and a leisurely bath, Sarah dressed in casual clothes, and went downstairs, carrying her tray. Remembering what she had been told regarding Mrs. Wilkin's kitchen, she carefully knocked before entering, placing the tray just inside. She then went to seek out Oliver. He and Dr. Lindsay were in the doctor's surgery, poring over some notes for the day. In a casual manner Oliver was asked if he would care to join the doctor on his visits, and meet some of the community. Jonathan would be coming too of course. It was all suggested in such a subtle way by the clever man, that Oliver had no idea that the offer had hidden motives. He agreed with enthusiasm, realizing that Sarah may like the first day to herself to explore old territory, and to make some enquiries on voluntary work in the area. The doctor looked up when Sarah entered, and gave a large knowing wink. Jonathan arrived, and the three men left for the mornings visits.

Sarah revelled in her freedom. Calling farewell to Mrs. Wilkins, she left the house and started down the lane. It being a Monday, she passed many on their way to the village centre. Mostly women, children in tow, pleased to escape the confines of their dwellings after the weekend, and meet friends and acquaintances for a gossip, Money was scarce. Although the war atrocities were less apparent here, its effects were the same. Food was rationed, and many a soul went hungry, so that her offspring could eat. There was a noticeable absence of young men, many women were doing their jobs. On the farms, delivering post, and of course driving ambulances, and other public means of transport. Sarah went on to the village itself. She went over to the village hall first, and read the notice board outside. One particular section caught her eye:

VOLUNTEERS NEEDED IN THE FOLLOWING CAPACITIES: CANTEENS: COUNCIL OFFICES: PARCEL DISTRIBUTION TO THE FORCES: INFANT CLINICS: HOSPITALS: PLEASE ENQUIRE WITHIN.

She went into the building. Looking around her, she made for the desk with ENQUIRIES shown above it. An elderly lady with spectacles was behind it. Sarah stood in front of her. She raised her head from studying a paper and smiled, transforming her face:

"How may I help you?" Her voice was quiet and efficient.

"I am here for a few weeks, and would like to help in some voluntary capacity if I can. I have done some nursing."

"Really. We can use your experienced help, I'm sure. Let me look. Ahh, yes. There is some help required at a welfare clinic on the outskirts of the village. Mostly weighing babies, and younger children, and distributing orange juice and vitamins. Do you feel you could manage that?"

"I'm sure I could. Not quite the work I have been doing, rather more pleasant I think. Thank you, how many hours a week will I be needed?"

"Just two days a week. Tuesdays and Thursdays from 10 o'clock to 3 o'clock. Here is the address, pop along tomorrow morning. May I have your name please?"

" Sarah Pearson. I'm afraid I am only here for a short time."

"Every little helps my dear. Thank you and goodbye."

The woman smiled and returned to her papers. Stepping outside into the sunlight, Sarah decided to visit the village store, and discover any changes, if any. The same bell sounded above the door as she opened it. Inside, there had been little change over the years. There were no longer candy jars, there being little or no candy. Shelves were mostly filled with jars of pickles, dried vegetables and fruit. Carbolic soap and washing soda stood next to candles and black lead polish. Sacks of salt, and sugar and flour with their measuring ladles, for precise apportioning of rations, were placed near to the counter. The back of the store still served as a post office. This was a single section, glass fronted, with a wooden door to one side for the use of the postmistress only. Though the grocery area and the post office were under the same roof, these days they were independently run. Mrs. Hicks ran the store with the help of her schoolboy son, who did all the local deliveries on his bike. They lived above the shop. Mr. Hicks had been killed in the first year of the fighting. The postmistress, Miss Fry, had once been a junior post office assistant in a larger town, before hearing of this senior vacancy, due to the retirement of old Mrs. Walters who had run the shop and the post office for many years. To her credit, Miss Fry was efficient, if somewhat direct in her manner. In her forties, she looked older, with hair drawn back into a severe bun at the back of her head, and round spectacles perched on the end of her rather thin nose. Her lips were thin and seldom smiled, and her face was entirely devoid of any cosmetic. She dressed plainly, with heavy suits and sensible footwear. She looked most unapproachable, but in fact was a sensitive gentle person to those who were fortunate enough to know her in any depth.

Desmond, Mrs. Hicks' 14 yr. old son had found a special soft spot in her heart. With him she became the benevolent maiden aunt, pinching his cheek, or tweaking his cap, and sometimes giving him a sixpence "for the good lad that he was." Sarah, not knowing this side, or in fact any side of this lady, went to the counter for some stamps. Miss Fry looked over her spectacles soberly. "How may I help you?"

"Three twopenny stamps please."

"Thank you, sixpence exactly please."

Sarah handed over a shilling piece, and received sixpence change.

Murmuring her thanks, she collected the stamps and walked over to the grocery section, where young Mrs. Hicks stood at the scales, carefully weighing small slabs of cheese, and wrapping them deftly into neat packets. She glanced up at Sarah and smiled: "Good morning Miss, can I be of assistance?"

"Thank you, yes. Have you any of today's newspapers left please?"

Reaching to the shelf at the back of her counter, Mrs. Hicks thumbed through several papers and magazines, most of which were already put aside for certain regular customers. At last she found one of the less popular national papers near the bottom of the pile. She held it up for Sarah to see:

"I only have this one I'm afraid. All of the others are ordered, awaiting collection."

"That will do nicely. How much please?"

"Threepence." She handed the paper over, and took the correct change. "Are you a visitor here? We don't get too many visitors these days."

"I am. I and my fiance are visiting with Dr. Lindsay for a few weeks. I did live here at one time though."

"Really, where abouts did you live?"

"Near to the Hall, if it still exists. We, that is my family and myself lived in Maple Cottage at the end of the driveway up to the hall. My father was gardener to the Lord and Lady there. Do you know if the cottage is still there?"

"How exciting for you, coming back and visiting old haunts. The cottage is still there, but empty, and very run down no doubt. The Hall was taken over by the military nearly two years ago, and set up as a headquarters, and a base for the wounded. The local hospital isn't big enough you see."

"Oh, I see. Perhaps I'll walk around that way, just for old times' sake anyway. Thank you for your help."

"You're more than welcome my dear. Hope to see you again. Remember me to the doctor. He's been a good friend to me and my boy in our times of trouble."

"I'll tell him I met you, and pass on your greetings. Thank you again."

Sarah left the store, and blinked as she came out into the bright April sunlight. Meandering over to the patch of green she came upon the rather imposing village clock tower, which remained accurate in its hour, despite several near misses from air attacks, and constant heavy military traffic shaking its foundations. It proudly displayed the time, and sounded each quarter faithfully throughout the village, and beyond. Sarah glanced up at the round face, showing twenty past eleven. She remembered it from her childhood, and marvelled at its continued existence. Finding a likely spot, she sat herself down on the grass. For a moment or two she sat, enjoying the comparative quiet of her surroundings.

Suddenly the peace was shattered by the approach of a large convoy of army vehicles, making their way from the outskirts of the village. The heavy transport thundered straight past the village green, where until a moment ago, Sarah had been quietly savouring the tranquillity. In a few minutes the platoon had disappeared as quickly as it had appeared, leaving a trail of dust and smoke behind. Though quiet once more, the illusion had been broken for Sarah.

Rubbing the dust from her eye, she rose and smoothed her skirt, walking back to the road. Looking around her to get her sense of direction, she followed a side road from the main village square. As she progressed, one or two familiar features caught her eye. Soon she came to the bend in the road which, when rounded would confront her with the cottage. She hesitated, part of her unwilling to face any change. Then determinedly she took firm steps around the bend. She stood, riveted, gazing at the scene before her eyes. Maple Cottage was barely visible, being almost buried in tangled undergrowth. Vines grew in grotesque fashion about her walls, and onto the roof. Moss had taken over the chimney pot, which leaned dangerously to one side. Slowly drawing closer, Sarah discovered the door, its paint peeled off, and hanging precariously on one hinge. Stifling a sob, she dragged it open and ventured inside. Adjusting her eyes to the dimness, she was aware of a cold dank feeling to the atmosphere. Slowly, her eyes became used to the gloom; and she stared around, arms hugged about herself against the chill. Sarah stood in what was once the cosiest, most loved room in the cottage, the kitchen. This was the room where everyone gathered, at mealtimes, around the range on long winter days. Mother did her sewing here, over in that corner seated on her high backed chair. Father would sit opposite her in his special chair at the end of the days work, supping his tea, his feet encased in his carpet slippers, whilst the young Sarah sat nearby reading her book or colouring. William would have gone to bed, and the room, full of flickering shadows, and the sound of soft laughter was the scene of family togetherness and contentment. Now, as she slowly cast her eyes around, she saw crumbling walls, adorned with thick hanging webs, spiders firmly established within. There was no furniture, apart from a wooden chair with one leg missing, and on the dust laden range sat a large iron pan, home for many a creepie crawlie this past year or so. Giving a final shudder, and wiping a tear from her cheek, she turned on her heel and hurried from the scene. It had been a mistake to think that there would be little change, a mistake to venture back. Her heart ached, and she shook herself in order to throw off the depression. Straightening her back, she strode off towards the centre of the village once more.

All this time, Dr. Lindsay, Johnathan and Oliver had been calling on certain patients in the locality. Oliver hung back hesitantly at first, relunctant to impose his presence on strangers, especially sick ones. However, the occupants of the houses they visited were also friends of the doctors, and insisted that all three came into the house. The teapot was warmed, and refreshed with hot strong tea, ready to be poured once the doctor had seen his patient. Most of the invalids were nursed downstairs, for convenience, and to save on the heating. Many were children, mostly infants. Under nourished and underweight, open to any infection, there was little the doctor could do, except reassure the anxious mother, comfort the child, and get Jonathon to mix a suitable mixture to soothe the cough, or break the fever, or ease the breathing. Diphtheria was the dreaded concern of mothers, and whooping cough also. Apart from this, many mild ailments required the doctor's attention. Boils were common, and anaemia, influenza, scarlet fever and the like.

The mothers had little time to be sick themselves, usually soldiering on until either their childs condition improved, or became so bad that the doctor had to visit eventually. The first two calls were to elderly inhabitants who had dwelt all their lives in the same houses, in this village. Edwin Stevenson was 82 yrs. old with chronic rheumatism. He never asked the doctor to visit, but was secretly pleased when he did so, at least once a week when he was able. Harriet, his daughter lived with him, and cared for him loyally. It had always been quietly under–

stood by her that when her mother died, she would look after her father. This had happened twenty years ago when Harriet had been a comely woman of 44 ; now, she was a washed out, stooped figure of a woman, looking older than her years. She never complained, carrying out her duty to her father day in, day out. His rheumatism had been really bad the last couple of years. Now, Harriet opened the door to admit Dr. Lindsay and his two companions.

She stepped aside, and they passed into the house. Old Edwin lay on a couch in the corner of the room. Although it was late spring, a fire burned in the grate, and the room was not over warm. Oliver looked about him. The room was clean and tidy, but poorly furnished. The floor covering was threadbare, and apart from a small wooden table and two roughly made wooden chairs, there was little else, just the couch in the corner, occupied by Mr. Stevenson. It was very gloomy, the only light from a small high window above the patient, and several patches of damp were visiable on the walls. Oliver turned his attention to what the doctor was saying: "Good day to you Edwin, how are the joints today?" "All right, I suppose." His voice was gruff and indistinct.

Harriet interrupted: "Terrible Doctor, they've been really troublesome, he's not had much rest from the pain."

"Have you been rubbing the joints with melted candle grease, like I advised."

She nodded, tucking back a strand of grey hair behind her ear. "I have. Twice a day. In the morning, when the pain is at its worst, and in the evening, before I settle him down. It does help for about an hour, then the pain comes back, bad as ever."

The doctor bent over Edwin, pulling back the covers to examine the offending joints. Jonathan gave assistance, and Oliver observed. Edwin's wrists were misshapen and inflamed.

So were his knee joints. He could scarcely bear the thin cover to touch them. Straightening the bedclothes gently, the doctor quietly consulted with Jonathan at the foot of the bed.

"What is it, what are you saying about me? Talking about me as if I wasn't here, speak up man!"

"I'm sorry Edwin, just professional chat. Nothing to hide, I assure you. My colleague and I just want to try and find some relief for you, from your pain. He is going to make you up some new medicine, which may help, I do hope so."

"So do I. All this medicine, none of it's much use. A waste of time, if you ask me."

"Well, just give it a try, you never know. It might surprise you. You take care of yourself too Harriet, now."

"She's all right, strong as a horse." Edwin muttered.

"She is a good woman, and you would be lost without her. Now, just remember that my man. Here is the mixture Harriet. To be taken in warm water, three times a day."

"Thank you doctor, and thank you for calling on us."

"Yes doctor, thank you indeed." Edwin echoed reluctantly. The doctor said his farewell to the both of them, and Harriet showed them to the door. Jonathon gave a small bow, and Oliver held out his hand. In some surprise, Harriet took it, and they shook hands agreeably.

The second visit was on an elderly married couple who had lost both sons. Killed in France within a distance of 5 miles and one week's duration of each other, the cable announcing both the deaths together. The old man, Mr. Miles had somehow kept his reason after the news. But his wife Joan sat herself down, after reading the cable, and handn't said a word since. This had been a month ago. Arthur Miles was at his wits end. Everything had to be done for Joan, down to the most personal requirements. He fed her, dressed her, toileted her, led her to and from her bed. And all the time, she remained silent. Not a tear was shed. Her face was as stone, her eyes dead. Dr. Lindsay had spent some hours trying to communicate with her, but she had drawn down a shutter between herself and the world, and sat wrapped in her own private grief and shock. On admittance, the doctor once more sat down, across from Joan, and began to talk to her softly. No response, not even a blink. Jonathan was in conversation with her husband, and Oliver, having been told something of the circumstances before their visit, stood beside the doctor. He caught the doctor's eye, and expression of bafflement. With a sign, Oliver conveyed the message that he would like to try and talk to Mrs. Miles if he could. Dr. Lindsay readily agreed, and moved aside. Oliver sat down. Taking the ladies pale cold hands in his own, he spoke softly:

> *"Dear Mrs. Miles, you don't know me. My name is Oliver. I was a soldier in France, where your sons lost their lives. I didn't know them, but I had many companions like them. I was fortunate enough to be invalided out in the first year of the war. Shell shock I think it was called. I am lucky I know, though sometimes I would like to be back in there doing my bit. Not that I proved to be much good when I was there, true. Now your sons, they were, are, heroes. They died, rifle in hand, fighting to the end. Not like me, smuggled out when the going was too rough. Be sad, cry for them, grieve as you should. But be proud of them, hold your head high. You have a good husband, he has grief too. Grieve together, then, get on with your lives, as both your boys would have wished."*

After his lengthy address, Oliver licked his lips nervously. Giving a comforting pat to the motionless hands, he sat back in his chair, closing his eyes in sudden weariness. A still clear voice broke the silence in the room :- "Dennis and Charlie." Joan Miles spoke through taut lips. Everyone in the room turned towards her in wonder. Her husband made to go to her, but was gently stayed by the doctor. Oliver leaned forward, his eyes fixed on her face. He touched her hand softly with his own. "I beg your pardon, what was that you said?"

She raised her gaze to his, her eyes deadened with grief. "Dennis and Charlie, those were my boys."

"I see. You must be so proud of them both, you and your husband."

Yes, we.... ohhh." Here she broke off, and buried her head in her hands, her body wracked with sobbing. Arthur strode to her and knelt down, holding her close to him, his tears mingling with her own.

The doctor silently beckoned the other two to follow him, and they went from the room, closing the door quietly behind themselves. Oliver was concerned. When they reached the car, he turned to Dr. Lindsay:

"I hope I didn't do any harm. Mrs. Miles was very upset, I think I should have left you to deal with it doctor, and not have interfered. I somehow had this idea that I might be able to help her. Sorry."

The kindly doctor turned to Oliver, putting an arm about his shoulder...

"My young friend. Jonathan and I were most impressed, and grateful for your intervention. For weeks, each day we have visited, taking it in turns to try and break through the barrier of silence Joan Miles had built. To no avail. Then what happens. A young stranger happens along, and in no time at all, does that very thing, in a couple of minutes. Now, she can grieve properly with her husband, and they can help each other. So, don't apologise dear boy, we all thank you very much, don't we Jonathan?"

"I'll say. You were a real expert."

Oliver flushed with embarrassment, and pride. It was decided that they should return home for some lunch. Oliver could make his own mind up, as to whether he wished to accompany them on any further visits today. Arriving back at Dr. Lindsay's house, Mrs. Wilkins gave several phone messages to her employer, then promptly served the three of them a light lunch in the parlour. Oliver excused himself after, saying he would take a rest in his room if that was alright. However, he would be pleased to join them tomorrow, if he wouldn't be in the way. His offer was readily accepted, and he went to his room, tired but content.

He must have slept. Light was fading when he opened his eyes. He rose and washed, then made his way to Sarah's room. Tapping on the door, he stood on the landing, smiling broadly as the door was opened. Sarah welcomed him, kissing him affectionately.

Drawing him into the room, she drew the curtains and switched on the lamp. "I looked in on you earlier, you were dead to the world, so I let you sleep in peace. You must have needed it. I just have to make myself presentable, then we must go down for dinner. How was your day?"

"Very good really. How about you?"

"The same. I am helping out at a welfare clinic tomorrow morning, just for a few hours, twice a week. You don't mind, do you Oliver?"

"I think it is marvellous. A welfare clinic shouldn't have too many handsome young men for me to be jealous of." She laughed gaily, pushing him gently away. She finished brushing her hair, touching her lips with colour, and pinching her cheeks. She linked her arm through Oliver's, and they went down to the dining room.

Throughout the meal, there was an exchange of news. Sarah informed the two men on her day's events. She admitted that she had taken a look at the old cottage, but left out the painful details, glossing over the subject lightly. On hearing

Oliver's praises sung by Dr. Lindsay, and listening to the full account of his actions, she clasped her hands together in satisfaction. "I knew it! I just knew it! No wonder you were so tired, you poor darling. Never mind, you must feel quite proud at your accomplishment, will you visit her again, do you think?"

"We will see her again tomorrow. Now she has started to speak, it will be a little easier to treat her melancholia. Oliver seems to have a soft spot in her heart, she may speak more freely to him. This will all help her condition. As long as you are strong enough to bear her mournful outpourings. It can be quite a strain, and you have to get yourself completely well yet. I can't take the responsibility for any regression in your state of health."

"No problem, I would like to help all I can." Oliver was resolute. After some lighthearted chat, all three decided it had been a long day, and retired to their rooms for an early night. In the early hours, there was a short violent air raid, resulting in the doctor, clad in his dressing gown, appearing on the landing, at the same time as Mrs. Wilkins, resplendent in curling papers and hair net, and Sarah rubbing heavy eyes, pulling her robe around her. They each carried a torch. Sarah and the housekeeper turned theirs off, leaving just the doctor's, its beam playing nervously into the shadows of the corners and recesses of the stairway. Oliver was noticeable by his absence.

"Oliver! I must go to him."

Sarah hastened to his room, her expression anxious. Inside, the room was pitch black, and she switched on her torch to get her bearings. In the circle of light, she made out the shape of the bed, and a figure seated there. Hurrying over, she bent and turned on the lamp at the bedside. Oliver sat on the side of the bed. His frame was rigid, hands clenched at his sides. His eyes were closed tightly, and drops of perspiration lay on his pallid countenence. Sarah touched his shoulder tentatively. He relaxed his body with a long shudder. Opening his eyes, he perceived Sarah's worried look.

"Are you all right darling? I think the worst is past now. It wakened us all."

"Thank you, yes I will be all right. It's only that whenever I hear loud explosions, or the sound of numerous aircraft, it fills my head until it feels as though I am there, with it, part of it. And my mind takes on horrific images, images which I would rather forget, but I fear will never be able to." He clung to Sarah, his strength drained from him. She held him close until she felt that he had calmed down. Moving slowly from him, she laid him back on the pillows, and pulled up the bedcovers. Although the all–clear had not been sounded, it seemed the worst of the raid was over.

"Would you like a cup of tea? I am going down to make some for myself, and can easily bring one up to you."

"No thank you dear, I think I will just try and go back to sleep now, I'm very tired." His voice murmured drowsily, and within moments he was in a sound sleep, his breathing quiet and regular, and his face content. Leaving the room quietly, Sarah found the doctor and his housekeeper still on the outside landing. Mrs. Wilkins had placed a tray of hot tea on a small table there. She quickly poured a cup for Sarah, bidding her take a seat on the linen chest, beside the doctor.

"Does young Mr. Oliver want one, do you think?"

No thank you Mrs. Wilkins, he has gone back to sleep."

Dr. Lindsay inquired on his condition, and as to how he had reacted to the raid.

'Well, he seemed more in control this time. The panic was there still, but he held it down, and actually spoke of his feelings during the raids. I think he still lives through his past ɔeriences, and those of his wounded companions. They are graved on his mind."

The doctor nodded, and took her hand to console her. Soon after this, the all clear sounded, and they returned to their beds.

The rest of the night passed peacefully. The doctor fell into a deep dreamless sleep. Mrs. Wilkins slept on her back, taking deep breaths, and letting the air out in whistles between her teeth. Oliver dreamed of his boyhood, and ran through fields of heather with his mother and father, in the wild, beautiful country of Scotland. And Sarah dreamed of Oliver. Tall and merry, with no battle scars on his mind. Laughing and carefree, hand in hand, the future bright and wonderful in front of them. In her sleep she smiled, in her perfect world.

11

TIME WELL SPENT.

Sarah settled in at the welfare clinic, arriving for her first spell of duty at the appointed time. She discovered the work there to be an enjoyable change from her usual hospital work. Much of the time was spent in weighing small babies, and children. She also helped to distribute orange juice and food supplements to the young mothers for their offspring. There were one or two other women helping out at the clinic, they were all very pleasant and helpful to Sarah, seeing that she was a cheerful and willing worker. Oliver frequently accompanied the doctor on his rounds, and proved to be both practical and sensitive in delicate situations.

Joan Miles continued to improve slowly. She now attended to her own needs, as well as looking after her husband. The doctor still visited each day, for a short chat, sometimes Oliver joined the conversation. Although she remained deeply depressed, and cried a great deal, she was coping with her life from day to day. Oliver, she had great regard for, and was able to relate, through him, to the loss of her sons in military action. Her bereavement caused him to give thanks for his own life, and so, each gained a little from the other's experience.

During the first week, any spare time found Sarah and Oliver strolling arm in arm around and about the village. Sarah discovered herself taking sudden cuts up bylanes, around corners, through fields, that she had long since forgotten, that had lain buried in the back of her mind for years. Now, with her man beside her, she remembered all the old familiar twists and turns in and about the locality. The day came when their steps led them up to the old church. Apart from some damage to the roof, which had been caused by vibrations from a not too distant bomb explosion the previous year, the building looked just the same as when Sarah had last been there. As there was no immediate danger from falling masonry, and a sad lack of funds amongst the community, repairs had been delayed until money and materials were more available. The villagers supported their church well, ensuring that the inside was kept clean and polished, and the hymn books treated with respect. A small group of women took turns to clean the silver cross, and candlesticks on the altar, and in the flower arranging. The main door was always left open, and Sundays found a full congregation morning and evening. Leading Oliver to the ground behind the church, she walked slowly through the gravestones, many of them leaning to one side, the inscriptions weather worn and faded with time. Others, quite recent, had now been added, their glaring whiteness distinct among those of their ancestors. The two halted before the plot, with its headstone containing the names of Sarah's mother and brother. Staring down, she held Oliver's hand tightly. The earth had been freshly dug and planted with bedding plants. Sarah smiled, the work of Dr. Lindsay no doubt. Later on, before they returned to Sidmouth, she would visit again, alone, and bring some nice flowers, and a vase. Giving a final thoughtful observation, she swallowed determinedly, and stepped back, before turning and walking away. Oliver followed a few steps behind her. He caught up with her at the front gate of the church. Turning her to him he drew her close in comfort. No longer able to hold back the tears, she let them flow freely. Taking the proffered hankerchief, she wiped her eyes, and blew her nose. After this she felt a little better. She smiled shakily.

"Sorry, I didn't mean to do that".

"It doesn't matter dear, it's quite understandable. Crying is supposed to release all your pent up feelings, it's good for you."

Sarah laughed; "Not much good for the make up though. What a mess! It must be difficult for you." She added this on a more serious note...

"What must?"

"Well, the fact of having nowhere to visit, to pay your respect to your parents, Nowhere to lay flowers, or mark a stone with their names. I feel very selfish, not thinking of your loss too. At least I have this spot to come to when I feel like it."

"At first, it really upset me. Though there was a service held at our church in Scotland, there could be no burial, no visible memory. I did have their names written into the church book of remembrance. And, when I really got to thinking about it, it wasn't so bad you know. They died together, and went to their watery grave together, what could be more fitting?"

"Yes my love, you are right. When you put it like that, it sounds so beautiful, Come now, I'm feeling hungry, I think it must be getting close to dinner time."

Arms entwined, they made their way from the church, and towards home. By the end of the first week, Oliver had been shown all the favourite childhood haunts of Sarah's. Most were unchanged, there being little war damage to date. The two of them walked up the driveway to the hall on one occasion. Here, the lovely grounds had been violated. Tall trees, and small copses of established greenery, shrubs and fashioned hedges, had been felled to the ground within the matter of days, to make way for lorries and armoured vehicles. A long wooden hut had been hurriedly erected on the site, and one or two tents had been raised here and there. Soldiers were everywhere. Groups of them sat around, enjoying some free time from their duty. The sound of a harmonica carried across to them, its sweet strains echoing some well known tune. Some of the drivers stood cleaning their machines, or checking over the engines. Grease covered, wielding a spanner or a screw-driver, they clambered over, and under their vehicles, whistling and bandying jokes about. A smell drifted from the direction of the wooden hut, apparently the cook-house. As Sarah and Oliver neared the large house itself, they were halted by two young guards, and prevented from going any further.

"Sorry Sir, and Miss, the house is out of bounds to the public, security reasons you see." The soldier who spoke was little more than a boy.

"Yes, of course. We understand. I'm sorry." Oliver spoke politely.

Taking Sarah's arm, he turned, and they returned the way they had come, past the busy groups of young men, each doing their small part, thankful to be on home ground, but in readiness to be sent at a moment's notice to less happy surroundings. In two days time, they could be entrenched in ditches on some foreign soil, shoulder to shoulder with a complete stranger, hungry, weary beyond belief, and in absolute terror of their lives though each of them knew this in theory, not one could envisage the actual conditions. Oliver knew the conditions. He longed to shout out to these young men, eager for action, warnings of that hell out there, and for them to be thankful for duties in their homeland. But of course he didn't. Instead, he and Sarah walked back down the driveway, away from the uniformed figures, back to the comparative peace of the village. Sarah was aware of Olivers preoccupation, and remained silent, her hand in his, until such time as his mood would lighten. In time of course, it did. Once out of sight and sound of military reminders, he regained his composure, and gradually relaxed into his usual informal style.

Time passed very quickly. Before they knew it, they were within three days of returning to Sidmouth. The change of scene had benefited them both, but Oliver showed remarkable signs of progress. Today would be the day of his final visit to Joan Miles and her husband.

Dr. Lindsay had continued his calls each day, Oliver accompanying him on a few of these visits. This day, he was with the doctor alone, as Jonathan was doing some long overdue paper work back at the surgery. Dr. Lindsay knocked on the door, and it was answered by Mr. Miles. "Ah, good day to you Doctor, and to you Mr. McGregor. Please come in." They entered. Joan Miles was in the kitchen.

"It is the doctor dear, and young Mr. McGregor."

The lady of the house emerged, wiping her hands on her apron. "Good morning doctor, and Oliver. Please, sit down, I'll make us some tea."

"I'll do that. You sit and talk to the doctor." Her husband disappeared into the kitchen, and busied himself with the tea making. Seating themselves, Oliver and the doctor waited for Joan Miles to settle herself. Although she sat opposite them in an ample arm chair, she could not fully relax. Perched on the edge of her seat, she clasped her hands together on her lap. She gave a faint smile to the pair of them, but each could perceive her restlessness, and the grey weariness of her face. The doctor spoke to her. "You look very tired Mrs. Miles, are you having trouble sleeping?"

"I don't sleep very well, no, not at all well really." Her husband entered the room just then, placing the tray of tea on the table, he interrupted:

"Never stops now Doctor, a week ago she wouldn't move, now, I can't get her to rest at all. Always dusting, and brushing and washing. Comes to bed about mid-night, tosses and turns until around 4 o'colock, then it all begins again. Theres no need of it. But something seems to drive her somehow. It worries me, I can tell you."

Dr. Lindsay nodded: "I think we may be able to help the good lady. Mrs. Miles, it is quite a natural thing to throw onself into a frenzy of activity, when suffering grief. It helps to some extent, to keep the mind and body busy. However, you must have some rest, or you will wear yourself into the ground. I can prescribe a sedative, that will ensure you a good night's sleep. This will make you feel a lot better during the day. Now then, I'll just fill the details in on the form. Either take it along to my surgery, where my colleague will make it up for you, or to the pharmacy, where Mr. Dodds will oblige, if he has all the necessary components, that is."

"Thank you doctor. I do feel so weary until I get to my bed, then, my mind races, and my arms and legs take on a life of their own." The doctor listened sympathetically:

"I'm sure that you will feel much less tired after a few nights rest. Now, I think we should be on our way, I have a number of calls to make. You realize of course that it is Mr. McGregor's last visit to you today, in two days time, he will be on his way home to Sidmouth."

Joan Miles and her husband both shook Oliver's hand warmly, and she gave him a swift hug of gratitude and affection. "I'll miss you, lad. You're a very special young man, you know. Your Mum and Dad should be really proud of you".

"I lost both of them a few years back." Oliver spoke without resentment. "But thank you all the same, it was very nice to have met you, and you too Mr. Miles. I wish you both well from here on."

They took their farewells and left the house. It was early afternoon, and a glorious day. Deciding to go for a stroll by himself, Oliver and the doctor parted at the village store, Oliver found himself wandering along a leafy lane, flanked by blossom filled trees. He came to an old bridge which looked rather unsafe. Taking the risk, he crossed it, and came to a farmyard of sorts. Crossing the cobbles and rounding the corner of the grey stone farmhouse, he suddenly came upon the prettiest of scenes. There, on the patch of green in front of the building was a young woman seated on the grass, a baby crawling at her side, an older child flying high and low on a garden swing, shrieking with delight as he got higher and higher. Under a low hanging tree, a man was seated in a deck chair, apparently the father, watching the antics from aside.

Shyly, Oliver cleared his throat and walked towards the group, reluctant in a way to interrupt the scene. They all turned their faces in his direction, and the woman rose to her feet to greet him.

"Good day to you. I'm so sorry to disturb you, I was just taking a walk, and came suddenly on your farm. I'm a stranger here you see."

"How do you do. We are all very pleased to meet you, you aren't disturbing us at all. I'm Margaret, Margaret Lawrence. This is Stan, my husband, and Geoffrey and Anne, our children. Please join us for a cool drink."

"Why, thank you indeed. That would be most welcome. My name is Oliver by the way. Oliver McGregor".

"Ah, a Scotsman no less, I thought that accent had a lilt to it. Nice to meet you. Please sit down." Stanley Lawrence waved his arm vaguely in the direction of the blanket, where the babe lay gurgling, her bare toes curling, her fingers crammed into her mouth. Oliver held his hand out to Stanley, then realized with a shock that the man was blind. His hand hung stiffly in mid air, until he remembered, and hurriedly brought it back to his side. Margaret appeared with a trayful of glasses, and a jug of lemonade. Placing the tray on the ground at a safe distance from the baby, she sat herself down and poured drinks into each glass.

"Geoffrey, there's a drink here for you, if you want it. Here, Mr. McGregor, or may we call you Oliver?"

"Thank you, you may certainly call me Oliver. This is very refreshing." He sampled his lemonade with satisfaction.

Margaret took a drink over to her husband, seated beneath the tree, she stood it beside him, within his reach. Turning back, she caught Oliver's gaze. He flushed, turning aside hurriedly.

"Stanley was wounded last year in Belgium. He was hit on the back of his head with a piece of shrapnel, which took his sight. He still has the shrapnel in his skull, it is too difficult to remove it, the doctors say. We feel so lucky that he is alive, don't we love?" Her husband reached out and took her hand.

"I'll say. I don't say it's easy mind, not being able to see the little ones. Anne, I've never seen, she was born about the time that I was sent home. But I can touch her, and cuddle her, and Margaret tells me how she looks. Geoffrey reads to me, and my wife treats me like a King, so, I am grateful to be alive, and here with them. How about yourself?"

Oliver paused: "I was invalided out too. Nothing so tragic as your own circumstances. My nerves went to pieces, I'm ashamed to say. *Shell shock..* I'm only just beginning to pick up. My fiance Sarah is marvellous, supporting me, and putting up with all my irrational fears. To this day, air raids or any loud uproar, especially gunfire, or explosions, drive me to abject dread, making me a physical wreck, until such time that they pass over. Can you understand that?"

"Understand it? I am just the same, aren't I Margaret? We are lucky, not too many raids hereabouts. But, whenever one occurs, I wake, sit up in a cold sweat, reliving that hell, we both know. Nothing can calm me, until the all clear has sounded, and the raid is past. Even then, it may take half hour or more for me to unwind enough to get back to sleep, isn't that right my love?"

"Don't I know it. Never mind dear, things'll surely get better for us."

Oliver spoke: "Personally I feel such a burden to my friends and family, also ashamed to think of all those young men at the front where I should be. It's different in your case, I mean, your eyes. You have been physically wounded. Me, I have nothing to show, just fall part, whilst an imaginary battle goes on inside my brain." His voice rose in anger and frustration, almost on the verge of tears. Margaret put an arm around his shoulder, in an effort to calm him down.

"There now, we do understand. You are not alone you know, and have no cause to feel ashamed, has he Stan?"

"Most definitely not. Come here and sit beside me for a while. Margaret has to see to the childrens tea, so we will have some time to ourselves."

His young wife scooped up her infant and went off into the house, closely followed by the boy. Once alone with Stanley,

Oliver blurted out his apologies. "Please forgive me. What must you think, a complete stranger unloading all his troubles onto you. Heaven knows, you have enough of your own."

"It's good to talk things through sometimes, and easier with strangers. Don't worry about it. You have my complete understanding and sympathy. I have no doubt you will enjoy a full recovery in time. I believe you mentioned that you are engaged? Is your young lady from around these parts?"

"Sarah, yes. She was brought up here as a child, then moved down to the South where we met. We are back here for a visit, returning home the day after tomorrow."

"Sarah. What is her surname? My wife has always lived in this area, and may have known her."

"Pearson."

"We'll ask her when she comes out here again."

"You seem to cope very well with your injuries, I do admire you. Your wife must be a great comfort, and your children."

"Indeed, yes they are. It's all a facade though, don't be fooled. Most of the time I am in the depths of despair, with persistent pains in my head. But, in front of Maggie, and the little ones I have to be cheerful. I just hope hat the piece of rock in my head stays still. It can't be removed, but if it

should shift, and press on anything vital, it could mean curtains for me. Then what would happen to my family. I try not to think in those terms, but you see if it was only myself, there would be no problem. It's Margaret and the children I worry for. I don't think we must feel shame. We did our bit up at the front. Personally I feel bloody angry at the whole futile business. It doesn't look any more hopeful yet either. Hasn't there been enough killing and maiming of young men, on both sides? I tell you, when it is all over, there will be a decrease in the number of men between the ages of seventeen and forty. Practically two generations of menfolk will have been lost. So, its up to you and me, and the likes, to keep the flag flying on the homefront, do you agree?"

Oliver grinned, between brushing a stray teardrop from his eyes. "You bet Stanley. Salt of the earth, you and I."

Margaret reappeared with a pot of tea, and was relieved to find them laughing.

"I thought you might like a cup of tea outside here, it's so lovely in the sunshine. Your're welcome to a bite to eat with us Oliver. I'm just about to heat a casserole dish up in the oven, it shouldn't be longer than half an hour, it you're not in a hurry, that is."

"It's very kind of you, but I must be making my way towards home. Sarah will be waiting."

Stanley broke in. "Do you recall a Sarah Pearson love? She lived around here as a child, and I thought you might have known her."

Margaret opened her eyes wide in amazement. "I do indeed. Little Sarah. I'm about four years older than her, if my memory serves me right. But I do certainly remember her, and her family as if it were yesterday. She lost her little brother and her mother too, within a short time of one another. The whole village grieved for them. The family was so well known and loved, you see. Is Mr. Pearson still alive and in good health?"

"Yes, he and Sarah are very well. They moved down to Sidmouth, to Mrs. Pearson's sister, and have completely settled there. I am now engaged to Sarah. I will tell her, and her father that I met up with you."

"Lovely. When is the wedding? Have you named the day yet?"

"No, not yet. But I am starting to think that it would be a good idea to have a date in mind."

"Don't hesitate." Stanley emphasised. "It's the best thing for a man, believe me. A housekeeper, cook, sweetheart and bed warmer, all in one. You can't do better than that now, can you?"

Margaret punched him playfully, and he rose from his chair. The two men shook hands firmly, and at length. Margaret reached up and kissed Oliver warmly on his cheek, and he left them standing, closely entwined, and waving their farewells.

He was thoughtful as he walked back home. His mind went over and over the last few hours. He recalled the unity and affection of the Lawrences. He called to mind their pathetic gratefulness at Stanley's return from front, albeit a damaged, broken man. At Stanley's enduring courage, and brave face admidst his loved ones. And finally he thought of that man's unselfish concern over the future of his family, not his own limited expectation of life, but that of his wife and children, should they be left to struggle and fend for themselves with little or no means. Still deep in thought, he came to the doctor's front gate. Straightening his shoulders, he took a deep breath and walked up the garden path to the house. He let himself in, and went directly to his room, where he sat for some time in contemplation. A rap on his door roused him from his reflections. Hurriedly pulling a comb through his unkempt hair, he smoothed down his tie, and answered the door. It was Sarah, face aglow and eyes shining. She beamed up at him, holding her cheek up for his kiss. In an instant, he clasped her close to him, planting frantic kisses on every inch of her sweet face, ending with a lingering brush of her lips. Sarah breathlessly disentangled herself, laughing and gasping in confused delight.

"Wait, wait...Oliver, just a moment, please darling. This is all rather overwhelming. Delightful, but overwhelming. Let me get my breath. Tell me, what brought all this on my love? It is not like you to be so demonstrative. I've no complaints mind, but I'm curious."

She walked with him into his room, and they sat on the side of the bed holding hands. Oliver looked down at her slender hand in his. He turned it over, studying the roughened palm, clearly used to hard work. He raised his eyes to hers, and smiled gently :

"I'm sorry dear, to have startled you. It is just that something occurred to me today, to make me realize how lucky I am, and how much I love you. Tell me, do you remember a girl named Margaret? I don't know her maiden name, but she is about four years older than yourself, and remembers you as a child."

Sarah frowned, trying to think back in time. Suddenly she recalled one young girl called Margaret Willis, daughter of a local farmer. Though they had not been actual friends, due to the difference in their ages, she had always seemed pleasant, calling out friendly greetings to Sarah and her family whenever they passed in the village.

"I think I know just who you mean Oliver. Her name was Margaret Willis. She seemed a very nice girl, although I didn't know her well. Did you meet her today then? How strange, after all these years. Tell me about it."

Oliver recounted, in detail, the events of the day, describing his unexpected discovery of the Lawrences. When he mentioned the matter of Stans injuries, Sarah exclaimed aloud in dismay.

He then went on to talk of his private chat with Stanley, and of his fears for the future of his family, and of his silent suffering and pain. Finishing the story, Oliver turned to her his eyes clear and earnest.

"With all their troubles Sarah, they remain so devoted to each other. I could see it, that hidden bond of family love. And I realized how very lucky I am, we are, compared to them. How do you feel about us setting a definite date for our wedding? I want us to be together so very much."

"Me too my darling. I long for that day too. Do you think a Christmas wedding would be possible? It could be a very quiet affair."

"That will be wonderful! As soon as we get home, I must concern myself with looking for some sort of work, and earn some money. I am quite good at bookwork, accounting and the like, I had good training for it back in Scotland. The thing is, who needs accountants these days, I wonder? Or I daresay I could work on the land, like your father. Whatever the job, if they'll have me, I'll do it. It would be nice to have some money behind us at the start of our married life. It's high time I snapped out of this state and got myself something useful to do, anyway."

Sarah gave him a hug. "We'll be all right, just you see. I have some money saved. Your aunt Celia has been very generous to me, since I started to work for her. Though she no longer has me in her service, she did give me sound advice in the past, on how to look after my earnings. So, you see, I have quite a nice little amount tucked away, for such an occasion as our marriage. It will start us off very nicely, maybe we can even rent some rooms. I shall look for some paid work, there must be something. And if you can find work as well, we shall manage very nicely. It is so exciting, isn't it darling? I love you so much."

"I know just how you feel, I love you too. Perhaps we should make our way down to dinner now, shall we take Dr. Lindsay into our confidence?"

"I think we must. He knows we're engaged anyway, and I just want to share our news. Are you ready then?"

Like two young children, they both went downstairs to the dining room where the doctor was already seated at the table, Mrs. Wilkins bustling in attendance to and fro from the kitchen. He rose as they came into the room.

"Good evening my friends, right on time. Have you both had good days?"

Sarah answered in the affirmative, and Oliver nodded too. They took their seats at the table, acknowledging Mrs. Wilkins as she served the soup.

We thought you would like to know that we have decided on a Christmas wedding."

Sarah gave her news breathlessly, adding , "You are the first to hear."

Dr. Lindsay rose once more, leaning across to kiss Sarah, and then give Oliver's hand a hearty shake.

"I am delighted my dears, delighted for you both. You make a fine couple, I know you will be very happy. Mrs. Wilkins."

He called his housekeeper back from the kitchen. She bustled in.

"Yes doctor, what is it?"

"Some of that good old port wine from the store, I think. We have something to celebrate. These two young people have almost decided on a wedding at Christmas."

"Oh, we have most certainly decided." Sarah said quickly.

"Not the exact day, but definitely around Christmas time."

"Very pleased for you both, I'm sure Miss Sarah, Mr. Oliver. I'll go straight away and get that port now."

"Bring an empty glass for yourself Mrs. Wilkins." The doctor urged her. He opened the bottle, and poured a generous measure into each of the four glasses in front of him, whilst Sarah and Oliver stood hand in hand, their faces shining with happiness. Handing everyone a drink, the doctor raised his glass.

"To Sarah and Oliver, health and happiness!"

"Sarah and Oliver." Mrs. Wilkins repeated. The toast given, the meal continued in a pleasant and easy atmosphere, glasses were replenished, the table was cleared, and the evening ended with hot coffee and cordial chat in the comfortable surroundings of the parlour. The doctor sank into his ample winged arm chair, puffed on his pipe, and stretched his legs out on his footstool, revelling in the pleasure. Sarah and Oliver sat opposite on the well worn sofa, spared from bygone days, it's pattern faded, its springs slack, it remained a restful comfy haven. For several moments silence prevailed. Oliver spoke at last, almost in a whisper :

> *"Doctor Lindsay, I know you are Sarah's friend, and of course mine. I want to thank you for that friendship, and for your hospitality to us both these past weeks. I have gained much from time spent with you, especially the time visiting your patients. They have taught me much about myself, and made me realize how fortunate I am, compared with them. Sarah, I know, has enjoyed the visit here, and we will both go back home refreshed and strengthened. I know I speak for both us us, when I say that it would please us very much if you were able to attend our marriage in December."*

The doctor leaned over and tapped his pipe out on the chimney breast :

> *"Young man, you know it has been a great pleasure to me to have you here. I must say I am most impressed with Sarah's choice of*

a husband. I am pleased that you have learnt that you are by no means the most unfortunate of persons. Indeed, I can think of many far worse off. However, you have had a terrible experience, which has left a permanent scar in your mind. It will heal slowly, but not quite completely. I fear that a small part of your mind will close itself off, keeping buried your most horrific visions of the past year. On the other hand, with this young lady's life perhaps, that part of you will be locked away for many a year, I hope. Now, you two, I must get my beauty sleep, so I bid you goodnight. I will certainly be at your wedding in December, wouldn't miss it for the world. Good night now. Pleasant dreams."

Sarah stood up and walked over to her old friend. She bent and kissed him affectionately on his cheek.

"Goodnight, and God bless you."

"Goodnight doctor." Oliver took Sarah's arm and they went from the room. Sarah lay in her bed, dreaming of the future, and remembering the past. Tomorrow would be their last day here. Time to say farewell to a few old familiar sights once again, and to several new friends made during the stay. She shivered delightedly. It would be nice to get back home again, to see father and Laura, and her friend Celia, and to acquaint them with their latest decision. They would be so thrilled, she knew. Oliver seemed so much better lately. Once they were married, she would give him all her time and her love, and ensure that he would regain his health completely, and be the laughing carefree young man of happier days. With this in mind, she sighed in contentment, turned over and went to sleep.

12

A BUSY SUMMER.

The following morning, Sarah and Oliver took an early leave from the doctor and Mrs. Wilkins. Goodbyes were said in the parlour. The doctor had his rounds to attend to, so had to decline accompanying the pair to the station. So whilst the ever obliging Jonathon waited outside the house in the car, hugs and kisses were exchanged between Sarah and her two old friends, and warm handshakes made between Oliver and the new found friend he had made, though Mrs. Wilkins insisted on a loud kiss, planted firmly on the young man's cheek. The car horn sounded outside, reminding them that they must be on their way, and with final promises from the doctor to attend the wedding at Christmas time, they tore themselves away, hurrying to the waiting car. Their last glimpse was of the housekeeper waving from the doorway, the good doctor smiling over her shoulder.

The journey to the station was smooth, and without incident. Within a reasonable time they found themselves on the first stage of the train journey bound for London. It was a quiet time, that few hours. The miles sped by, and Sarah and Oliver enjoyed the compartment to themselves, she leaning her head comfortably on his shoulder. Once or twice, she dozed off, in the pleasant rhythmic motion of the train, while Oliver quietly enjoyed the passing scenery.

Too soon, London was reached, and they climbed down from their train into the clamour and din of the busy station. However, Oliver, taking the heavier of the two cases, placed his spare hand beneath Sarah's arm, and skilfully guided her through the throng to the platform where their second train was due to arrive. He seemed calm and composed. With several minutes to spare before catching their train, he deposited Sarah on the end of a platform bench, and hastened away, returning moments later with two cups of tea. She accepted hers with a grateful smile, noticing that his hand shook slightly, and that his expression was rather strained. Military uniforms were much in evidence all around them. Although managing to keep his composure, Oliver evidently found it a strain.

Soon, the large engine steamed into the platform, and there was a rush toward the carriages. Sarah and Oliver managed to scramble in, and found a place on the luggage rack for their two cases. Quickly, the compartment filled. Kit bags and helmets filled every available corner, spilling over into the gangway. Suitcases rested on top of each other, serving as a card table for two young soldiers at the far end of the carriage. No sooner were they seated, when out came a deck of cards, and they continued to play throughout the journey. Apart from one dapper little man engrossed in his newspaper, the rest of the occupants were soldiers. Sarah studied them from her seat in the corner.

Next to the gentleman and his paper, sat a nervous youth, a cigarette dangling from his lips. When it was finished, he immediately lit another from it, ensuring a continuous drag, and exhalation. The atmosphere became very dense, and smoke filled. Oliver opened a window to its full measure, but it gave little relief to the conditions. No–one had the heart to request the young man to put out his smoke, he seemed in such desperate need of them. Next to him with his head at an impossible angle to his neck, a soldier slept. Oblivious to everything about him, he sat, his eyes closed, a contented look on his face, the occasional snore issuing forth. Beyond him sat the card player, who was opposite to his card playing friend. Then came a lad, seated next to Oliver, who seemed much like Oliver himself had been, when he first came home from the war. He sat, straight in his seat, his hands tightly clasped on his lap. His face was empty of any expression, though his lips were tight, and his eyes were deep, dark pools of blackness. Sarah realized that Oliver was aware of this young man, in close proximity to himself. And Oliver could observe them all, especially the last, with compassion and understanding.

The train continued on its way. The surroundings became uncomfortably warm and murky. Smoke swirled about the air. Sarah fanned herself with her handkerchief, and Oliver loosened his collar. Everyone else seemed unaware of any discomfort. The reader read his paper yet again, seeking for any titbits that he may have missed. The sleeper slept on, his head falling farther and farther forward onto his chest. Cigarettes had at last run out for the smoker, and he restlessly gazed about him, licking his lips, and twisting his hands together. The game of cards went on, amid good natured banter. And the haunted young man next to Oliver had finally fallen into an exhausted sleep. He was hunched forward, his head resting on his hands which lay on the top side of his kit bag.

Outside, the countryside was gradually changing in appearance. The gloomy greys and browns of the war strewn cities, were softening into the greens and reds of the approaching suburban areas. Rows of tall narrow houses gave way to more rambling, less crowded dwellings. Scattered villages nestled among the soft hills, and suddenly between two craggy mounds Sarah glimpsed the silver flash of the sea. She felt a surge of emotion, realising that this was her home now, everything and everyone she loved, was here. Leaning forward, she greedily drank in the passing views. The train was gradually losing speed, drawing near to its destination. Fellow travellers were responding to the slowing down of the engine. Opposite, the gentleman reluctantly folded his paper, and resigned himself to watching the scene outside the window. The pack of cards were taken in, and tucked away, until required again. The sleeping soldier woke himself up with a final loud snore. Straightening up, he gingerly felt his neck, and rubbed it to relieve the stiffness. The smoker moistened his lips, set his cap to rights, and anticipated his next cigarette. The young soldier with the darkened eyes slept on, exhausted. Oliver very gently touched his shoulder to rouse him. He reacted immediately! Jerking his head up, his eyes flew open in confused panic. His kit bag fell over, and his cap slipped to the floor. Oliver retrieved it and handed it over with a smile. The young man took it without a word, his eyes boring into Oliver's.

"We've reached our destination I think. I'm sorry to have woken you from your sleep. Please forgive me." Oliver spoke quietly.

"Thanks; thanks very much indeed." His tone was clipped, but he managed a small smile. With a final grind, and rush of steam, the great train came to a halt. Oliver bade Sarah remain in her seat, until the other occupants had gathered their belongings together, and left the compartment, giving them more space. There was much hoisting of bags, shouldering of rifles, straightening of caps, before the door was finally opened, allowing an exodus onto the platform. The last one to leave was the small man, his paper tucked possessively beneath his arm. He glanced at Sarah and Oliver, touched his cap politely, and went, leaving just the two of them.

Oliver quickly retrieved the suitcases from the luggage rack, and alighted from the train. He paused to give Sarah a helping hand down. They both breathed in the fresh air, relieved to be out in the open.

Outside the small station, Matthew's van was waiting. He stood alongside, puffing on his pipe. He held out his arms, and Sarah rushed into them, laughing.

"Father! It's good to see you. I have missed you. We didn't expect to be met. We could have made our own way."

"Yes indeed we could. But it is good to see you Mr. Pearson, and as Sarah said, good to be home."

Oliver helped Matthew with the cases, loading them onto the back of the van, and they all climbed aboard. In the matter of minutes, Laura's house came in view, and as the van pulled up at the front gate, she and Celia bustled out of the house, and down the garden path. There were greetings all round, before everyone crowded into the house, all laughing and chattering at once.

Welcomes complete, the tea was brewed, and the company settled back to enjoy exchanging news, and a cup of tea. At this time it was right to give the family word of the forthcoming wedding. As expected, the news was received with delight and excitement, the two women already making plans in their minds for the occasion. The improvement in Oliver's health was noticeable. Celia was especially gratified. She wondered how such a change could have come about in such a short time. He was more aware, and communicative, and also there was an air of wisdom and maturity about him, that was new. Although still youthful, he had gained years in a few weeks, and was now a man. She was just thankful that he seemed to have recovered his spirit and enthusiasm.

Later that evening, Oliver and Celia walked the short distance to her house. It would be necessary to re-open it at some time in the future, as Laura's house was scarcely spacious enough for all of them to occupy. Sarah and Oliver intended house (or room) hunting almost immediately, planning to have a suitable place to move into, directly following their marriage. In the meantime, they resided at Laura's, under rather crowded conditions. Oliver slept on the downstairs settee in the parlour, Matthew retained his own small room, Celia also had a room to herself, albeit tiny. Sarah slept on a small pallet in the corner of Laura's bedroom. The arrangement, though not ideal, was adequate, in the short term anyway.

Life took on the normal day to day duties almost at once. Celia, now had to be content with an easier life. She did light housework and cooking at Laura's, and produced the odd item of knitting in her contribution to the fighting forces. Matthew continued labouring hard on the land. He was looking older these days, of course, since he was in his forties. Even so, he was tanned and lean, and experienced satisfaction from his work. He had made many friends and was well looked after at home. Laura had reduced her hours spent at the hospital, in order to spend more time with her friend, Celia. However, her days were still full. She visited those in the area, who had misfortune in their lives. Perhaps they were homeless, due to bombing, or short of food and clothing, due to poverty. Maybe there had been death, either of a loved one serving in the forces, or from illness in the home, due to malnutrition, and lack of medicine.

In each case, Laura tripped in, smiling her merry smile, murmuring words of comfort and encouragement. She usually managed to provide a few items of clothing and some food supplements to help that family through the following day or so. As well as this, she continued to give an hour or so to the hospital each week. Her health remained good. Even so, she was now in her late fifties, and clearly showed exhaustion at times. Sarah drifted back into her hospital work, being thoroughly welcomed by all her colleagues. However, she needed to find some work with wages, so started to seek in the local papers and advertisement notices in the newsagents. One day, she observed a requirement for an assistant librarian in the town, no experience necessary, though an interest in books would be an advantage. Making a phone call, using the specified number, she got through to a helpful gentleman, who, after a few basic questions, offered her an interview in two days time, at the Library.

Meanwhile, Oliver was having little success in his job hunting. It seemed there was little call for "battle fatigued" young men to be occupied in the community. Most office jobs, which would have suited him well, were run on a shoe string, by the smallest possible amount of staff. If staff weren't on the premises, then the office was closed, until someone was there to open it up again. Shops were mostly run by mature gentlemen, or women supplementing their earnings, whilst their men were away. Almost at the point of defeat, he was strolling past the local press office one day, when an advertisement was actually being placed in the window of the premises. Pausing to examine it, he read that they required an apprentice printer, to start immediately. Without hesitation, he entered the shop, causing the bell to sound as he opened the door. An elderly, ink stained individual shuffled from the back room. He wore a grubby work jacket, and round spectacles. A pencil protruded from behind his ear.

"Mornin', what can I do for you?"

"I've just seen the advertisement in the window, and would like to apply, if I could." Oliver spoke hesitantly.

"Name?"

"McGregor. Oliver McGregor".

"Wait here if you please."

He disappeared through a second door, after knocking first. In a minute he emerged once more, and beckoned Oliver over. Holding the door open, he ushered Oliver into the room, closing the door behind him. He discovered himself in a small office, dominated by a large desk, behind which sat a stout gentleman with a heavy moustache. He was writing, and didn't look up immediately. Oliver gazed about him, twisting his cap in his hands.

The main feature about the office was its total lack of tidiness. News sheets and papers were strewn around every–where. Books lay in piles on chairs, and even on the floor in one corner of the room. The waste basket was full to overflowing, its contents spilling out onto the floor. The desk itself was no exception. Besides a typing machine, and a telephone, which was hidden beneath sheaves of papers, pens and pencils lay at random with a brass paper weight, which had nothing under it, and a dubious looking blotter, which had seen better days. By the typing machine was a large mug of tea. Taking a loud gulp from the cup, the man at last looked up at Oliver, and smiled.

"Good morning to you Mr. McGregor. Please sit down."

Oliver searched for a vacant spot to sit down.

"Oh, just move those books lad. I'm afraid it's a case of organised chaos in here. Would you believe, I know where every tiniest scrap of paper is. Well, most of the time. Now, you are interested in the job?"

"I am yes. I haven't any experience with printing, though I have worked in an office."

"The job in question is in the printing workshop. Experi–ence isn't needed, as there is a senior man who you would be working with. Tell me, how is it that a personable young man like yourself is seeking work?"

Oliver explained his situation, he skimmed over his dis–

charge from the army, explaining the circumstances leading up to his present need for a job, in preparation for the forthcoming wedding. He finished speaking, and waited for a reply.

Mr. Harris had remained silent throughout Oliver's speech, his chin resting on his hands, his eyes narrowed. Sometimes he nodded slightly. He liked this young man, and could easily imagine the whole story, filling in the gaps of the account. He thought long and deeply, then suddenly gave a wide smile, stood up and leaned across the desk to shake Oliver's hand.

"Welcome young man, to *The Tribune*. Now, I daresay you will want to know about wages?"

They shook hands, and Oliver voiced his thanks at Mr. Harris's decision. Wages were discussed, which sounded quite generous to Oliver, and he left, on the understanding that he would report the following morning at 8 o'clock. He couldn't wait to get home and tell Sarah of his success. He fairly sprinted the distance of the few hundred yards between the printing shop and home. It was only when he had almost arrived at the gate, that he realized that Sarah would be at her hospital duties for at least another two hours. Rather than sit aimlessly around at home, in the impatient state of excitement he felt, he decided to walk.

He made his way down to the seafront, and stood, surveying the ocean shimmering in the sunshine before him. He recalled happy times gone by, during his first visits to Sidmouth. Outings with Sarah and his aunt, silly capers, and warm balmy days, strolling the promenade savouring a bag of greasy chips, or licking a giant cornet. He licked his lips almost expecting to taste ice cream there, though, in fact, all he did taste was salt from the sea. Gazing about him, he took in the sight.

A few early beach lovers were already comfortably

positioned on the shingle. It seemed as though the day would be getting progressively hotter, and even now, there were some individuals in the sea. Some strips of beach had been closed off, and barbed wire was visible in several places, also many penny arcades were shuttered up, which had been filled with happy holidaymakers in years gone by. However, one or two small gift shops still flourished, and the ice cream parlour still sold cornets, and wafers, as well as candy floss and even sticks of rock (if one had sufficient left on their rations, to enable them to purchase one). Even as he stood, the ice cream cart, bell sounding, slowly came to a halt at the head of the steps leading down to the beach. From nowhere and everywhere, people, mostly children descended on the spot, emerging triumphantly clutching their "goodies" in their hands. Being tempted, Oliver strolled along to the vender, and bought himself a cornet. Sitting down on the sea wall, he lazily wiled away an hour, licking leisurely at the ice cream, and watching all the activities around him.

The beach was filling up, and way out on the sea, a small fleet of fishing boats made their way in to shore, with their night's haul. Suddenly, amid the peaceful setting, the silence was shattered by the loud wail of an air raid warning. Immediately, hoards of semi clad persons rose from their positions, and flocked onto the promenade in one large throng. Some were still wet from their interrupted bathe, and clutched towels about themselves. Mothers tried to hurry little ones along, lifting the tiniest in their arms. Buckets and spades were dragged behind, or left abandoned, to be found or covered by the tide at some later date. Ice creams were dropped, half eaten onto the shingle. Children wailed indignantly at being dragged from the beach. In no time at all, the stretch of shore was completely deserted, the crowd having headed for the communal shelter in the town. Oliver thought it best to return straight home. Before he reached the house, a distant rumble heralded the approach of several aircraft. Hurrying into the house, he made for the centre, which happened to be the dining room. Calling as he went, he ascertained that he was alone in the house. Laura must be out on one of her charity visits, perhaps his aunt was also visiting, socially. Or maybe she was out shopping. Whatever, no one was in the house but himself.

By now the distant rumble had become a menancing row. Sound filled the air, the heavy drone caused vibrations all around. Crouching down beneath the table, Oliver covered his ears, closed his eyes and prayed. A loud detonation shook the foundations, causing two dinner plates to fall from the dresser, and shatter on the floor. After what seemed an age, the sound of the passing planes faded, until it seemed far enough away for Oliver to risk uncovering his ears. Sweat glistened on his brow, and his hands shook. Slowly, he emerged from his shelter beneath the dining table. The all–clear sounded. Mopping his face with his handkerchief, he brushed himself down, and set about clearing up the broken china from the floor.

Sarah came home soon after, and found a composed Oliver with a pot of freshly brewed tea, awaiting her. Over a cozy cup of tea, Sarah learned of Oliver's lone experience during the raid. She wished she could have been there to help him, though quite honestly, it seemed he had coped very well. Then, he discovered that the loud explosion had been a bomb dropped just off shore, causing almost complete destruction of the fishing boats and their crews. He cried a little then, remembering their calm, innocent beauty of an hour ago. Sarah held him close in comfort.

"What else did you do today, dear?"

Oliver remembered suddenly his good news.

"I got myself a job."

He spoke shyly. At Sarah's exclamation of delight, he described the events of the morning and the promising chance of earning a moderate sum toward their wedding.

The following morning, Sarah had her interview at the library. She arrived to find a number of young girls, also in line for the post, so she wasn't really very hopeful.

Sarah was the third girl called in. Her interviewer was the chief librarian, Mrs. Ryan. This lady was an experienced librarian of many years. Her husband was in the Navy, and her son in law too. She and her daughter shared a house on the edge of town. Her daughter Mary had a 10 month old baby girl Emily. Mrs. Ryan had always worked, apart from the time spent in rearing her daughter. When war had broken out, Mary had been sixteen, and engaged. A hasty wedding was arranged, before the departure of William, her son in law, and David her husband to the front. Quite naturally, Florence Ryan drifted back into work. She had a love of books and literature, and found her work satisfying. She studied the young woman in front of her.

"Miss Sarah Pearson, am I correct?"

"Yes, that is right."

"What makes you think that you have any special qualities that would benefit this job?"

"I have no special training as such, but love books very much, I always have my nose in one." She finished with a laugh.

"What have you been doing up until now?"

"I spent some time as a lady's companion. Now, I am a volunteer worker at the local hospital."

"I take it you are not married?"

"No, but engaged. We hope to marry at Christmas. My fiance has just found work. I would like to earn some money too."

Florence Ryan nodded. "Very commendable. Your young man, he is not at the front?"

"No, he was invalided out some months ago."

"I'm sorry to hear that. Now, I must say that you appear to be the ideal person for the position, however I still have quite a few young women left to see, so cannot give you an answer today. But you will be hearing from me, one way or the other during the next day or two. It was nice to meet you, thank you for your application."

She stood, and shook hands with Sarah across the desk. Ringing a small bell at her right hand, she summoned in the next candidate.

Sarah left the building feeling rather dejected. She felt that she could have made more or herself, and been more enthusiastic in her manner. But, she had been honest and polite, so would trust in good fortune. There would be other jobs if this one passed her by. Stepping out, she returned to the hospital, and donned her cap and apron before entering the crowded frenetic confines of the ward.

Two days later, a letter on the mat confirmed that she had the position. She gave a whoop of joy, waving the letter in the air. Her work at the library would commence the following Monday. It was now Thursday. Oliver had been at his situation for two days, and loved it. He worked in a friendly environment, amongst typical west countrymen. Their lighthearted banter, and cheerful instruction relaxed him, enabling him to grasp knowledge of his duties without too much difficulty. He learned how the lay out of a page was decided, and how to set up the machine and rollers to set it in print. The office employed three young reporters, two men and one woman, who trod the streets, days and night, in all weathers to bring in a story. The story, if accepted by the office would be prepared by one or the other of the two journalists, who typed it up, and passed it on for the editor (Mr. Harris) to approve or dismiss. If approved it went through to the printing room, where Oliver helped to ensure its prominence and inclusion in the pages of *The Tribune.* His days work was from 8am. until 6pm. and the first few days exhausted him in mind and body. Gradually though, as he became accustomed to his work, it took less out of him. In fact, he actually benefited from it, coming home in the evening, ink stained and weary, but content, and full of the days happenings at the workshop. The family were delighted to see how he flourished.

The next Monday Sarah reported for work at 9am. at the library. She had promised at the hospital to go in and help them whenever she had some spare time. The library closed at 4pm. so it was possible that she may be able to do an hour at the hospital, before going home for her meal.

She found the work at the library soothing and fulfilling. Her duty was to sort any new books in, or returned volumes, and replace them in their correct place on the shelves, ensuring those were dust free. She also checked any old volumes which would need rebinding. She quickly adapted to the work, and made friends with a young woman colleague called Vera, who worked at the desk with Mrs. Ryan. They dealt with the incoming and outgoing books to the townsfolk, filing their cards and collecting payment on overdue books.

Vera was 22 yrs old. She had a mother and three sisters, she was the eldest of the three. Her father had died several years ago when Vera had been 10. Life had been hard, though they had never gone without, their mother taking in washing to keep the girls clothed and fed. Now, she looked an old woman at 39, and Vera was determined to pay her back for her years of struggle. The oldest sister was 19, and was training to be a cook, her apprenticeship was nearly up, then she would be able to contribute to the household funds. Vera was trained in library work, and received a fair wage each week. She had no regular boyfriend, but seemed to prefer to spend her spare time at home with her mother and younger sisters of 14 and 13 yrs. She and Sarah liked each other on sight.

Jane's wedding was to take place in a week's time, Sarah and Oliver had a printed invitation to the wedding, and to a standing buffet afterwards at the bride's home. Laura and Celia helped Sarah make up a length of material supplied by Jane, into a bridesmaid's dress. The pattern was simple, especially for anyone as clever with a needle as Celia. It was the colour of peach, and it shimmered and fell in its satin folds to her ankles. The neck was sweetheart, and the sleeves fully puffed. White gloves and shoes, and a crown of white and pink flowers were to complete the outfit. When Oliver saw her in the gown for the first time, on Jane's wedding day, he was speechless in admiration and choked with emotion. She looked a picture!

It was a beautiful day for a wedding. Cloudless blue sky, golden hazy sunshine, and the bells peeling out from the bell tower in the old church. Jane and Ted came out into the sunshine from the church. Dorothy and Sarah posed with the newly weds for the photographs, then they were joined by the respective families of the bride and groom for the family study. Later, at Jane's house, over an informal buffet and drink, there was time to chat. Sarah with Oliver at her side firstly congratulated Jane and Ted, who were soon to leave on their honeymoon to Cumbria, then she made her way through the small groups of people to Dorothy, Oliver following close behind.

"Sarah! And Oliver! Wasn't it beautiful! I can't believe that Jane is actually married. Your turn next, so Sarah tells me Oliver. Hope I'm invited."

"Of course you are. It is to be a small affair, but I would like you to come, and be a bridesmaid. If Jane can manage it too, that will be delightful."

Oliver nodded in agreement, his arm about Sarah's shoulder. He was relaxed and happy.

The celebration progressed, and later in the afternoon, Jane and Ted emerged from upstairs, ready to leave for the honeymoon. Ted looked proud and protective of his new wife, who in turn dimpled and sparkled with joy. As they made to step into the car, after farewells had been said, Jane turned and threw her bouquet directly to Sarah who caught it easily. The couple drove off, and the company gradually broke up, and went their separate ways. Oliver and Sarah dawdled home, savouring the happiness they felt, and impatient for the time when it would be their turn to be wed. Sarah buried her nose in the flowers, and dreamed of how it would be.

13

APPROACHING THE BIG DAY.

Summer 1916. War still raged, despite frequent predictions that it would soon end. Every so often, a particularly violent raid would occur at home, maybe to remind everyone of the fighting and bloodshed still going on at the front. There was a unity of the people in Britain, which was apparent in war time, whilst not particularly evident otherwise. The Christian side of folk showed itself in many ways, from taking a family into ones home, who had suffered the bombing of theirs, or perhaps sharing a meagre ration of food with someone even less well off.

Second hand clothes and goods went from family to family, as they were grown out of, or as the need arose. Voluntary work flourished. Women with a sense of vocation, who had never had the opportunity to prove their worth, found themselves running canteens and restaurants as part of a team, helping out in clothes distribution centres, helping in the hospitals, and driving ambulances. At food offices, issuing ration cards, or at clinics lending a hand to weigh infants, and supply vitamins and orange juice to grateful mothers. Women also were found doing their men's jobs, whilst they were absent from home. Delivering coal, and sweeping the streets, to name but two.

The long days of Summer drifted into Autumn. In July Sarah celebrated her 20th birthday. Oliver had reached the age of 27 back in May. Toward the end of September, the weather changed for the worse. It continually rained, the air had a chill to it, and Sarah came down with a severe cold. It started one particularly dismal day, when she got a soaking on her way to work in the morning. Having no change of clothes, she remained in damp skirt and footwear for some time, until eventually it dried on her. By the evening, her throat was sore, and her eyes heavy. Laura cosseted her that evening with hot rum and milk, and rubbed her chest with wintergreen. She still had a most disturbed night, tossing and turning, hot and cold in turns. By the morning, her temperature had risen, her head ached, as did her back and legs, and her nose streamed constantly.

Laura rang the library, informing them that Sarah was unwell, and that she would keep them posted as to her condition. She then set about ensuring the wellbeing of her niece. Extra pillows were found, and placed at her back in the bed. She was plied with cold drinks, and bathed regularly to cool her down. Laura made up a mustard inhalation, and stood over her whilst she breathed in its fumes. She emerged from beneath the towel, flushed and moist, her brow bathed in sweat. Her breathing was eased somewhat from the treatment however, and she lay back on the pillow, closed her eyes, and slept.

Oliver returned home during his lunch hour, anxious to check on her condition. He found her resting peacefully, her hair damp and tousled across the pillow, her arms flung wide on the bed. Laura reassured him that she was comfortable, and that her temperature had dropped a degree. Hopefully, it would'nt be necessary to call the doctor in.

The cold lasted nearly a week, leaving Sarah with a troublesome cough. On the sixth day, Laura helped her out of bed, and down to the parlour, where she had lit a small fire. Although the rain had ceased, the air had an Autumnal nip to it, and the evenings drew in early. Eventually, Laura decided to get the doctor in. Sarah's cough persisted, and she remained very weak and tired. He called one Monday morning, and gave her a thorough examination. His name was Dr. Gordon. After his check–up, he sat at the table, and wrote out a prescription. Turning to Laura, he spoke:

"Miss Fairchild, you did well to call me in, that is a nasty cough your niece has. I have prescribed an expectorant, which she should start to take today, directly you can get it made up, then as directed. Also, a mild tonic, which should put the roses back in her cheeks, and give her some energy. Good day to you, and to you Miss Pearson, I'm sure you will feel yourself in no time at all."

He raised his hat, as Laura saw him out of the front door.

The mixture was made up and administered as instructed, and by the following weekend, an improvement was apparent. Sunday, the day being fine and bright, Sarah, with Laura's leave, wrapped up in warm attire, and accompanied Oliver to the morning service at the church. It felt good to be out again, and when they returned to the house some two hours later, she had roses in her cheeks, and a sparkle in her eyes. Laura had prepared a hearty meal, and Sarah tucked into it, along with the rest of them.

After lunch, Matthew took an afternoon nap, in between reading the newspaper. Celia helped Laura clear the dishes and wash up, Oliver fetched in some logs, and replenished the fire, and Sarah sat, surrounded by cushions, her feet raised, in the large armchair by the fireside. Later, with the wireless playing soft music in the background, she and Oliver played draughts, whilst her aunt and Celia knitted and gossiped, and father enjoyed his paper, and his pipe.

Sarah returned to her work on Wednesday, still a little weak, but feeling stronger each day. Her cough had disap–peared, and she slept through the night now. Everyone was pleased to see her at work. She had quickly proved her worth with her friendly, cheerful manner, and her willingness for work. There was quite a bit to catch up on, and by the end of the day she was weary, ready for home. She was pleased however, to be back at work, and earning some money.

Both Oliver and herself were searching for possible accommodation in their spare time, to move into after the wedding. October came, and went very quickly, they were well into November, when they found exactly what they had been looking for. Ground floor rooms, with a small back yard. Without more ado, they took the rooms, and paid advance rent for them. There were three in all, with a tiny kitchen and bathroom also. A large front room led off from the hallway, just inside the front door. Through the second door was a small dining room, beyond which was an even smaller kitchen, with an exit onto the back yard. Opposite the doorway to the dining room was the bedroom, next to that, the tiny, but adequate bathroom. Partially furnished, there was plenty of scope for added furnishings of their choice.

Sarah hunted the many secondhand shops in the area, for knick–knacks, and oddments in the way of china, chairs etc. She dicovered a handsome rocking chair, which she thought ideal for Oliver. She brought it home, and Oliver painted it, and polished it, before actually sitting in it, and pronouncing it perfect. Between them, they collected various items from different sources, and with all the linen and cutlery, and books gathered over the years, they soon had the rooms dotted with their own personal effects. Celia gave them a giant patchwork bedspread, which she had made herself, many moons ago. It was a riot of colour, and looked as new. Laura supplied many unused items for the kitchen, including several tea cloths, a carving set with a platter, and a handsome set of kitchen scales.

Matthew put together some simple items of furniture, a couple of stools, a sewing table for Sarah, to set her machine on, and a shelf unit for the many books.

At last it was complete. Standing with Oliver, after much arranging and re–arranging the belongings about the rooms, she surveyed the final result, her arm about Oliver, his about her. She gave a deep sigh.

"Isn't it wonderful?"

"Our own home, yours and mine. Yes, it is wonderful."

"To think, in a few weeks time, we will be living here. I will be cooking your tea, whilst you rock in your chair and read your paper."

"Sounds delightful." Oliver laughed.

They gathered up their dusters and brushes, putting them in the cupboard under the staircase, then they let themselves out of the front door, locking it carefully behind them.

The wedding was to be on December 18th. Jane was to be matron of honour, and Dorothy a bridesmaid. They were both to wear blue, and Laura and Celia were busy with the gowns. Sarah had taken up the offer of wearing Celia's wedding dress, which just needed a few alterations to it. It had been cherished over the years, in layers of tissue paper, and sprinkled with lavender, and rose petals. Taken out from time to time, and shaken out of its folds, it was a beautiful dress. Celia was so thrilled that Sarah had consented to wear it. Pale cream satin, it had long slender sleeves, ending in lacy frills at the wrists. The neck was high, also a circle of delicate lace. The bodice was gathered at the waist, and studded with many tiny pearls. The skirt was straight, falling in gradually widening layers at the ankle line. The week before the big day, all alterations were complete, and Sarah had the final fitting, Celia and Laura hovering around like mother hens, making the final nips and tucks, whilst poor Sarah stood on the chair, being pulled this way and that. But it was worth it, oh yes! When she finally stepped down, and made a twirl before them, she was a vision! Her blonde hair shone, its soft waves thick and abundant. Her eyes sparkled, her skin glowed, and her lips were parted, as she laughed and posed, the dress shimmering about her, hugging her slim figure to perfection. Celia and Laura were speechless with delight. Suddenly, Oliver's voice was heard in the hallway.

"Wait, wait! Stay there a moment. You can't come in just now, do you hear? Give us a moment."

Laura hastily stood guard by the door, and Celia helped Sarah get out of the dress. It was removed from sight, and Sarah donned her blouse and skirt. Finally, Oliver was allowed in.

On December 15th. the snow fell. Lightly at first, gradually thickening, it floated steadily down, onto a crisp white carpet, covering the ground in all its beauty. On the eve of the wedding, Sarah left work early. It was Friday. The world was white and silent. Traffic was almost non–existent, the road being almost unsurpassable. A few brave pedestrians battled against the ever driving snow flakes, heads bent forward, muffled beyond recognition, they trod firmly on their way. A glimmer of lights shone bravely from shops, in anticipation of the Christmas season. Come nightfall, they would be extinguished, in accordance with blackout regulations, it was now 3–o–clock in the afternoon.

Sarah hurried on her way home. Tonight, Oliver and Celia were staying at Celia's house, honouring the traditon of the groom spending his wedding eve away from the bride.

She arrived home, and found the house empty. Drawing the blinds, she put a match to the ready laid fire in the parlour, and went to find out what could be had for the evening meal.

She discovered some fresh fish which Laura had been able to get that morning, and some flour and onion. Soon, she had fish pie slowly baking in the oven, and potatoes boiling. Climbing the stairs, she slowly peeled off her clothes, and ran a warm bath. Lying back in the steamy suds, she thought ahead to tomorrow, her big day. She was so excited, and longing to be wed to Oliver. The water cooled, and reluctantly, she clambered out, rubbing herself briskly with the towel. Downstairs, the fire had caught, and blazed merrily in the hearth. From the kitchen, an appetising aroma drifted. Settling herself by the blaze, she awaited her father and Laura.

Laura came first, bringing a cold gust of wintry air with her, into the hall. She shed her heavy clothes, and joined Sarah in the parlour. They were talking cosily together when a loud bang of the front door announced Matthew's arrival. Sarah went to help him off with his boots, and topcoat. Rubbing his hands, he followed her into the parlour. After a general thawing out at the fireside, they all made for the dining room, where Sarah served dinner.

The evening was spent in close unity around the fire. There was no great need for words that evening. Each was lost in their own thoughts, as darkness deepened, causing the firelight to send flickering shadows on the walls. Matthew and Sarah sat close, her head resting on his knee as of old. Although he was happy for Sarah, he couldn't help a certain heaviness of his heart, at the thought of losing her to another man, albeit Oliver, whom he admired greatly. How wonderful if Elizabeth could have been with him to see their little girl married. He sighed deeply. Sarah and Laura looked at him.

"Now now, Father, none of that. I won't have you sighing on my wedding eve. Actually I know just how you feel, because I feel it too. Not for tomorrow and the future of course, that will be wonderful, but just for all the past times, and the good, and bad moments that we have shared."

Laura nodded, taking out a hanky, and blowing her nose noisily. "Yes my dears, we all have a few sad thoughts, with the passing of time. All I can say is, that my life took on new meaning when you both came to live here. You are my family. And tomorrow, Oliver too will be part of that family. You are not losing your daughter Matthew, you are gaining a son."

"I know. I know. I'm not really unhappy, just a bit maud-lin' you understand. Now, how about a nice hot drink? You must get your beauty sleep tonight my lady, so must I if I'm to do you proud tomorrow, when I accompany you up the aisle."

Sarah laughed, and kissed him assuring him she had every confidence in him for the morrow. Laura made some hot cocoa, which they savoured lingeringly. Then they exchanged fond goodnights, and went to their beds.

Saturday dawned, grey and leaden. But by the middle of the morning, a few blue patches showed between the clouds. The ceremony was to be at 12.30. The morning flew by. Jane and Dorothy arrived at 10.30. They donned their blue dresses, and spent ages making up their faces, and curling their hair at Sarah's dressing table. Laura was attending to Sarah. Once the gown was on, she set to work on her hair. For the occasion, she piled it high, securing it with tiny ornamental combs. Then she carefully placed the floral coronet, setting it amongst the soft waves. A heavy veil hung down from the headpiece, Sarah threw it back, whilst she made up her face. She was wearing the necessary "something borrowed" from Jane, a fine cotton un-derskirt with figured embroidery at its hem. The "old" wedding dress from Celia. A blue silk garter from Dorothy, and a pearl pin at her throat, which was new, bought by Laura as a special gift.

At last, the car arrived for the bridesmaids. Laura had already left, after a tearful parting from Sarah. Sarah stood alone, gazing into the mirror. She was pleased at her appearance. There was a tap at the bedroom door, and Matthew entered. Resplendant and handsome in a dark grey suit, his white collar stiff and gleaming. His silver grey hair was slicked back neatly, and he smelt of cologne. They stared at each other, father and daughter. Love filled their eyes, and they held hands, drinking in each others every feature.

"My dear, you look so beautiful. Very much like your mother, with your hair up like that."

"I'm glad. You look very handsome too, all the ladies will be giving you the eye. I love you Dad."

"I love you as well. Now, lets put this veil down, here are your flowers. The car will be here in a minute. How do you feel?"

"Wonderful!"

Outside, there was the sound of a car pulling up in front of the house. Willing helpers had cleared a path in the snow from the front door to the road, and when Sarah stepped out of the door on her father's arm, the sun was bravely shining. Neighbours cheered them into the car, and Sarah waved back.

In a few moments they were drawing up before the church. The bells were ringing. Matthew handed his daughter down from the car, and they went forward into the church entrance where the bridesmaids waited. Matthew and Sarah stood in line, Jane and Dorothy behind, as the organ sounded, announcing their arrival.

14

DOMESTIC BLISS.

Looking back, Sarah would recall that momentous day in her life with pride and delight. The walk down the aisle on the arm of her father, strong and tall beside her. Oliver standing, waiting for them, stepping forward to claim her, smiling warmly. At his side, Ted, Jane's husband, the best man. The ceremony, with its vows, and the blessing, and Oliver placing the ring on her finger. Then, signing their names in the marriage book, and finally, the big moment, when they walked proudly arm in arm, back up the aisle, Sarah's veil thrown back, her eyes bright. Oliver, her husband now, smiling broadly, and acknowledging friends seated in the church. Sarah spotted Dr. Lindsay and Mrs. Wilkins, dabbing furiously at her eyes with a hanky.

Outside the church, the sun shone feebly, though the air remained chill, and the snow underfoot was crisp and hard. Photographs were taken in the shortest possible time, to allow the swift dispersal of the family and friends to a warmer situation.

Everyone gathered back at Laura's house for sandwiches, wedding cake, and a glass of wine. There were about a dozen in all, and the occasion was happy and lighthearted. Several presents were laying on the table, beside the wedding cake, and after the guests had each been given a slice of the cake, Sarah and Oliver opened their parcels.

There was a blue and white tablecloth, a mantleclock, a brass plant holder, some glassware, a standard lamp, and a set of cooking pans. Dr. Lindsay had given them 20 guineas. Laura gave them a combined dinner and tea service, Celia two sets of bed linen, and Matthew also gave them 30 guineas. Thanking everyone, the pair felt very fortunate, and lucky with the gifts. They circled the room, hand in hand, personally thanking the guests, and chatting. Gradually, by about 4 o'clock, most of the visitors had taken their leave. Soon, Dr. Lindsay and Mrs. Wilkins were the only two left. They were staying at Lauras for the weekend, travelling back home on Monday. After a cosy cup of tea around the fire, Sarah went upstairs to change out of the wedding dress, and collect her case, before she and Oliver left for their house.

She came down, and entered the parlour, having changed into a soft blue woollen dress, and a red coat. Kisses and hugs all round, until at last she and Matthew stood together. Holding her close, with his other arm about Oliver's shoulders, he spoke firmly.

"It's been a wonderful day my dears. I must say, I feel a little shaky at present, but very happy for the pair of you. Remember Son, you look after my little girl now. Run along the pair of you, God Bless you both. Will we see you at Church tomorrow?"

"Yes father, we'll be there. Thank you for everything. Goodnight, and God bless."

Sarah gave him a warm kiss, Oliver shook his hand, and they left the house. It was snowing heavily again. Their feet sunk into the newly fallen white blanket. Laughing gaily, and clutching each others arms, they struggled on to their abode, just a few streets away.

In about 15 minutes, they stood outside the front door to their lodgings. Oliver fumbled in his pocket for the key, and inserted it into the lock. The door creaked open and before Sarah realized what was happening, Oliver had swung her up into his arms, and carried her inside, in the true tradition. Amid squeals and giggles, he at last set her down on her feet, and they retrieved the cases from the snow outside.

The parlour was comfortably warm. Matthew had been round earlier and put a match to a small fire in the grate. He had banked it well, and it still glowed, filling the room with wel-coming soft light. Oliver threw some wood on to the embers, and soon the flames were dancing cheerfully. The two removed their heavy coats, and hung them in the hall, before returning to warm themselves by the fire. A good bottle of wine stood on the table, with two glasses. Oliver opened it up, and poured them each a glass. There was food in the kitchen cupboards, as Sarah had done some shopping over the last few days, and the stock was well provided. Neither felt hungry for the moment, content with being alone, in their new intimacy of husband and wife, and sipping at the fruity red wine, left for their enjoyment.

They lay together, arms about each other, sipping, and gazing into the coals of the fire. There was no need for words. Olivers passionate kisses, and Sarah's response to them were indications enough of their thoughts. Bed time came. Sarah slipped off to her toilette, whilst Oliver banked up the coals, and switched off the lights.

The bed was warm still, from hot water bottles placed there earlier, and Sarah jumped in, burrowing into the covers. When Oliver entered the room, she welcomed him to her.

Their love came naturally to the two of them. It was deep and passionate, and an exquisite experience to both. Oliver was both tender and fervent, he worshipped this beautiful woman, and was appreciative of the fact that she was his, and his alone. And so, he treated her gently and with some respect. Sarah, however responded amorously to his lovemaking, clutching at him, and avidly returning his embraces. At length, they lay, pleasantly replete, arms flung wide, gazing in languid wonder at each other. Sarah chuckled, Oliver smiled back, and they kissed lovingly. Cuddling close together, they slept, the sleep of the contented.

Christmas was around the corner, and whatever the situation caused by the war, everyone made an effort to celebrate in some form or other. Shopkeepers endeavoured to make their shops look as gay as possible. Paper chains were looped, and hung around the store, and maybe an artificial tree would adorn a corner or a window, with glass baubles, and coloured strands among its branches. Grannies and aunts got on with their knitting of bonnets and gloves, and scarves for the children of the family. Mothers contrived their coupons, and wangled candy bars, or sticks of licorice, to help fill up a corner of the Christmas stocking, for their offspring. And the children whispered and giggled, with their plans, busy with scraps of material, and ribbon, or with their paints and squares of card. There was a frequent rustling of paper, amid frantic efforts to conceal their secrets, whenever grown–ups or other interlopers entered the room. Putting on expressions of wide–eyed innocence, they pretended candour, denying with their chatter and activity any thought of intrigue. Once more left alone however, they lost no time in returning to their festive undertakings.

Celia's house was to be used by the family over the Christmas period. The place needed a good warm through, and despite her gratitude to Laura for taking care of her for the past several months, she did miss her own four walls. During the summer months, she had not been idle in regards to keeping an eye on the place. With the help of two of her friends, curtains and carpets had been cleaned, furniture and silver polished, bed linen laundered, and the kitchen scrubbed, its pots and pans left shining. The cooking range was black and gleaming, ready for use at any time. Over the last few weeks Celia and Laura had been gradually restocking the large larders. There was now a reasonable store of bottled fruits, home–made wines, dried goods such as flour and rice, jars of chutneys and jams and marmalade. Later on in the week they would be bringing some eggs, the plum pudding and mince pies (already made at Lauras), vegetables and whatever meat they could acquire from the hard pressed butcher. Today found Celia once more on her way to her home, in her basket some potted shrimps, and some apples stored from the summer in Laura's attic. She intended to move in on 23rd December, and make final preparations in readiness for her Christmas day visitors. Laura and herself would be cooking the Christmas lunch, and no doubt everyone would get together to help with the washing of the dishes. After the departure of the others, later that evening, she could enjoy some solitude, by her own fireside, in her beloved parlour. On 27th. December she would return to Laura's, just for a few weeks until the spring, when she would move back here for good.

Nearing the actual building now, she stood and surveyed it, the wind whipping her coat about her legs. Some of the windows were still boarded up; they could be dealt with later in time, no hurry. Matthew and Oliver had cleared the garden of rubble earlier in the year, and given the outside walls of the house a coat of paint. The conservatory was completely destroyed, but in the main, the rest of the house was in good shape. With a determined glint in her eye, Celia secured the scarf more warmly round her collar, jammed her hat down over her ears, and bent forward into the wind, her slender form battling with the elements.

Sarah and Oliver still had their heads in the clouds. Sarah sparkled and blossomed, setting off for work each day, having ensured that Oliver had eaten an adequate breakfast. He in turn whistled his way through work, joking and chatting to his colleagues. At the end of their working day, they would sit and eat the meal prepared by Sarah, before settling for a cosy evening by the fire, listening to the radio, or talking, or even just relaxing in each others arms, enjoying their domestic bliss.

Both of them finished early on Christmas Eve.The library closed at 1.00pm. and the printing room shut down a 3 o'clock. Oliver hurried home to find Sarah finishing some gift wrapping. The fire was glowing, making a welcome sight, after the swirl–ing snow outside. Laura and Matthew were coming for tea, about 4 o'clock. Matthew would now be off work until after the Christmas break, and Laura had a few hours off today, all day tomorrow, and then she would work for an hour or two at the hospital on Boxing day. They had decided to call in on the newly weds, at Sarah's invitation, for a cup of tea, and maybe a cake or a scone, before making their way home.

Oliver had just removed his overcoat, and was in the process of thawing out at the fireside, when the front door bell rang, announcing the arrival of the visitors. Sarah hurriedly cleared string and paper from the floor, set the kettle onto the fire to boil, and went to answer the door. Her father and Laura came into the hall, their muffled figures well powdered with snow. Matthew stamped his feet on the doormat, whilst Laura gradually removed the layers of clothing wrapped about her. Sarah relieved them both the scarves, hats, gloves and coats, hanging them all on the hallstand, and placing the wet footwear beneath to dry off. Then she kissed her father and her aunt. Their faces felt icy cold, and they followed her thankfully into the front room, where Oliver already sat, now completely warm and confortable in his armchair. He made to rise in greeting, but Matthew bade him remain seated.

The guests found a spot to sit near the warmth of the blaze, and Sarah knelt and filled the pot from the singing kettle. She placed a small table within reach, with cups, saucers and plates set out. A plate of cakes, and some scones fresh from the oven gave off an appetising smell. Pouring four cups of tea, and adding milk and sugar to everyone's taste, Sarah then offered round the scones, asking that her guests help themselves to jam as they desired. She then curled up at Oliver's feet, her head resting against his chair, and sipped at her tea. Laura complimented her on the scones, and Matthew let his eye travel about the room, taking in the warm bright colours of Sarah's choosing, enhancing the room. Gaily printed chair backs and cushions were evident, the latter scattered casually about.

A bright rug lay in front of the hearth, and a dark red chenille cloth covered a round table in the corner of the room, on top of which stood a brass vase, filled with bronze chrysanthemums. Several objects and ornaments of brass adorned the room, gleaming brightly in the soft light of the fire. He glanced up at the mantleshelf, where Sarah's treasured family photographs stood, now in frames carefully chosen especially for them. His gaze fell on the picture of the four of them, before the untimely death of his young wife and son. He sighed to himself. It seemed an age ago. The distance of years seemed greater, with the intervention of the war taking precedence over all else. And now, here was Sarah his daughter, a young wife herself, difficult to believe. He came quickly out of his daydreams to the sound of Sarah's voice in conversation with her aunt.

They were discussing arrangements for the following morning. Everyone would be meeting for the early church service, and then go on to Celia's for the rest of the day. Apart from a few last minute items, all the gifts were already at Celia's, ready for opening after Christmas lunch. The clock struck the half hour after 5 o'clock, and Laura reluctantly made a move to rise from the comfort of her chair.

"I'm sorry dears, I feel we must make a move before the weather sets in too badly, don't you agree Matthew?"

Matthew nodded, stretching his limbs, and getting to his feet. "Yes, you're right of course. I must say I'll be sorry to leave the comfort of this fireside, you really have made it very cosy."

"It's a credit to you both, you have made it into a lovely home. You will always hold this place dear to you, in years to come when you have moved on, this will remain in your memories specially, as your first home together."
Laura spoke warmly.

Oliver and Sarah accepted the complimentary words graciously. They were constantly filled with delight at their little home, but it was nice to know the appreciation of others, especially the family. They both saw their visitors from the room, and helped them with their tedious piling on of the heavy apparel once more. They all said their goodbyes, and the door was opened to reveal a scene of wintry wonder without. The sky was filled with twinkling stars, the snow had ceased to fall, but lay deeply all around, white and shining, silent and unspoiled. The air was keen and exhilarating.

Matthew and Laura linked arms for support, and plodded away down the road, turning once to wave farewell to Sarah and Oliver, huddled together in the doorway. Then, closing the door on the night, the two turned back into the warmth and intimacy of their first Christmas eve in their own home.

The night was undisturbed by raids. Sarah woke up, unsure of the hour. She switched on the lamp at the bedside to look at the time. It was just before 6.30. For the next half hour, she lay awake, but relaxed, beside Oliver who still slept deeply. At 7 o'clock, she crept out of the bed, and went to the kitchen, and filled the kettle. The small range in the kitchen was unlit, but ready laid with paper and wood. She put a match to it, and it crackled into life immediately. She set the kettle on top, and laid a tray with cups and saucers, adding a tiny gaily wrapped gift beside. Going into the front parlour, she checked on the fire there, hoping it would still be alive, but the ashes were grey and cold – it would have to be relit later in the day. Drawing back the curtains she looked outside. It was'nt snowing, but the white, thick blanket lay still across the earth, promising further falls to come. Above, the navy blue sky was scattered with the same stars. As she stared in wonder, the sound of the church bells rung out, heralding Christmas day. Fastening her robe more securely about her, she returned to the kitchen and prepared two cups of tea. The range now glowed brightly, and gave out a pleasant warmth, making the room homely and comfortable.

As she entered the bedroom, Oliver was just stirring from his slumbers. He opened his eyes as she slipped into bed beside him. She smiled, and tenderly kissed his mouth. Drawing back, she gazed at his sleep filled countenance, and his tousled hair.

"Happy Christmas darling". She spoke softly.

"Mmmm, that was a wonderful awakening, Happy Christmas to you too." He reached and stole another kiss from her.

"Here's a nice cup of tea for you, a special treat, don't expect it every morning, mind." Sarah reached over and brought the tray onto the bed. Struggling to sit up, Oliver took the cup, thanking her with his eyes. She then drew his attention to the small package left on the tray.

"For you darling, an extra gift from me."

Putting his cup to one side, he concentrated on opening the gift. Inside the paper was a tiny box, which when uncovered revealed the finest gold tie clip. Sarah had found it in a back–

street shop when she had been furniture hunting, it had winked up at her from its black velvet bed, beneath the glass topped counter. It looked tasteful, and she wanted it for Oliver. Enquiring as to the cost, she learned that it was priced slightly more than the pair of candlesticks which she had originally gone in for, so without more ado, she purchased it. Now looking at Oliver's face, she knew she had chosen her gift well. He was delighted with it, and a little later, dressed for church, he allowed Sarah to fasten it on to his tie.

The service was heart–warming and satisfying. The church was packed, and looked festive with greenery and flowers. A life sized stable scene, with the Holy family and worshippers, together with cattle and sheep, and a donkey, all in beautifully modelled clay, was situated just inside the main door, for all to enjoy. After leaving the service, Sarah and Oliver, together with Celia, Laura and Matthew made for Celia's house, still under the spell of the stirring sermon, and the resounding carols.

Celia proudly led the way to the front door, and turned the key in the lock. A rush of warm air greeted them, as the door opened. She still had a store of unused fuel, and a pile of logs at the back of the house, and so had lit every fire possible, and the kitchen range too, filling the house with a pleasant feeling of good cheer. Passing from the hall into the parlour, they were faced with a riot of colour. Celia had worked hard to make this a happy time: she had decorated a good sized branch of pine tree, brought in from the garden yesterday, its dark green leaves were threaded with silver and white garlands, and a shining star adorned the very top. Vases of holly filled various corners of room, and brightly coloured chains hung across the ceiling. The fire crackled in the hearth, and an appetising smell drifted from the kitchen.

They dined at half past one, savouring roast ham with onion sauce and mustard, roast and boiled potatoes, carrots and parsnips, complimented by a glass of homemade wine, made by Laura from pure grapes, several summers past. Plum pudding and custard followed this, followed in turn by groans of excess indulgence. Laura and Celia were praised for the delicious spread, and after a short interval, allowing the feast to be comfortably digested, Sarah with the help of her father and Oliver made short work of clearing the table, and washing the dishes. Celia and Laura collapsed gratefully into the fireside chairs. In the parlour the radio was turned on, the sweet sentimental music filled the room, the fire spat and crackled, and the silver strands glinted on the tree. It was nearing 4 o'clock, and the daylight fading fast, before the job of opening presents was tackled. Sarah thought of the previous year, when Oliver had still been troubled in his mind, and quietly gave thanks for his continued recovery, and for the fact that as his wife, she was able to care for him.

The gifts were only small in value. Times were hard, luxuries were not often to be found in the shops, and when they were, there were very limited supplies. However, the majority of people managed to acquire little items, which gave pleasure to whoever received them. Both Celia and Laura were better off than most, having ample means, and no dependants. However, a fair sum of money had been spent on the wedding, and the gifts, so there was not too much to spare on expensive presents at this time. Everyone however was happy with the gifts that they were given. Sarah and Oliver went home that evening with more useful household items, towels, a handsome mirror (from Matthew) which would be just right for the hall, pastry set and mixing bowl from Laura, and acondiment set and soup dishes from Celia. All things useful to them, and given with much love. In return they had given a pipe and tobacco to Matthew, lace handkerchiefs and perfume to Celia, and slippers and woollen stockings to Laura who hated the cold.

Oliver gave Sarah a silver backed set for her dressing table, and he received a leather blotter pad and a heavy glass ink stand. All in all the day passed most enjoyably. They all left about 9 o'clock that evening, thanking Celia for the marvellous day, and all her efforts to make it so. There were no stars this night, and light flurries of snow were falling. It was pitch black, every house light blacked out with heavy curtains, and no street lamps, in accordance with restrictions. The way home was familiar, and negotiated with not too much difficulty. Laura's was reached first, goodnights were said, and kisses given all round, before Sarah and Oliver went on their way, leaving her father and aunt at their front door. They, in turn reached their front door, and entered the house. The front room fire had gone out, and the room felt a little chilly at that time of the evening. However, the kitchen range was still glowing red, so Oliver drew the curtains, and he and Sarah finished their evening, sipping hot drinks around its cheerful warmth, seated on wooden stools made for them by Matthew.

Early the following morning a lengthy and violent air attack shattered the peace of the town. Walls shook with the reverberations, roofs and chimneys toppled. Several houses got hit by bombs, and at least two families, with young children, perished in their beds. The church steeple was struck directly, and in the morning was seen to be lying at right angles to the building, resting on some nearby trees.

Sarah was woken by the noise, and straightaway reached out toward Oliver's side of the bed. Her arm felt the empty pillow. Scrambling out of bed, she grabbed her robe. Taking the candle and lighting it, she went in search of him. Hearing a sound from the kitchen, she went forward to investigate. A loud boom filled the air, and caused her to stop and grasp the wall to steady herself. The house shook, and there was a sound of breaking china. Taking a long deep breath, she continued on to the kitchen. Opening the door she strained to adjust her eyes to the gloom. Holding the candle before her, she shed some light around. Oliver sat at the kitchen table, his eyes closed tightly, his hands clenched in front of him. Sarah moved to the window, to make sure that the curtains were drawn, then she lighted the gas mantle, filling the room with a soft yellow light. Blowing out her candle, she placed the half filled kettle on the range, poking a blaze into the coals beneath. Going to Oliver, who sat unmoved, she took one of his hands in her own, pulling a chair up to sit beside him. Her face was calm and compassionate, her chin firm, and her eyes wide and steady. She looked lovingly at Oliver who still had his eyes closed. His face was ashen, and his lips tight together.

Another nearby blast caused the whole house to tremble in its foundations. In the distance, shouting and screaming could be heard, amid the sound of sirens and the clanging of the fire engine bell. Sarah made herself concentrate on the plight of Oliver. She squeezed his hand, and he returned it with such pressure that she had to stop herself crying out with the pain.

"Oliver, darling, please open your eyes. I'm sure the raid is nearly over, it seems to have been going a long time. I will make us some tea dear. How long were you sitting here? You should have woken me, I would have sat with you. Oliver?"

He opened his eyes and looked at her. Releasing her hand, he buried his head in his arms on the table and wept, loudly and wretchedly. Sarah leaned towards him and gently raised his head, leaning it against her shoulder. She then placed his arms around her, and hers about him and there they sat, for some while, giving each other strength and solace. At last the clamour outside seemed to have ceased. Slowly, Sarah drew away from him, and observed that he had regained much of his composure. He even managed a shaky attempt at a grin. Sarah smiled back.

"I am such a fool." He spoke angrily.

He was silenced with a long kiss, and told not to speak such rubbish. The kettle was rescued from the stove, before boiling completely dry, and Sarah made a strong pot of tea, ensuring that Oliver had two spoonfuls of sugar in his cup. Everything remaining quiet the two decided to try and get some rest for the last few hours of the night. Turning the lamp down, and closing the fire, they made their way back to bed by the light of the candle. The bed was now very chilly to get into. They shivered and drew close together. And so they slept. Wrapped in each others arms, sleep stole over them, filling them with warm contentment. They remained in this same position until finally they both awoke with pangs of hunger, ready for breakfast, and a new day.

15

FAMILY TIDINGS.

It turned out that the raid which had caused so much of an uproar in the town that Boxing day morning, was the tail end of a major sea attack. The newspapers were full of accounts over the following days. Many ships had been sunk, together with their crews. The attack had been prolonged, with a bombard–ment from the air, and an undersea assault from German U–boats.

A few days after Christmas, Sarah and Oliver took a walk about the town, and saw the extent of the damage. The morning was sunny with a blue sky, the white snow giving off a brilliant glare, that dazzled the eyes. They drew near to the church, where so recently, so much joy had been shared by them, and many others at Christmas. Several labourers were attempting to render the fallen spire safe. They were hoisting it with ropes, piece by piece from its precarious position, and lowering it to the ground behind the church, until such time that funds, or cir–cumstances would enable its replacement in its rightful place. There was a great breach in the church roof left by the fallen steeple. This had been roughly patched up with heavy canvas as a temporary measure. Houses that were familiar to them had been completely destroyed, and rubble from collapsed build–ings were strew about the streets.

Laura had suffered little damage to her house, though a vast section of brick wall between her and her neighbour had toppled, completely burying her bed of roses, and flattening two handsome young spruces, planted just that last summer.

Celia had suffered more window breakages, due to the vibrating of the building, but no more.

The New Year of 1917 arrived with no great celebrations taking place. Everyone wished for the end of the war now. Sickened by the continual battle, and killing of their young men, and weary of the want and deprivations at home. There was great discontent, and impatience growing among the people, anger at the countries' leaders, and their apparent failure to bring this bloody war to a swift end. The whole country still mourned the vast number of casualties suffered in the Battle of the Somme the previous autumn, where about 400,000 men had either been killed, wounded, or taken prisoner.

Life went on in the usual way for Sarah and the family. Oliver became more like his old self, in his new found happiness with Sarah. In March, she found out that she was to have a baby, due in October. She waited for exactly the right moment to tell Oliver, choosing one Friday evening after their meal, when the dishes had been cleared, and they were seated in comfort by the fire. Oliver was reaching the paper, Sarah was knitting the first of many small items in preparation for the happy event. She looked over at Oliver.

"Oliver, I was feeling a little peaky for a time, so I visited the doctor on Wednesday." Oliver frowned over the top of his paper.

"You didn't say anything to me, you should have told me."

"I didn't want to worry you darling, besides everything was fine."

"Well, what was the trouble? Sarah! What did the doctor say it was"

"He said...that it was quite a common complaint, and that I was likely to be putting on a fair bit of weight."

"Really? How strange. What's the complaint called?"

"It's called....... "Being Pregnant" I think, yes that's right." Sarah went on with her knitting, glancing at Oliver from lowered eyes, appearing to be intent on her task. Oliver slowly lowered the paper, his mouth fell open, and his eyes stared across at her.

"What do you..... you mean that....you..and I...., a baby?"

Sarah dropped her knitting, and went over to him at last, placing his paper to one side, she settled herself on his lap, and put her arms around his neck.

"Yes my love, a baby for you and I. Are you happy at the news?"

"I'm so very happy my darling, I don't know what to say, I'm lost for words. "

Oliver was filled with emotion, his eyes were moist, and his voice gruff. They hugged each other closely, making plans and dreaming dreams. The evening drew on, the fire died down, darkness came, and still they sat, unaware of anything but themselves, and the wonderful secret they shared.

The next day the rest of the family were told the news. Celia was overjoyed, and couldn't wait to start sewing and crocheting baby things. Laura too was happy, offering to help Sarah shop for necessary items like a pram, cot and highchair. With all the organizations that she was involved with, she was most likely to come across such things in the course of her charity work. Matthew simply held his daughter close, and grasped Oliver's hand warmly, when told the happy news. He told them that he would, that very day open an account and start saving for his grandchild, and that he couldn't wait for October to come.

Oliver had been moved to a higher position at his work, which was lucky, giving him a small rise in his earnings. One of the older men had retired through illness, allowing everyone to move up the ladder. A new young lad was taken on to fill Oliver's old post.

Sarah continued at the library, though Mrs. Ryan strictly instructed her not to lift heavy weights, or climb to high up the ladder to the bookshelves. Her pregnancy gave her a bloom and a quiet glow of happiness. Her health was good. She tried to eat the right things as far as possible, and had a particular craving for beetroot and pickled onions, which Oliver pandered to, but found difficult to understand.

The Allies had now been joined by the United States in the fight against Germany. They were able to help with supplies and money, though needed time to prepare their troops for Europe. On the other hand Russia had gone through such hardship, large numbers of its peasants having joined the army, and had so neglected the cultivation of the land, that there was much unrest amongt the common people in that country. In March 1917 revolution broke out. Soldiers joined the workers in the uprising. The Tsar, Nicholas ll was dethroned, a temporary government taking over. The revolutionaries included names which were to go down in history as leading Bolshviks (the name given to the workers' political party) Lenin, and Trotsky.

All ships travelling to or from any allied ports came under special attack during the early part of 1917, following German instructions. In consequence vessels leaving Britain for distant lands, were quite often not seen again. Supplies from abroad became particularly scarce that year.

The struggle went on at home to feed and clothe oneself, and the family. The summer months were easier to get by in, but everyone dreaded another winter of shortages.

Sarah and the family continued to cope fairly comfortably. Matthew was able to bring home vegetables grown on the farm, which were straight away prepared for preserving and pickling by Laura and Celia for the coming winter. That year was a particularly happy one for Oliver. His health was good, and he was overcoming his intense dread and panic during the raids. He had mastered his job well, and made some worthwhile friends in his colleagues. Mr. Harris was well pleased with his progress, even tentatively suggesting another bonus in the new year.

Also, in that year of 1917, Oliver put himself forward for the occasional game of cricket in the local team. In his teens he had played for his school, proving that he was no mean hand with a bat. So, quite often, on a sunny Saturday afternoon, Sarah would pack a picnic tea, and accompany him to the cricket green on the edge of town. He, respendent in his whites would help his team, with a splendid innings, and a not too bad effort in the field. Sarah sat in her deck chair, shaded by a large brimmed straw hat, waving and clapping at the right times. She was finding life a little uncomfortable these days, seeming to grow larger by the minute. She had now had to give up work, as her ankles swelled alarmingly, if she did not rest them frequently, and her actual shape and size proved a hindrance when moving in and out, between the shelves. This August was extremely hot and oppressive, and she didn't exert herself more than necessary.

Most of the items needed for the infant had been obtained. There was a smart navy blue bassinette, brought into one of Lauras distribution centres, when she herself was there. She knew the family from which it came, and was assured of its careful use, so she took it upon herself to put it to one side for Sarah's approval. Sarah herself had purchased the cot from her employer's daughter, whilst still working at the library. She had mentioned to Mrs. Ryan the fact that she was in need of a cot, and that lady stated that her daughter was about to sell hers in order to replace it with a bed for her fast growing infant. Sarah visited her with Oliver, and the transaction was made to everyone's satisfaction.

They had also acquired a "kiddy car" a small chair on wheels, with a tray secured in front, decorated with rows of large wooden coloured beads, enabling a bored child to wheel itself around the floor in safety, and occupy busy hands with sliding the beads to and fro on their frame. A high chair was another of the several pieces obtained. It stood together with the pram, cot and kiddy car in the corner of the bedroom, beside a large wooden linen chest full of baby requisites. Tiny cotton vests, and flannel bodices, minute woollen bootees and mittens in all the prettiest colours imaginable, more than enough gowns for night and day wear both, and shawls and bonnets beautifully crocheted and embroidered by Celia and Laura. They had both been busy all summer with their needles. Finely hemmed blankets for the cot and pram, embroidered pillow cases, with fancy frills and bows. Celia had excelled herself in producing a thick quilted eiderdown for the pram in pale cream silk. She had salvaged the material from an ancient gown in her wardrobe, beautifully preserved, but quite out of style. The pram cover was filled with pure lambs wool, making it extra cosy for winter days.

August came to a close. Early in September, Matthew received a letter from Dr. Lindsay saying that Mrs. Wilkins had passed away after a sudden illness. He now had a younger housekeeper, Mrs. Watts. He was finding it difficult to adjust to her rather bossy manner, though she made up for it by being an excellent cook, and keeping the house immaculate. On hearing the news, Sarah burst into tears, being inclined to emotional outbursts of late. She had no great attachment to Mrs. Wilkins, but it was just another slice of the past taken away.

Autumn was all around now. The red and gold leaves were aflame in all their glory, the days bathed in rich sunshine, tinged with the keen touch of the seasonal change.

Everyone was prepared for yet another hard winter. Most food was home produced where possible. Allotments were encouraged, and were worked on by members of families, ensuring vegetables for the winter months. Larger plots of land including farms were given over to agriculture, employing women (land girls) and men not conscripted to the fighting. There were jobs too in the munition factories. Here again many empoloyees were women.

The newpapers were filled with gloom. Bombing had been particularly heavy that year over the big cities. London had suffered immensely, large German planes bombarding it, mostly by moonlight, but often in the daytime too. Sarah continued to keep in good health. She took gentle walks most days, and rested each afternoon with her feet raised to relieve her ankles. September progressed on into October. The baby was due on the 17th, but in fact made an early appearance on October 12th.

Laura was in residence with Sarah and Oliver, in order to assist during, and after the birth. On the night of the 11th October, after a pleasant evening meal, herself and Sarah were clearing the dishes ready for washing, when Sarah grimaced, and learned over, clutching her stomach. Oliver leapt to her side, and assisted her to a chair. Once seated she felt easier, and passed the discomfort off as indigestion. The rest of the evening passed without incident, though Laura and Oliver watched Sarah carefully for further signs. The midwife lived a few doors away, and had been alerted, in case the need came to call her out.

At 11 o'clock, all three retired for the night, Laura sleep–

ing on the pallet, beside the front room fire. She was shaken awake by a frantic Oliver at the unseemly hour of ten past three. The room was chill, the night black and starless. Laura instructed Oliver to run along to Miss Davies the midwife , whilst she went to Sarah, assuring her that everything was in hand. Water was placed on the range to boil, and clean linen was laid on one side for the midwife's use. She came within minutes, trying to calm a distraught Oliver. Passing him over to Laura, she went straight to her patient, asking that boiling water be brought to the bedroom. Whilst Laura attended to this, Oliver paced the small kitchen, his face pale and tense, wincing whenever he heard Sarah cry out from the bedroom. For a while there was silence, which in its way was worse. Then once more, intermittant sharp cries, which became more prolonged as the time passed. Laura glanced at the kitchen timepiece, it was twenty five minutes past seven. She brewed some hot coffee, and passed a cup to Oliver, laying her hand on his shoulder in reassurance. He looked at her and gave a strained smile.

"Why is it so long? Surely it must be soon now. Poor Sarah! I feel so helpless. I tell you Laura, this is worse for me than any air raid."

Laura smiled.

"It's not long really Oliver, some women are in labour for many hours before the actual birth. Sarah has been just....about four and half hours up to now. She is strong, don't worry too much. Only think of the reward at the end of it."

He nodded and sighed in resignation. Daylight came. Laura built up the fire, and made yet more coffee, and some toast, though neither she nor Oliver could find a taste to eat anything other than a few nibbles. At a quarter to ten the bedroom door opened, and the rosy faced Miss Davies appeared, damp curls clinging to her forehead. She smiled broadly.

"You have a baby girl Mr. McGregor. Your wife and the baby are both well, and you may go in and see her. She is very tired now, so don't stay too long. Congratulations!"

Oliver shook her hand, his face a mixture of laughter and tears, then he left to go to Sarah, whilst Laura offered the good lady a well earned cup of tea, and took note of her instructions. She promised to visit again that evening.

Gently opening the bedroom door, Oliver crept in, and crossed the room to where Sarah lay, eyes closed, on the bed. She was pale, and shadows lay beneath her lashes. Her hair was brushed, and lay shining about her on the pillow. She smiled contentedly in her rest. Oliver went to her side, and sat carefully on the side of the bed. She opened her eyes, and held her arms out to him.

"Darling Oliver! See what I have for you. Look here, our little girl."

He peeped over the far side of the bed into the cot there. It was hard to see the baby, as she was heavily swathed in layers of covers. So, rising, he walked around the bed to where she lay. Leaning over, he gently pulled a corner of the cover away from her face. His daughter had the look of an over anxious wizened old pixie! Her face was red and wrinkled, her eyes screwed tightly shut, and her lips pursed together. Her brows were drawn together in a worried frown. Of course, Oliver saw the most beautiful of babies, in his awesome state of proud parenthood. One tiny hand was visible above the bed clothes. He tentatively introduced his finger, stroking the pink palm. At once the perfect little fingers curled around his own, possessively. He was overcome with happiness, and surprised at the strength of that clasp. He turned back to Sarah, his eyes brimming with love and pride. Bending to her, he kissed her lips tenderly.

"She is so beautiful my love. I am so proud and happy at this moment. We must think of a beautiful name for her. But now, I will leave you to get some rest, you have worked so hard. Sleep now. Thank you darling, I love you, and our baby so much."

He kissed her again briefly, and took his leave. Laura went in for a short visit, taking a peek at her great niece, and giving a warm kiss of congratulations to Sarah. Then, the new young mother was left with her baby to regain her energy and strength in an undisturbed sleep.

Miss Davies came again that evening as promised, staying with Sarah while she fed her baby, gently instructing and encouraging her. Sarah got a great feeling of contentment feeding her little one. The baby lay content in her arms, eagerly sucking in a regular manner. The whole procedure went smoothly, after which Sarah winded her, and changed her nappy, before placing her back in her cot. Oliver stood to one side whilst all this was going on, determined not to miss one moment of it.

After the midwife had departed, Matthew and Celia visited. Celia spent a few minutes with Sarah, and cooed over the baby, before leaving Matthew with his daughter. He was delighted with his grandchild, secretly pleased that it was a girl. He saw some resemblance to Sarah as a baby, and told her so. Later that evening Oliver and Sarah talked cosily on the bed, their offspring sleeping soundly in her cot. Sarah brought up the subject of a name.

"Have you any ideas?" Oliver asked her.

"Well, I did think Alice was a pretty name, or even Lucy, or Ellen. What do you think?"

"Alice sounds just right. Alice...Alice....Alice McGregor. Perfect."

And so, Alice it was, and on December 18th. she was

christened so, on their first wedding anniversary, in the church of their marriage. Christmas was wonderful! Despite hardships all around, they all had a really enjoyable family Christmas. The snow fell, carol singers sang gustily at the door, and inside, the tree stood glorious, bedecked with adornment, the fire crackled in the hearth, and the air was filled with appetizing aromas from the kitchen.

Celia did the honours again, inviting everyone to her house. She was now in residence there, had been for a few months. The windows had been repaired, the rooms once more were warm and welcoming, complete with the sound of chatter and laughter ringing throughout them.

Alice of course was the centre of attention. She had altered quite a bit since her birth. Her eyes were deep blue still, and tried hard to focus on things that glinted or shone in front of her. The redness had gone from her face, it was now a delicate shade of pink, and her mouth was small and rosy. She smiled often, and was an easy baby in every way, being content and well loved. Her wispy hair at the moment was blonde, but of course would most likely change over the next month or two. Sarah bloomed, and Oliver and herself doted on their daughter, spending ages just looking at her when she lay asleep, marvelling that she was theirs alone.

January 1918 was a dark, damp chill month. The snow was wet and slushy, but hung around reluctant to go. The winter wind was not so much clean and cold, but more bleak and penetrating. There was much illness about at that time, and it wasn't until the end of the month, when watery sunshine struggled through the gloom, and the slush had more or less disappeared, that Sarah ventured out of the house with the baby. Snugly wrapped in her warmest clothes, and covered with layers of covers, topped with the quilted cover, she lay in a cocoon of warmth beneath the hood of her pram. Sarah took her for a short outing into the town, around four corners, and finished up at Laura's.

Laura welcomed them in delightedly, helping Sarah into the hallway with the pram. Alice was still asleep, so they left her, and went into the parlour where a fire burned brightly. Laura had been reading, and about to make herself some coffee. Sarah said that she would be pleased to join her. They spent a cheerful half hour gossiping. Laura told Sarah to take care of herself, as she looked a little pale.

"I haven't managed to get out of the house for some time. It was good to get some fresh air today, I think that will bring some colour back to my cheeks. Oh to feel some warm sun again, I'm not too fond of the cold weather."

"Me neither." Laura agreed.

Spring arrived. Food rationing had been intensified in February, and meat, butter and margaine were doled out in meagre quantities to the individual.

Oliver received a letter from Scotland in April. It was from a solicitor. A close friend of his parents, chosen by them to be Godfather to Oliver had died, naming Oliver in his will. It was necessary to journey up to Scotland to go over some details with the solicitor, and to ascertain the extent of the inheritance. It had been hinted that the amount was quite substantial.

He left Sarah and Alice one bright sunny morning in May. His heart was heavy at the parting, it being the first separation from Sarah since their marriage, and the first ever from his daughter. After a prolonged farewell, he took up his suitcase and walked across to his waiting taxi cab. He turned with a final wave. Sarah blew a kiss, and lifted Alice's hand in a goodbye gesture.

16
DREAMS DENIED, ARRIVING FULL CIRCLE.

Oliver expected to be away for just a few days, but it so happened that the inheritance bequeathed to him was quite a small fortune, and involved much signing of papers, and meeting with solicitors was necessary. The few days lengthened into a week, at the end of which Oliver telephoned to Celia's, where he spoke to Sarah. He explained that he hoped to be home during the following week, that several hundred pounds had come their way. and that he missed them both so very much. Sarah said that they missed him too, and rewarded him with a cheerful gurgle from baby Alice. They exchanged loving words together, before he rang off. Sarah had no idea that this would be the last time that she would hear his dear voice. Two days later, she got the telegram saying he was dead.

He had, after all, proved himself a hero. The night following his phone call to Sarah, he had gone for a stroll after his evening meal in the guest house. The evening was pleasantly warm, after a bright sunny day. He meandered in and out the cobbled streets, deep in thought. His and Sarah's future was looking rosy now. The money was going to give them a good start. Alice would want for nothing, and once this war was over, they could find a small cottage somewhere, with a garden for the baby. Sarah could grow some flowers, and life would be just grand.

Suddenly, the warning sounded, sending the few people that were about, hurrying and scurrying toward the communal shelter in the town. Oliver followed. The raid didn't last too long, soon the all clear siren announced the passing of the aircraft. Everyone emerged from the shelter and went on their way. The air was full of smoke, and the darkening sky was aglow from a large fire burning a street or two away. Oliver walked towards the noise and clamour to see how much damage had been done. On reaching the scene, he discovered the partly ruined structure of an old house, surrounded by the total destruction of its neighbours. Firemen were not yet on the site, and crossing over the charred debris of fallen masonry and beams, he approached a gathering of people, silhouetted against the still lively flames. One woman was screaming and struggling to escape the grasp of two captors, holding her arms firmly. Oliver learned that the woman's baby son was still in the burning house. She was desperately attempting to go back for him, but her friends were insisting that it was too late, and too dangerous, and held her fast. The firemen no doub't would make the attempt, but they hadn't yet arrived, probably being employed elsewhere for the time being.

After only a moment's hesitation, Oliver moved. He took off his shirt, soaking it in a trough of water standing nearby, and dashed forward to the burning building, wrapping the wet shirt about his head, as he disappeared into the house.

The atmosphere was thick with fumes. Holding the moist material firmly over his mouth and nose, Oliver pressed onwards, and upwards, climbing the stairs to where the child's bedroom was likely to be. There was no sound at all to tell him whether or not the little boy was alive. He struggled on, choking beneath the cloth. He made out the shape of a door in front of him, and threw himself against it, sending it crashing in. Entering the room, he stumbled towards the dim outline of a cot. The room was hot, and getting hotter by the minute, he could see the starry sky through a large hole in the ceiling, and the whole building was heaving and crackling all around. He reached into the cot with his free hand, finding a tiny still form there. Enveloping the infant beneath the fast drying protective shirt, he turned back to leave the room, but found a sheet of flame confronting him. He made to rush through it, but missed his footing and fell, hitting his head and passing out. Minutes later the fire brigade tore onto the scene outside, straight away getting into action, and gaining control over the final pockets of fire. Oliver, with the little boy still clasped to his chest was discovered some twenty minutes later. They were both dead.

A day or two after the telegram, Sarah received a letter from the fire service involved. It stated that Oliver had proved himself to be a true hero, putting his life at risk for the sake of saving another. It was a tragic outcome, both lives having been sacrificed, but nevertheless, a brave act, to be a proud reminder to his wife and child. They enclosed a silver badge, engraved with his name, the date, and a brief acknowledgement of his attempt, from the fire service.

It was fortunate for Sarah that she had baby Alice to tend to at that time. When she was busy with the baby, she could almost believe that everything was right with her world. But at night time, when Alice was asleep, and the flat was filled with emptiness, with reminders of his being all around her, that was bad. She sobbed until there was no tears left. She slept, an exhausted sleep, clutching his pillow to her. Laura stayed with her for several days, ensuring that she ate something, and giving help with the baby. The whole family were devastated. Oliver's remains were conveyed by train to Sidmouth, and on June 15th, he was buried in the churchyard, in the shadow of the church of his marriage, and of Alice's christening.

Despite the continuation of the war, this now took second place in Sarah's life. To her, nothing seemed important now, except her baby. Alice thrived. She now had some teeth, and enjoying chewing on her bone teething ring. Her hair was definitely showing signs of becoming red, like Oliver's, but her eyes were her mother's, as was her smile. She crawled every-where, and needed constant watching, as she moved so quickly, and would easily get into bother.

Now that Oliver had died, the inheritance automatically came to Sarah. She was not at all interested in it at first, refusing to discuss it. Matthew took her to one side, pointing out the advantages of the money for herself and the baby, and she soon admitted that it would give them security for the future.

With the passing of summer, it seemed that at last things were looking up for the Allies. The Americans, French, Aus-tralian, Canadian and British forces made a successful advance with troops and tanks in Amiens, driving the Germans back, eventually to the opening lines of battle of 1914.

Clear up operations were still going on at home. It would take years for the big cities to be rebuilt, they would never look quite the same. September was here once again, with the be-ginnings of a brilliant and beautiful Autumn. Sarah scarcely noticed it, totally involving herself in the care of Alice, now approaching her lst birthday. Each day would find mother and child taking the air, usually in the early afternoon. Sarah would stroll slowly to the promenade, or to the park, find a seat, and sit watching, whilst her active daughter teetered around on her newly found feet. Sometimes they would go down to the beach. The weather was still pleasantly warm, and the baby enjoyed watching the sea breaking onto the shore, and the many seagulls swooping around and about the ocean. She now said the odd simple word, the most common being "mum mum", she also said "Gan" , " dad", "cat" and "dog".

Sarah kept Oliver's photograph in a prominent place at home, showing it to Alice often, and encouraging her to say

"Dada". The lst birthday was celebrated quietly at Laura's, with just the family there. Alice blew her candle out on the cake, with Matthew's help, and enjoyed feeding herself with some cake, finishing up with much of it on her tray, her feeder, all over her face, and in her hair. Everyone chuckled at the sight, even Sarah, who laughed seldom these days. Later, when the baby had been settled down, in a state of contented weariness, Laura and Celia cleared the table. Matthew sat, his arm around Sarah, curled up at his knee. He spoke.

"She's a beautiful child. Takes after my side of the family, no doubt. She does you credit my dear."

"I know. She means everything to me, now that....Oliver has gone. I get so frightened sometimes, I can't think ahead anymore. I feel I should be thinking of our future, but I can't see it at all."

"You will pet, you will. I felt the same when your mother died, you know how I was. But, we come through. We are never quite the same, but we do come through, believe me."

Sarah nodded, her eyes full.

"I feel so much pain inside me. I sometimes wonder if it would be a good idea to move away from this place and all its memories."

"The memories would still be there my love, even if you did move."

"Yes, but, there wouldn't be familiar sights and places that hold such vivid reminders, and cause me such distress."

"No....I suppose not." Matthew agreed.

"Anyway, I have been thinking, that when the war is over, whenever that may be, I will seriously consider moving. I might even go back to Suffolk. There are friends there. I'm sure I could find a suitable place to live, now we have the means, it may even be possible to buy a small cottage. I still miss that

little village sometimes, you know."
"Me too. Sidmouth is beautiful, and has been good for both of us, but I'm Suffolk born and bred, and it will always be home to me."

Sarah kissed him tenderly, then went to take her leave of her aunt and Celia, before wheeling the pram containing Alice, out of the hall, down the garden path, and on the way to home.

On 11 am. on 11th November the Great War came to an end, the German Government having signed the Armistice six hours earlier, admitting their defeat. Despite the loss of about eight and a half million fighting men, including five million fighting for the Allies, in addition to twenty–one million wounded in battle, everyone was relieved by the settlement. Victory celebrations went on all over Britain, and at last it seemed possible to look to the future.

There was so much to be done. The re–building of towns and cities, the building up of the industries once again, the re–settlement of men returning from the front, some of them emotionally or physically impaired. If possible, they would have to be found some form of employment, as well as receiving necessary care and treatment for their particular disability. The time ahead would not be easy. On top of all this, there was much sickness and even death, from an epidemic of influenza which swept throughout Great Britain and most of Europe during the last few months of 1918. Lack of nutritious food, due to shortages and delayed implementation of rationing, to provide fair portions, no doubt was partly to blame for this critical situation.

Matthew, Laura and Celia ensured that Sarah and Alice were provided for that difficult winter. Fresh vegetables, and hot nutritious meals were regularly brought around to the flat for both to enjoy. Sarah did her best caring for her daughter, but her grief prevented her thinking rationally at times, and the ready cooked meals arriving from the family, kept her and the baby healthy that winter.

Christmas came, and went peacefully. There was little celebration in the family, as nobody really felt like celebrating. A tree was decorated for Alice, and simple presents were exchanged, but no great essence was brought to the occasion. 1919 was similarly greeted, quietly and peacefully, with a mixture of sadness and hope.

Sarah continued to drift, lavishing all her care and affection on to Alice. More and more her thoughts turned to a change of scene, constant vivid reminders of moments shared by herself and Oliver occurring frequently.

March brought signs of Spring. The snow had completely disappeared, and glimpses of a watery sun gave promising warmth to the buds of new birth, struggling to emerge. One bright, pleasant afternoon, Sarah sat in her yard, behind the house. Alice pottered about with a coloured ball, and some building bricks of wood, which she loved to knock down, once they were built. Matthew was visiting. For a while both sat silently, watching the antics of Alice. Then, Sarah spoke:

"Father, do you remember my speaking to you about moving away from here, from Sidmouth?"

"I do indeed."

"Well, I have decided to do it. Alice is young, and I would like to settle down somewhere before she has to start her schooling. I think maybe I will write to Dr. Lindsay, and see if there are any likely flats or small cottages for sale up there. We could move into something temporary for a while, until something suitable came along."

"You are determined then, in your plan to move away?"

"Definitely. The more I think about it, the more it seems

the most sensible idea. Of course, we will both miss you Father, very much. It would be really wonderful if you could come with us. I don't suppose that's possible."

Matthew puffed long and thoughtfully on his pipe. Then, removing it, he turned to his daughter, his eyes shining.

"Why didn't I think of that? There is no real reason why we cannot all go back to the village. I can still find work of a kind, wherever I go. Your aunt and Celia will miss us of course, but they are good friends, and can always pay us a visit. Yes my dear, I would love to come with you both, if you really want me."

Sarah hugged him close in delight, then swept the startled Alice up into her arms, smothering her with kisses.

Laura and Celia proved to be most understanding, when the plan was disclosed. Celia was undecided on how she was to manage the large house by herself – now that she was getting on in years, it was really too large for one person, though she avoided the thought of selling it. In the end, it was determined that she and Laura would run it as a small holiday guest house during the season. Laura would live in at Celia's for the few busy months during the summer, helping with the cooking, and the comfort of the guests, returning to her own modest house out of season. The residences were very close to each other, and both ladies were on the telephone, so communication was no problem.

Dr. Lindsay replied to Sarah's letter promptly. He stated that there were very few residences for sale at that particular time, although it was interesting to note, that their old cottage, derelict and run down, still stood uninhabited. However, there were sure to be some temporary rooms for their use, until something better came up. In fact, he added that they were welcome to reside with him for the time being.

Sarah was very excited at the news of the vacant cottage, and asked her father how he felt about the idea of trying to buy it, painting it throughout, repairing the damages, and generally making it a home for the three of them. To her relief, he was most enthusiastic, for she had been worried that he would be against the idea of living there once more. But he urged her to get in touch with the doctor, and find out anything she could, regarding the present owner, agents etc. This was done, and before long came the information through the post.

It seemed that the cottage was still part of the estate belonging to "The Hall". During the war years the hall had been taken over and used by the military, the grounds ravaged and churned with armed vehicles and tanks. While just down the lane at the end of the drive, hidden in a leafy grove, stood the cottage. Each day it was passed by, virtually unnoticed by conveys of lorries and military personnel. It had been uninhabited now for several years, the last occupants being those who took the place over when Matthew and Sarah left all those years ago.

The large Hall was now the property of the local government, and was for sale. The cottage was also for sale, in its own right, and with all the details at his hand, Matthew journeyed up to Suffolk, to spend a couple of days, looking over the place, and starting transactions with the agents. It had been nearly ten years since Matthew had stood on Suffolk soil, and he had a lump in his throat as he stepped down from the train, and gazed about him. He took a lift from the waiting horse drawn cab outside the station, and as they slowly rumbled along the lane toward the village of his youth, he saw little apparent damage to the surrounding countryside. The fields were all neatly ploughed and planted with crops, and cattle and sheep stood contentedly in the green pastures. At last, they rounded a bend in the road, and there below them, snug in the valley was Stowmarket, his village. Groups of red roofed tiny dwellings, occasionally interspersed with roofs of thatch. Thin spirals of smoke drifted upwards from the numerous chimneys. Matthew picked out the church, standing slightly apart from the closely formed village, and behind, in its own grounds, the hall, where he had happily worked for so long. He couldn't make out the cottage yet, but it didn't matter because by this time the cab had pulled into the village square, and before he knew it, he was standing, his bag beside him, the conveyence disappearing down the lane.

Straight away he made his progress to Dr. Lindsay's house, as the good man had invited him to do. The door was opened by a tall good looking woman who he found out to be the housekeeper, Mrs. Watts. It seemed strange, not to be smothered in Mrs. Wilkin's embrace, as always used to be in times before. He pulled himself together, and was especially pleasant to the latest housekeeper.

He was shown into the parlour, which was exactly as he remembered it, and clean and shining under Mrs. Watt's care. A fire burned in the grate, and he sat down to await the doctor's arrival. He was brought tea and scones, and made most welcome. After a short while, he heard the front door open, and the loud voice of the doctor in the hall. Moments later, the door of the parlour was filled with his stout form.

The two men greeted each other with much warmth, the doctor bidding his guest resume his seat by the fire, whilst he made himself comfortable in the other chair, gratefully accepting the appearance of a fresh pot of tea, bourne in by Mrs. Watts.

News was exchanged, Dr. Lindsay voicing his sadness at the news of Oliver's death. Matthew had informed him by letter soon after the actual event.

"He was such a pleasant young man, so right for your Sarah."

Matthew nodded, tapping his pipe thoughtfully on his chin. "I know, I know. I just wish I knew the reason. The reason that such a caring, gentle person had to die so young."

"Many young people have died with little apparent reason over the last few years. At least he and Sarah were able to have a few precious months together, and Oliver had the joy of seeing his child born. More than a few couples had, no doubt." Dinner was served, and after a late evening glass of the doctor's old brandy, Matthew retired to his bed.

The following morning, after breakfast, he donned his hat and coat and left the house for the agents office situated in the main square of the village. On reaching the premises, he was greeted by Mr. Frost the manager, and was handed the keys of the cottage, for his inspection and perusal of the same. He left the office, the keys clutched tightly in his hand.

Within ten minutes, he was standing in front of a ram–shackle, neglected dwelling, scarcely recognisable to Matthew, prepared as he was from the doctor's description of the prop–erty. Moving aside tangled growth from the leaning gatepost, the wellworn sign, *Maple Cottage* confirmed that this was indeed the right place. In a dazed state, he moved forward to the front door, bare of paint, wood rotten and warped by weather and clime. Shakily, he inserted the large key in the keyhole, and turned it, the door creaking open. He stepped into the past.

Time fell away as Matthew stood, peering into the old familiar corners of the past. He noticed not the dust, and cob–webs, nor the bare boards, and broken panes. Instead, he saw the gleaming hearth, embers glowing within the dark confines of the range. He smelled the wholesome aroma of the cooking pot, and heard the kettle singing on the fire. Furniture and

fittings were visible as he remembered. The house lived.
It took several moments for the illusions to disappear, leaving Matthew feeling weak and confused. Slowly the rooms became cold, and empty, apart from beetles and spiders. Cold air whistled through breaks in the windows, and dust lay thickly everywhere. Supporting himself on various spines and columns, outstanding from the walls, he came to rest on a fallen beam, to one side of the old range. Resting his head in his hands, he pulled himself together. Slowly he raised his head and gazed around. Gradually he realised that the place had great possibilities.

Transactions were agreed, the agents being more than relieved to be rid of what they considered a worthless pile of bricks. Matthew straightaway contacted Sarah, notifying her of the purchase. After a few more local plans and words with electricians and plumbers in the area, he made the journey back to Sidmouth.

On his arrival, he walked the short distance from the railway station to Sarahs rooms. She had just put Alice down for her afternoon sleep, so was able to give her father all her attention. That evening the family met up at Celia's for the evening meal, and to discuss plans, arising from Matthew's trip. It was decided that he would make periodic visits to Suffolk, sometimes staying for a while if required. He would look in on the workman, and in fact tackle some of the straightforward tasks himself. He proposed to travel up again in two weeks time.

Summer was right around the corner, and at last the people were beginning to feel carefree and hopeful for the future. There were many young men who would never taste the fullness of life, again, their minds twisted and warped, trapped forever in the horrors they had experienced. They numbered heavily in the hospital wards, together with the permanently disabled physically, either disfigured through loss of limb (or limbs) or perhaps scarred from severe burns. Rehabilitation was attempted, but all to often, the victim finished up an immobile prisoner in his own home, being a full time job for his hapless family, or remaining in some kind of clinical establishment cared for by overworked nurses, who although dedicated to their task, had little time for more than a hurried straightening of covers, or mopping of a fevered brow as they hastened about their many duties.

After two further visits to Stowmarket and the cottage, Matthew estimated that Sarah, Alice and he should be able to move in by the late Autumn. Restoration and repairs were going well. Basically the cottage was still sound. Carpenters were replacing the cracked stone flooring with wooden floorboards, and renewing warped and rotten doorposts and window surrounds.

Slates were replaced on the roof, and fresh wiring was installed to convey electricity to the house. A small outhouse adjoining to the main building was to be made into a bathroom. The plumbers were already busy with the zinc bathtub, connecting it, and fixing taps and a water heater on the facing wall. Matthew kept an eye on the workmen, but soon found that they were good, reliable men, and worked well as a matter of course.

He began to set about some painting. Firstly, he whitewashed the outside of the cottage, and painted the door green, in accordance with Sarah's wishes. Then he started on the inside. Working from the upstairs down, he put a basic coat of colour on all the walls. If Sarah wished a different shade, she could decide on it when she got here. The walls and ceilings were clean and fresh, and the woodwork rich and smooth within a week or so. The bath was installed, and in the house the range looked as new after several polishings with blacking. There was a new kitchen sink, and the copper was tested and pronounced serviceable. Matthew knocked up one or two small items of furniture, which included a worktable in the yard for his use, and a swing for Alice under the apple tree.

Summer was at its height when next he travelled down to the family. The baby was a healthy golden little girl, in and out of the sea almost every day. Her hair was a mass of russet curls, and every so often, when her head was turned a certain way, the resemblance to Oliver was uncanny. But her eyes remained Sarah's, and the smile which betwitched everyone, that too was so like her mother's. Matthew was entranced with his grand-daughter. She changed each time he was absent for a week or two.

Sarah looked well enough, she too was bronzed from the sun, and days spent on the shore with Alice. She laughed and played with her daughter, and made frequent visits to Celia's and Laura's. But, the light was gone from her eyes, and she had lost some weight, and womanhood had come upon her, the young girl gone for ever. The plans for the move filled her mind these days, and she could not help but feel some excitement as completion of the repairs drew to a close. In late August, Matthew made his final inspection and returned in triumph.

The move could take place within the month. Now, there were things to do at Sarah's end. Packing cases were carefully filled with wrapped ornaments and photographs, and the few dainty pieces of crockery and glassware that she possessed. Less delicate objects were parcelled into large cardboard cartons, whilst soft furnishings were rolled up, or folded into two trunks of Celia's, brought down from her attic. The move was arranged for the final week of September. The weather was golden and mild, with a hint of frost in the mornings. Matthew hoped that they would have a good day for the actual move. Sarah would be travelling up by train with the baby, and Laura, who was going to help them settle in, staying for a few days the other end. Matthew would accompany the removal truck and would be starting out two days ahead with them. They had a long road journey before them, and would take breaks in the passage on route, putting up overnight in one of the many inns they would encounter.

During the week before leaving, Sarah handed over the keys of the rooms, and moved in with Celia until the time of departure. All the belongings were stored at the warehouse belonging to the removal company, ready for loading and transference on the appointed day. Sarah took the opportunity of visiting most of the many friends and acquaintences she had made, in this last week, Celia being very happy to mind Alice for an hour or two. Sarah's friends were sorry to see her go, but wished her and the baby well for their future. She was unable to see Jane, as she and her husband were away on a holiday at that time, so Sarah wrote an affectionate letter to both her and Dorothy, who was still nursing, giving them both her address, and a firm invitation for a future visit.

On the eve of Matthew's journey, everyone went to Celia's for lunch, it being a Sunday. After the meal, they adjourned to the parlour, where Matthew lit his pipe, and caught up on his newspaper, Alice drowsily played in her playpen with a favourite rag doll, and a wooden cart, and the women gossiped over a cup of tea. All to soon, it was time for Matthew to leave. He had a busy two days ahead of him, and had to be up early the next morning. He took a long affectionate farewell of Celia, and kissed Sarah and the baby :- "Goodbye my dears. I look forward to seeing you both on Wednesday. Have a good journey now."

"You too Father. Goodbye."

"Goodbye Matthew, God Bless you. I shall be up to visit, never fear."

Celia gave him a last hug, before he and Laura went out of the front door.

Wednesday dawned, another hazy pleasant promise of a day. Celia accompanied her friends to the station, and waved her hanky until the trains carrying them turned the corner and she was lost to view.

It was a long journey, Sarah was glad of Laura's company. Alice slept some of the time, but got restless towards the end of the last lap. Sarah couldn't help but think back to her last time on the train, making this same trip with Oliver. It all seemed so long ago. She snapped herself out of this frame of mind, and concentrated on Alice, being held to the window by Laura, in order to see the passing fields full of cattle and sheep. In another half hour, they should reach their destination, and find Matthew waiting with some transportation to take them on the final leg of their journey.

He was there. Eagerly scanning the travellers as they stepped down from the train. Then, he caught sight of Laura, handing down Sarah, who held the baby in her arms. He hurried forward to assist with the cases. Greetings over, they walked through the station, to where a shiny black automobile stood waiting to take them to the village. Doctor Lindsay had kindly loaned it to Matthew for a few hours. Passengers aboard, Matthew cranked the engine, which loudly caught, and spluttered into life. He hastened around, and into the driving seat, and soon they were steadily rumbling over the last mile or two to the village, and home.

Laura was taking great interest in the scenery about her. The countryside had its own beauty, though entirely different from that of the South, which she was used to. Within a matter of minutes, they were entering the market square of the village. Slowly the car moved up a side lane, over a bridge, rounded a curve to the right, and there it was, Maple Cottage! Its newly painted white walls contrasted with the surroundings reds and browns of the autumn foliage, and the smart green door with its heavy black knocker was there, in front of them, waiting to be entered. Matthew handed Sarah the key. She stepped forward hesitantly, inserted the key, turned it, and pushed the door open, entering the cottage.

Warmth greeted her, Matthew having lit the range already. Behind her, Laura took in the brightness and comfort of the newly decorated room. Sarah was bemused. She had not believed that the workmen could work such wonders with the run down premises. The paint gleamed, and the woodwork glowed richly in the softening light of the afternoon. Matthew meanwhile, secured Alice beneath one arm, and the baggage beneath the other, in an attempt to deposit both safely inside the house. Alice was grateful to be free from the confines of travel, and wriggled in his grasp. Once lowered to the floor, she gleefully tottered to each corner of the room, delighted in her limited taste of freedom.

Sarah and Laura discarded their travel stained clothes, and thankfully sat down to Matthew's fresh pot of strong tea, and a plate of cakes. Alice guzzled a cup of milk, and gnawed on a crusty slice of bread and butter. Half way through this, she stuck her thumb in her mouth, and fell asleep in the chair. Sarah gently picked her up, easing her day gown over the red curls, and putting on her warm night gown. Taking her upstairs, she lay her down in the crib next to her own bed. Kissing her lightly on her cheek, she went downstairs to join the others.

There were still packing cases to be emptied, but, it had

been a long day, there would be time enough tomorrow. Having returned the doctor's car, Matthew came back and sat around the range with his daughter and Laura, content with a fresh pipe and a pint of ale. The women were very weary, and it was only

Around the corner and there was Maple Cottage

just coming up to 9 o'clock, when Laura showed signs of how tired she was, scarcely able to stifle a number of yawns. Matthew hastily made up the spare pallet in the corner of the warm room, and he and Sarah said their goodnights, and went up to their rooms, Sarah giving him a fond kiss goodnight at the top of the stairs.

It was easy to settle into the cottage. Laura left for Sidmouth after a week, seeing that they were quite comfortable, and satisfied with the situation she was leaving them in. There were tearful farewells at the station, with repeated promises of a "not too distant visit from herself and Celia".

****

Although Sarah had been grateful for Laura's assistance, she couldn't help but feel quite pleased to have her home to herself at last. Matthew had already found a few odd jobs in the village, and was out most days, coming home in the evening to a hot meal prepared by Sarah. The local people were very friendly, especially when told that the family had lived in the village originally. Doctor Lindsay was a regular caller, and he and Alice became the best of friends. He would lift her high in the air, then bring her down to sit on his knee, telling her tales and singing her songs, enjoying the wideness of her eyes, and the dimpled smile, as she attempted to sing along to the simple melodies.

The months passed. Winter was over, spring on the way. One morning Sarah rose earlier than usual. Alice still slept, Matthew was out already. Sarah dressed quietly and went downstairs, letting herself out of the back door. The small patch of garden was wet with dew, and the sun was only just rising over the distant hills. Going to the far edge of the garden, Sarah gazed into the dark blues and purples of the far horizon. Oliver was as clear in her mind as if he actually stood beside her. She hugged herself tightly to prevent herself reaching out for him. The sun rose. Another day. Alice called out from within the house. Turning back, she felt Oliver's presence about her, and his approval of the cottage, and his warmth and loving strength, forever protecting her and Alice.

She smiled through her tears, murmured his name, and hurried in to tend to their daughter.